THE EARL
PLAYS WITH FIRE

Chapter One

London—1816

'Have you heard the latest?' The voice came out of nowhere.

Christabel Tallis, aimlessly fanning herself, stopped for a moment and glanced at the mirror which hung on the opposite wall. She knew neither of the women reflected there. Perched uncomfortably on one of the stiffly brocaded benches that lined the Palantine Gallery, she had been wondering, not for the first time that morning, why she'd ever agreed to her mother's suggestion that they meet Julian here. Lady Harriet had insisted they attend what was billed as the show of the Season, but for Christabel the delights of London society had long ago palled. The salon was overheated and far too crowded, and her delicate skin was already slightly flushed.

'About the Veryan boy, you mean?' one of the women continued.

The name hovered in the air, menacing Christabel's shield of calm detachment. The buzz of inconsequential chatter faded into the distance and every fibre of her body became alert.

'He's hardly a boy now, of course.'

'Indeed no. How long has it been? Lady Veryan must be overjoyed that he is returning home at last.'

Suddenly Christabel longed to be far away from this conversation, away from this room. A shaft of sunlight streamed through the gallery's long windows, breaking through a lowering sky and burnishing her auburn curls into a fiery cloud. The warming light was gone almost as soon as it appeared, but to her it seemed to beckon escape. Escape to where, though? To a country of grey slate and blue seas, a landscape of moor and rocks? To Cornwall, to home? But that could not be; she knew well that her future lay elsewhere.

'One can only hope that he actually arrives,' the woman opined in a hushed voice.

The other shuddered theatrically. 'I understand the journey from Argentina is very long and most dangerous.'

'My dear, yes. You must remember *The Adventurer*—just a few years ago. It sailed from Buenos Aires...'

The women moved away and she heard no more. That was sufficient. Richard's name reverberated through her mind. After all these years—five, six it would be—he was coming back. Her deep green eyes stared into the distance and saw only memory.

She was seated on a stone bench in the garden of the Veryan town house, the lush fragrance of rose blossoms tumbling in the air. Richard was standing straight and tall in front of her, his mouth compressed and his face white and set. She had just told him that she could not marry him and was offering his ring back. She could not marry him because she was in love with Joshua. And Joshua just happened to be one of Richard's closest friends. What a wretched business that had been. She and Richard had drifted into an engagement, more to please their parents than from any passionate attachment, and Joshua was the result. The family estates bordered each other and she'd known Richard all her life. It felt natural to be planning to spend the rest of it together. But her visit to London to buy bride clothes had vouchsafed a different perspective: Cornwall and their shared childhood vanished in a sea mist. Instead there was a thrilling round of parties, balls, picnics, assemblies and, at the end of it, Joshua. No, she couldn't marry Richard. She was too young and too passionate and friendship was not enough.

'Miss Tallis, please accept my sincerest apologies for arriving so late.'

A well-dressed man in a puce tailcoat and fawn pantaloons stood before her. He took her shapely hand in his, kissing it with elaborate courtesy, and bowed politely to Lady Tallis, who had broken off her conversation with a chance-met companion just long enough to smile benignly at the man she hoped would become her son-in-law.

Sir Julian Edgerton's pleasant face wore a rueful smile. 'I fear the Committee took longer than expected. There is always such a deal to do for the Pimlico Widows and Orphans. I hope you'll forgive me.'

'Naturally, Sir Julian, how could I not? You lead a truly benevolent life!' Christabel's musical voice held the suspicion of a laugh, but her face was lit with the gentlest of smiles.

'Now that I am here, may I get you some refreshment?'

'What a good idea! It's so very hot in this room. Lemonade, perhaps?'

'It will be my pleasure,' he said gallantly, 'and when we are once more comfortable, would you care to make a quick tour of the paintings with me? I am anxious to hear your views. You have such a refined sensibility.'

She sighed inwardly, but nodded assent while her mother beamed encouragement. She knew Lady Harriet was counting on Sir Julian's proposal. At nearly twenty-five Christabel was already perilously close to being on the shelf and she could no longer delay the decision to marry. Sir Julian might not be the most exciting man of her acquaintance, but he was solid and dependable and would make a restful husband. More than that, he would be an adoring one. And she could trust him. After the bruising experience of her girlhood, such a man was surely worth any amount of excitement.

If she made this marriage, it might help repair some of the destruction she'd wreaked all those years ago. Her parents had loved Richard as a son and his dismissal had hit them very hard. As for Richard, she was sure he'd remained heart whole. He'd never loved her with the passion she had craved. Instead he'd been angry and humiliated. It was the gossip he had loathed, being on everyone's tongue, the jilted suitor. Within a sennight he'd escaped England and was on a boat to Argentina. Lord Veryan had told the world it was needful that his son administer the family's growing estates in South America, but the world had known the real reason for Richard's sudden departure. So he'd escaped, but she'd paid the price for her indiscretion. Jilting a man three weeks before the wedding was the height of bad *ton* and scurrilous gossip had swirled around her head for months. It was difficult to recall six years later just how vulnerable she'd felt. Today she was an acknowledged leader of fashion, an ice-cold beauty who'd remained impregnable despite countless suitors. But then she'd been a raw, passionate girl, in the throes of a thrilling infatuation, and unable to dissemble.

'I'm afraid the lemonade is as warm as the salon.' Sir Julian had emerged from the crush and was at her elbow, proffering the glass he'd procured with some difficulty.

For a moment she looked blindly up at him. Past distresses were crowding in on her and, for the second time that morning, she looked for escape. She needed distraction, needed to be on the move.

'I think I would prefer to view the pictures after all, Sir Julian.'

She rose from her seat as she spoke and, smoothing the creases from her amber silk walking dress, took her suitor's arm. They began slowly to stroll around the gallery. As always her elegant figure drew glances of frank admiration from those she passed and Sir Julian, feeling pride in his possession, held her arm even more tightly. While they walked, he spoke sensibly about the paintings they inspected and she tried hard to conjure interest in his carefully considered opinions. He was a good man, she told herself severely, and she must not hanker for more. That way lay disaster. She had learned that lesson well. It had taken little time to discover that Richard was worth twenty times the man who'd displaced him. The relationship with Joshua had petered out, destroyed by her guilt and his inevitable betrayal.

'I must say that I find these colours a little too forceful. They jangle the nerves rather than soothe.'

Sir Julian was standing before a group of canvases whose landscapes pulsated with lurid crimsons and golds, an anarchic depiction of the natural world.

'What do you think, Miss Tallis—am I being old fashioned?'

'Not old fashioned precisely, Sir Julian, but perhaps a little traditional? One needs to open one's mind to different possibilities,' she hazarded, thinking that just one of the pictures on her bedroom wall would be enough to keep her awake at night.

'As always you are right. I will look with your eyes and endeavour to see these canvases anew.'

Why did he always have to agree with her? Richard would have mocked her pretensions, laughed openly at her and they would have ended sharing the joke together. But Richard's companionship was long gone. How strange to think that he would soon be in England, but this time returning as the new Earl Veryan. It was three months since Lord Veryan's life had been brutally cut short by a riding accident. Richard would have left for home the minute he'd received the dreadful news, but a long and treacherous journey meant his father had been buried while he was still on the high seas. At the funeral Lady Veryan had been beyond grief; it was certain to be a very sad homecoming for her son. Her escort continued to talk, but Christabel's thoughts were elsewhere, straying inevitably towards a lone man adrift on a distant ocean. With a great effort she forced herself to return to Sir Julian and his enthusiastic recital; the small successes of Pimlico's deserving poor had never seemed less riveting.

A few hundred miles away, the new Earl Veryan gazed blankly over the sea as it threaded itself swiftly past the ship. He was deep in thought and not all of it was pleasant. The last image of his father played through his mind, the stocky figure waving from the dockside, a bright red handkerchief in his hand, growing smaller and smaller as the ship made its way to the open sea. He had been away from England for too long; he had not been there for his father when he needed him. Now at last he was returning home, but to an unknown life. The Great Hall would no longer echo to Lord Veryan's greeting and the task of administering a large estate was now his. He knew himself well capable, but he was sorry to be leaving Argentina behind. The country had been good to him. A rugged outdoor life had taught him authority and decisiveness. It had honed him physically and created an inner strength he'd not known he possessed. And life there had not been all hard work. The social round was lively and largely free of the stifling conventions of London society, and the tall, handsome Englishman was a popular guest. There had been music and laughter and plenty of beautiful women happy to engage in a light flirtation or more. He'd enjoyed their favours freely and indifferently, determined to consign love to the vault of history and simply enjoy the physical pleasures of the moment. It had become a way of life for him, demanding little emotion and no commitment.

The moon cut a path across the surface of the small waves so bright that it made him blink. His eyes focused on the expanse of ocean, at the different shades of silver and black stretching to the horizon, then to the lanterns which hung above him, swinging comfortingly to the rhythm of the ship. The crew were engaged elsewhere and he had the deck to himself. He wondered if he dared to smoke a cigar, a disastrous habit he'd contracted in Argentina, but decided that he'd better keep that delight for later. Dinner would be served soon and he did not want to escort Domino to the table smelling of tobacco.

The boat gave a louder creak than usual with the sudden

swell of the ocean, but the vessel soon recovered its peaceful passage. A sailor appeared from the deck below and waved a greeting.

'Fine weather, sir, and the forecast's good. Should be a quiet landfall, I'm thinking.'

It had not always been so calm; they had suffered tempests aplenty since leaving Buenos Aires and there had been times when he'd wondered if they would ever make it to land again. But it was tranquil now and he had leisure to think. The grey eyes were expressionless, his dark straight brows furrowed. The meeting with his mother would be painful, he knew, but there would be joy too. To be home again; to feel Cornish air on his skin once more and to awake to the sound of Cornish surf breaking on the rocky cove below Madron Abbey. He saw in his mind's eye the winding path from the house across the green headland and then the sudden dramatic fall of cliffs tumbling into the wild seas. He'd walked that pathway so many times in memory. In just a few weeks he would be walking it in reality.

Immediately the ship berthed in Southampton, he would post up to London and ensure that Domino was safely consigned to the care of her aunt. The sooner he could do this, the sooner he could travel on to Madron.

'There you are, Richard. I've been looking everywhere for you.'

The speaker was a diminutive brunette who barely came up to his chest. She raised a pair of soft brown eyes to his hard grey ones and smiled sweetly. Richard smiled back in response.

'Not quite everywhere, it seems. I'm not exactly invisible.'

'I didn't expect you to be behind the lifeboats! Were you

thinking of leaving the ship without telling me? Or, more like, you were just about to smoke one of those noxious cigars of yours.'

He looked guilty and she crowed with delight, clapping her hands together and doing a little dance around him.

'You see, I know you so well.'

He doubted that, but it would hardly be surprising if she thought so. They'd been cooped up together in this small vessel for nigh on a month. When he'd first been asked to escort the Spanish ambassador's daughter to London, he'd been aghast. His mind was beset with worries over his mother and grief for his father and he had no wish to assume the responsibility of a seventeen-year-old girl.

But Señor de Silva had been persuasive. Domino had been invited by the English branch of her family to spend a Season in London and then to make the journey on to Spain and her paternal home in Madrid. Alfredo de Silva was insistent that his daughter should experience something of European society.

'Argentina is pioneer country, you know, Richard, not the place for a young girl.'

'She seems to have thrived on life in Buenos Aires,' Richard protested, trying to escape the fate he saw coming.

But Señor de Silva was adamant. Domino must be launched on society and not in a rough-and-ready place like Buenos Aires. As a considerable heiress, and charmingly pretty, his daughter could look to the highest for a husband.

'It's a very long journey for a young girl. There are dangers.' Richard made a last attempt, but to no avail.

'Yes, yes, I have considered well,' Señor de Silva reassured him. 'The time is right—Napoleon is captive and confined on the island of St Helena where he can do no further harm. Domino will be able to travel in safety to England and then on to Spain. And you will be with my darling to protect her on the long journey.'

And so he'd agreed with reluctance to chaperon the girl aboard ship. He would see her safely on land and delivered to an aunt in Curzon Street, but after that his role would end.

Domino was speaking again. 'When we get to London, Richard, will there be many parties and balls?'

'Almost certainly,' he smiled teasingly. 'Otherwise why would you leave all your admirers in Buenos Aires and come to London?'

'My father says I must make good use of my time there. I can have fun, but I must make sure that I meet lots of gentlemen too. Eligible gentlemen.' She rolled the syllables off her tongue and pulled a face.

'That will be for your aunt to decide. She is your chaperon and she'll tell you who is eligible and who is not.'

'Are you eligible, Richard?'

'For you, no. I'm far too old and a deal too worn.'

'How old are you?'

'Twenty-eight.'

'That's not old. My father was ten years older than my mother. And I like the way he looked in his wedding pictures. Worldly and experienced.'

She looked up at him trustfully, the melting brown eyes smiling a clear invitation. He was taken aback. This was one outcome he had not foreseen. He'd no wish to be part of any emerging adolescent fantasy. He knew too well the pain which could accompany the insubstantial dreams of youth.

The image of a pale-faced girl with a torrent of red curls

and glinting green eyes swam suddenly into his vision. He was startled. It was years since he'd thought of Christabel, really thought of her. It must be that he was nearing England, coming home after so many years. She would be settled amid the London society he hated, probably married with a pair of children to her name.

He didn't know for sure. His parents, mindful of his feelings, had never kept him informed of her whereabouts or her doings. And he had not wanted to know.

It had been enough to know that she had betrayed him, and with a man he'd considered one of his closest friends. That moment when he'd realised, known for certain that he'd been blind and a fool, came rushing back to him. The whispers which he'd ignored, the sympathetic looks which he'd refused to see, and then the two of them—Christabel and Joshua—a secret smile on their faces, secret murmurs on their lips, emerging from the darkened terrace into the lighted ballroom, walking side by side, bound together as one. The sharpness of that moment still cut at him. He'd looked around the room and realised that every pair of eyes was fixed on him, wondering what he would do, what he would say. He'd left the ball abruptly, incensed and distraught in equal measure. The next day she'd told him. A little late, he'd thought bitterly, just a little late. Three weeks to their wedding and she was sorry, she loved another. Sorry! Sorry for betraying him with a fly-by-night, a professional second-rater who'd pretended friendship only to get closer to his prey. And she, she'd been willing without a second thought to betray people she had professed to love and to expose him to the most shameful tittle-tattle.

He had drifted into the engagement with Christabel. Their two families had been friends for as long as he could remember and as youngsters they'd been constant companions. It wasn't difficult to do what their parents had been dreaming of, not difficult to imagine a life lived with each other in the Cornish homeland they shared.

But in the end it had not felt that way. He had begun the affair in nonchalance and ended in love. He had wanted to marry. He had wanted her: her russet curls tickling his chin as they walked together in the gardens, the sensation of her body moulding to his as they dared to learn the waltz together, the softness of her skin to his touch, the softness of her mouth to his lips when he'd first ventured to kiss her. It had been a revelation. Now standing on this weathered deck, the empty ocean spread before him, her beautiful sensual form seemed to envelop him once more and he felt himself grow warm and hard with longing. He cursed silently. To feel passion after all these years was ridiculous. Surely it was only an image of the past that aroused such feelings, only an image, not reality that still had the power to hurt.

'Are you all right, Richard? You look quite angry.' Domino's eyes held a troubled expression and he pulled himself back abruptly to the present.

'I'm fine,' he replied easily, 'I'm not at all angry. But we mustn't stay on deck any longer—it's grown far too cold for you.'

'But I love it here. The moonlight is so beautiful, isn't it?'

He had to agree. The moon had risen fully now and the world was bathed in silver. Against his will his mind refused to let the memories go, for it had been a night like this when they'd gone swimming in the cove. Forbidden, thrilling, an intimation that Christabel was no longer the child she'd once been. And he had gloried in it. The water contouring itself around her slim form. The long shapely legs glimmering through a gently rippling surface. All he'd wanted to do was wind himself around her and stay clasped, fast and for ever.

'Dinner is served, Lord Veryan, when you're ready.'

Neither of them had heard the captain as he approached from the saloon behind. They had been caught up in their own thoughts, standing motionless before the beauty of the ocean.

'Thank you. We'll come now,' Richard replied swiftly and offered his arm to the petite young lady beside him.

'Lord Veryan? That sounds so grand, Richard.'

'It should do. Take heed and obey!'

She giggled and made haste to the table that had been prepared for them. The smell from the kitchen was not encouraging. She pulled another face and her eyes glinted mischievously. Her aunt would have to stop her showing her feelings quite so evidently, he thought. It would not do to be too natural in London society. In his experience the Season involved nothing but artificiality and sham. He heaved a sigh without realising he was doing so.

'Something troubles you, Richard? You're not looking forward to going home?'

'Indeed I am. I'm going to the most beautiful place on earth. How could I not be looking forward to it?'

'More beautiful than Argentina?'

'To my mind, Domino, but everyone thinks their own home is the best in the world.'

'Tell me about Cornwall.'

'Let's see, what can I tell you? It's wild and free. Its colours are green and grey—granite cliffs and slate-roofed houses, but rolling green fields. Above all the sea is blue within blue and never still. I can hear the sound of the surf breaking on

the beach from my bedroom window and smell the salt on
the air.'

'You make it sound a paradise. And what about your house?'

'The Abbey is very old and built of grey stone. It has mul-
lioned windows and a massive oak front door studded with
iron. Every room is panelled in the same dark oak.'

'That sounds a bit gloomy—but perhaps abbeys always
are?' Domino puckered her forehead in disappointment.

'It could be, but in the summer the garden is a cascade of
colour—some of the flowers as vivid as those in the tropics
because Cornwall is so warm—and in the winter, the rooms
are lit by the flicker of open fires and the house is filled with
the sweet smell of burning apple wood.'

'Ah, then it does sound wonderful after all. And do you
have many friends there?'

'A few.' His tone was indifferent.

'No one in particular?'

'No one,' he reiterated, this time with certainty. And the
image of flying red hair and shining emerald eyes was once
more banished from his conscious mind.

Christabel returned early that night from a supper party
and sat quietly in front of her mirror while her maid carefully untangled the knot of auburn curls. The evening had
been insipid and she'd been glad of the excuse of a headache
to leave for home. Although her face had maintained a calm
detachment throughout the day, her mind was troubled. Ever
since hearing his name that morning, she'd not been able to
put Richard out of her thoughts. There'd always been a part
of her, buried deep, that held his memory, but the passage of
the intervening years had soothed the raw pain of his depar-

ture and the collapse of the world she'd trusted. She'd done all she could to forget him. Now a random conversation between two unknown women had brought his memory throbbing back to life.

She scolded herself. He would be so changed that she would hardly know him, nor he her. In all probability he would sail into Southampton with a new Lady Veryan on his arm. They were bound to meet again at some time in the future, given the proximity of their homes, but not for many months. He would be certain to post down to Cornwall as soon as he could, to be with his mother. And she, where would she be? No doubt by the end of the Season preparing to be Lady Edgerton, and packing her valise for a protracted stay at Sir Julian's Berkshire estate. She sighed involuntarily and Rosa stopped brushing her hair for a moment, thinking that she had hurt her mistress. Christabel was smiling at her reassuringly when the bedroom door opened.

'I'm so glad I've found you still up. I wanted a brief word with you, my dear.'

She nodded dismissal to her maid and looked warily at her mother. She knew well the likely nature of the brief word.

'I was so pleased today at the gallery to see you on such good terms with Sir Julian. You do like him, darling, don't you?'

'Yes, of course, Mama, what is there not to like?'

'I mean,' her mother said doggedly, 'that it's not simply a case of not holding him in aversion—you do *positively* like him?'

'I think so.'

Lady Harriet tried to restrain her irritation with this lovely but obdurate daughter. 'You don't sound very certain.'

'That's because I'm not. Sir Julian is kind and charming and obviously a very good person, but perhaps he's just a little too good for me.'

'Stuff,' her mother exclaimed unexpectedly. 'How can you talk so, Christabel! You deserve the very best.'

Her daughter remained silent, gazing gravely at her reflection in the mirror.

'Are you still thinking of that business with the Veryans?'

Even her mother, she noted, did not dare to speak Richard's name. Lady Harriet came close and put her arms around her daughter.

'Bel, my darling, that's over and has been for years. It's nonsense to let it determine the rest of your life. It was a bad affair at the time, but you must put it out of your mind and make a fresh start.'

Whether it was her mother's hug or simply because she'd had a jarring day, she couldn't say, but Christabel found herself dissolving into tears.

Lady Harriet soothed her lovingly and then spoke to her as if to a weary child. 'The time has come, Christabel, to make a sensible decision which will affect the rest of your life. You have received many offers of marriage and have refused them all. In a few months you will be twenty-five and in our society that is not a good age to be single still. If you really dislike the idea of marriage to Sir Julian, you know we will not try to persuade you otherwise. Your father and I have profited from painful experience. But if you feel you could live comfortably with him, then I would urge you not to wait too long. He is obviously deeply in love with you and you have only to "throw the handkerchief"—a vulgar saying, I know, but a perfectly true one none the less—and he will pick it up with alacrity.'

'I know, Mama.' Her daughter's woebegone expression raised a smile on Lady Harriet's face.

'Do not look so miserable about it. You will have a splendid life. You will never want for anything and will have a man by your side whose only wish is to make you happy.'

How to tell her mother how she felt? How to explain it even to herself? Her head told her that a tranquil life with Sir Julian was the best possible compromise she could make, but her heart murmured traitorously that tranquillity would not satisfy. What did she want, then? Gaiety, exhilaration, adventure even? But she knew her mother was right. She was a mature woman and she must behave like one. That meant making a sensible decision about her future.

Thinking that her homily had gone home, Lady Harriet continued. 'Promise me, my love, that when the moment comes you will listen to whatever Sir Julian has to say and consider his words favourably.'

'I promise, Mama.'

She made the undertaking in good faith. She must try not to disappoint Sir Julian, nor let her family down again.

Her pledge was put to the test the following Saturday morning. She was quietly engaged with Rosa, selecting dresses from her wardrobe that needed attention and listing the new gloves and slippers she must purchase now that the Season was well advanced, when the second footman appeared at her bedroom door.

'Milady would like to see you in the drawing room, Miss Christabel.'

She wondered what was toward and made haste downstairs. Her heart sunk when she saw Sir Julian perched rather unsafely on one of the decorative but spindly chairs her mother had recently hired for the drawing room.

'Miss Tallis, how good to see you. And how well you look in that ensemble.'

She looked blankly at the old dress she was wearing and wondered if her potential spouse needed glasses.

'But then,' he continued, 'you always contrive to look amazingly elegant.'

Her mother beamed appreciatively. 'Sir Julian has been speaking of the new floral exhibition in Hyde Park. It sounds truly magnificent and has been especially designed as part of the celebrations arranged for the French Royal Family.'

'In fact,' Sir Julian interjected eagerly, 'they are actually to celebrate the Prince Regent's own assumption of power, but since his father is so very ill, it would be bad form for him to broadcast it, I dare say.'

Christabel looked from one to the other in some puzzlement, wondering where she fitted into this conversation. Her mother was at hand to help.

'Sir Julian has very kindly called to discover if you would care to see the display. I know you have no engagements this morning, my dear.'

Sir Julian added his voice to the petition, 'I hope I do not importune, Miss Tallis, but I would welcome your company. And I am sure you will be charmed, knowing your highly developed sense of beauty. The southern tip of the park is a sheer blaze of colour.'

Christabel had no alternative but to agree, only stopping to change her gown and unpack the new bonnet which had just been delivered by Celeste, her favourite milliner. It was a charming confection, a light-green cottager style tied beneath the chin with an enormous chiffon bow. It set off to perfection a gown of pale primrose silk. If she was to be wooed, and she had no doubt that this was Sir Julian's plan, she would at least look the part.

Hyde Park was unusually busy for a Saturday morning and for some time they had little leisure to converse, their attention distracted by the need to avoid a constant parade of slowly moving barouches and their elderly occupants, baby carriages with their nursemaids and schoolboys bowling their hoops. It seemed the whole world and his wife had come out to play this early April morning. And it wasn't hard to see why. The sun streamed down from an almost cloudless blue sky and spring was in the air.

Richard was also in the park that morning, carefully shepherding Domino through its north gate towards Rotten Row, which was already busy with riders. It would be a good opportunity, he thought, for the young girl to experience one of the more popular pursuits of London life. Annoyingly he had been forced to kick his heels in the capital for some days while legal papers were being prepared for his signature. But he could at least enjoy this heaven-sent morning.

He glanced sideways at his companion, an amused expression on his face. She was in high gig now that he'd unexpectedly remained in town and her aunt had agreed to his chaperonage. Lady Blythe's horror at the notion of a male escort the younger side of thirty had evaporated the moment Richard presented himself in Curzon Street. His manners were excellent and he showed an avuncular affection for Domino that not even her worst nightmare could translate into any threat to her charge. She was only too pleased to accept his protection for her young niece whose company she was already finding exhausting.

They had hired hacks from the stables around the corner from Aunt Loretta's house, but had almost instantly regretted it. Neither had any hesitation in characterising their respective mounts as out-and-out slugs. Domino had already begun to feel irked by the restraints her aunt had found it necessary to place on her; after weeks of confinement on board ship, she was restless for the kind of unfettered gallop she had been accustomed to in Argentina. Her horse was unlikely to provide that. Yet the morning shone with perfection and the greensward stretched invitingly in front of her. She could not resist the attempt, and before Richard could stop her she had dug her spurs hard into the horse's flanks. Startled out of his wits, Firefly was for once in his life true to his name. He shot off across the park at breakneck speed to the shocked outrage of those sedately taking their morning promenade. Forced to ride sidesaddle, Domino crouched low over the horse's neck in order to keep her seat, with her hair streaming inelegantly behind. After a frozen instant of shock Richard urged his mount into an unwilling gallop and rushed after her, fearful for her safety and intent on stopping her from creating the kind of scandal of which she had no notion.

Firefly hit the dust of Rotten Row, choking nearby strollers and scattering them to the winds as they leapt for safety, just as Sir Julian had worked himself up to the point of a declaration.

'I shall be leaving for Rosings in the morning, Miss Tallis, and had hoped to depart with one very important question answered. It is a question dear to my heart and only you can settle it. I do not, of course, require an immediate answer, but I would be truly grateful if you would agree to think over what I have to say. You see, Miss Tallis, Christabel—'

He was forced to break off mid sentence and take drastic action as Firefly thundered towards him and his lovely companion. In a trice he had swept Christabel up and literally jumped her out of harm's way. A second later another horse galloping headlong in pursuit caught up with the runaway and grabbed hold of Firefly's bridle.

'Never, ever do that again!'

Richard's voice expressed his cold fury. Badly jolted by the headlong flight of her horse and realising that she had committed a serious social sin, Domino slipped from the saddle, her face white and frightened. She had never seen Richard so angry and she wasn't certain whether she should shout or cry. He gave her no chance to decide. Turning to the couple who had narrowly escaped Firefly's thundering hooves, he bowed in apology. Sir Julian inclined his head at the irate stranger before him. He had no idea of his identity for he had been travelling on the Continent when Richard Veryan had first come to the capital.

'Please forgive my companion,' Richard offered stiffly. 'She is a visitor to London and unaware of the rules governing riding in Hyde Park. I trust that you have received no harm.'

'I'm glad to say that we haven't,' stuttered Sir Julian, now very shaken by the incident, 'but your charge—for I take it that she is your charge—needs to be given a summary lesson.'

'She shall have it,' he said crisply, glaring at Sir Julian with annoyance. Domino had put him in the wrong and he did not like it.

He turned to apologise to the woman he had only glimpsed from the corner of his eye and for the first time in the encounter was struck dumb. For what seemed endless time, he stood motionless and without expression, absorbing the picture before him, hardly believing what he saw.

He had not visualised the moment when he would meet Christabel again. He'd made quite sure that his imagination never strayed into such dangerous territory. But if he'd been tempted to speculate, it would not have felt like this. He would have felt nothing—the meaningless liaisons of years would have done their work—and any carefully suppressed images that still remained in the recesses of his memory would have, should have, shrivelled in the cold light of reality. He ought to feel nothing. But that, it seemed, was not so. He stood and looked and his heart received a most painful jolt.

She was even more beautiful than he remembered. The glinting green eyes and the sensual tumble of red locks against translucent skin were arousing all his senses. He looked searchingly at her ungloved hand. Astonishingly she was not married, at least not yet. That popinjay with her was no doubt the intended.

Christabel had known him immediately. He was still the same tall, athletic man that he had always been, but he seemed stronger now, more muscular, his face lean and tanned. There was an authority about him that had not been there before. His grey eyes as they fixed her in an unwavering stare beneath black, straight brows were lacking in all emotion. There was no warmth, no answering response to her tentative smile.

His voice was as indifferent as his expression. 'Miss Tallis? Your servant, ma'am.'

How hateful of him to speak to her thus, stiff and formal as though they had met for the first time only yesterday. Sir

Julian looked questioningly between the two of them and Christabel forced herself to perform the social niceties.

'Sir Julian, may I introduce Earl Veryan. Lord Veryan, Sir Julian Edgerton.'

The two men eyed each other askance, instinctively hostile. Domino, abandoned at a distance, walked her horse towards them and Richard was compelled to make her known to her erstwhile victims. She smiled sunnily at them.

'I'm so sorry, please forgive me for frightening you.' Her accent was marked as though she hoped that this might produce a swifter forgiveness.

'I don't know the rules,' she continued, 'and Richard never told me, did you, Richard?' And she smiled up at him, her eyes glowing with affectionate entreaty.

But Richard was still looking at Christabel and saw those extraordinary green eyes half-close. Was that perhaps unhappiness at Domino's youthful adoration, an attempt to erase a discomfiting image? It seemed unlikely given her ruthless rejection of him. Yet undoubtedly she'd flinched at Domino's display of fondness. The girl meant nothing to him, but Christabel was not to know that. He hoped that she was suffering at least a little of the agonising jealousy that he'd once known.

He was shocked by the vindictive thought, shocked that his emotions were surging out of control. That he should be so susceptible, so easily disturbed, after six long years was dismaying. He schooled his face to remain expressionless as he bowed his formal farewell, but his mind was deep in tangled thought. He walked swiftly away and Domino had almost to skip to keep up with his long stride.

The unexpected meeting had unnerved him. He'd felt his

body invaded by unwanted desire and his mind battered by conflicting impulses. He was bewildered by his reactions for they made no sense. But of one thing he was certain. He could not allow himself to be drawn to Christabel again; he had to overcome a weakness that had come out of nowhere. As he walked a vague sense grew upon him that if he could prove to himself, prove to the world, that her beauty was only skin deep, she would cease to bother him. The veriest shadow of an idea began to form in his mind.

Chapter Two

Christabel allowed herself to be escorted home, Sir Julian steering her expertly along the pavement while remonstrating at length on the licence given the very young these days. She hardly heard him for her mind was in turmoil. The unexpected meeting with Richard would have been difficult enough but his cold aloofness had at first amazed her and then upset her deeply. Years had passed since she'd broken their engagement and she'd imagined that whatever anger he'd felt towards her would have cooled long ago. But it was clear that it was not so. Those steely grey eyes had expressed—what, indifference, aversion, even enmity? Richard, of all people, the boy who had meant most to her for most of her life.

Sir Julian continued his monologue as they made their way through the busy crowds that thronged Mayfair that morning.

'I am only glad, Miss Tallis, that you sustained no lasting injury. How I could have reconciled myself to that I do not know. It was I who invited you to view the floral display—if it had not been for me, you would never have been in danger.'

She roused herself to reassure him. 'Please don't blame

yourself, Sir Julian. The incident was in no way your fault. You could not have foreseen such a thing happening.'

'That is true, but I still feel a heavy responsibility. And tomorrow I must go away. I cannot delay my visit to Rosings any longer. I have already put it off once and my bailiff remains most anxious to consult me.'

'Of course, you must not delay. Why ever should you? As you see, I am perfectly unharmed. My nerves may be a little jangled, but they will soon recover.'

'Miss Tallis, you are a pearl among women. Others would have had hysterics. You are so cool and admirable under adversity.'

Sir Julian's fussing was becoming an irritant. She might well have succumbed to hysterics, but not from the possibility of being crushed by a runaway horse. She could hardly admit that the shock she'd sustained was in encountering Richard's hostility, and she was desperate for her well-meaning companion to drop the topic. Thank goodness he was to journey to his estates tomorrow and she would be free of his company for the next few days. But how dreadful that she should feel this way about the man she was considering taking as a husband.

'I shall be back very shortly—' he had almost read her mind '—and then, Miss Tallis, I hope to renew our conversation which was so violently terminated.'

They had reached the house in Mount Street that Lady Tallis rented every year and Sir Julian bounded up the white stone steps and knocked sharply on the front door with his cane. Christabel wasn't sure if this was to impress since there was a perfectly good door knocker. However, he was beaming down on her with a gentle kindliness and she tried to look suitably grateful for his care. As soon as she could, she would send him on his way and seek refuge in her bedroom. She needed time to think, time to digest all that had happened that morning.

The bright blue door of Number Six finally swung open after an unusual delay and the two of them made to enter, but were pulled up sharply on the threshold by a scene of rampant confusion. The hall was overflowing with trunks, cases, holdalls of all kinds and a decidedly sulky-looking parrot in a white ironwork cage that Christabel recognised instantly.

'Sophia? Sophia is here?'

'Yes, Sophia *is* here.'

A strident voice emanated from behind the furthest stack of parcels. The young lady who emerged, smiling triumphantly at her sister, was not ill favoured, but against Christabel's pure beauty she appeared unexceptional.

'What on earth are you doing in Mount Street? Why have you left Cornwall?' Christabel exclaimed.

Before her sister could answer, a cheery male voice called out from the adjoining library, 'Hey, Sophy, you could hang the bird here.'

'Benedict? He's here too?'

Christabel was dumbstruck at this sudden eruption into her life of the two siblings she had supposed to be fixed at Lamorna Place for the next few months. Lady Harriet floated into the hall, waving her hands ineffectually over the assorted baggage as though by doing so it would miraculously order itself and march away.

'Christabel, my darling, I'm so glad you're back. The servants are being amazingly slow at sorting this mountain and I need your help.'

'I'm not surprised they're slow—why on earth is there so much?'

Sophia drew herself up with an indignant puff and was just about to launch into an impassioned response when she spied Sir Julian hovering just behind her sister. Christabel had not introduced him immediately and he took the chance to excuse himself, saying in a rather nervous voice that he could see the family was extremely busy at this time and he would take his leave.

'May I call on my return, Miss Tallis?'

'Yes, of course, you may.' It was her mother who replied so readily.

Sir Julian bowed himself elegantly out of the door and down the steps, but not before he heard Sophia's accusing voice. 'Why didn't you introduce us to your fiancé, Christabel?'

The door shut behind him.

'He is not my fiancé.'

'That's very strange. We understood that you were engaged. That's why we're here, isn't it, Benedict?'

Benedict smiled in a superior fashion. 'It may be why you're here, but I'm here to have fun,' he returned.

'Mama, may I speak privately with you for a moment?' Christabel asked in a tight voice as she ushered her mother into the library.

Lady Harriet looked flustered. 'Shouldn't we get the hall cleared first, my dear? The house is at sixes and sevens and the staff really do not like it.'

'In a minute, Mama. This is more important.'

Once in the library, she wasted no time. 'Why are Sophia and Benedict here?' she asked, fixing her mother with a minatory look.

'They are family. It is quite natural that they should come to stay with us,' her mother responded defensively.

'But why now, Mama? You know that it was decided they would both remain in Cornwall for the next few months.'

'That was certainly the initial plan, but things have changed a little.'

'What things precisely?'

'Sophia is eighteen and should have the opportunity to partake of at least some of the Season.' Her mother appeared unwilling to answer her directly.

'She was eighteen when we left Lamorna, so I ask you again—what has changed?'

'Sir Julian has changed.'

'What do you mean by that?'

'I mean that he is ready to make you an offer, Christabel. You cannot deny it and if, as I hope, you will see fit to accept him, Sophia must be introduced to the *ton* at the earliest possible moment so that she, too, has the chance of contracting an eligible alliance.'

'But it was agreed that she would come out officially next year.'

'That was before we knew about Sir Julian.'

'What do we know about Sir Julian? Sophia said that he was my fiancé. Why should she say that?'

'He is—almost,' her mother ventured.

'He has not asked me to marry him.'

'But he will. And I cannot think why he did not do so this morning. It was clearly what he intended.'

Christabel ignored this and pursued her own enquiry relentlessly.

'Have you told Sophia that I am engaged?'

'I may have mentioned in letters to your father that it was possible you were on the point of accepting a proposal.'

'And Papa has repeated this to Sophia?'

'He may have mentioned it.'

'May have? He obviously let it slip and, knowing Sophia, she will have plagued him to death until he agreed that she could come to London. Isn't that so?'

Her mother hung her head guiltily.

'I thought so. And I am to be coerced into agreeing to this marriage so that my sister can have her way.'

'No one is talking of coercion, Bel. You know that you must be married, if not to Sir Julian, then to someone else. We've had this conversation a hundred times before. And it's only fair to Sophia that she be allowed her place in the sun.'

'And is Benedict also to be allowed his place in the sun?'

'Don't be foolish. Benedict is still a stripling and only just down from Oxford. Your father thought it wise to let him gain some town bronze before he settles to learning the management of the estate.'

'What you mean is that he also plagued Papa until he was allowed to come.'

'He will be here only a month, my dear, and someone had to escort Sophia. I cannot understand why you are so cross.'

Christabel took a deep breath and said with deliberation, 'I am cross because I feel my hand is being forced. I understood that we would be here on our own for this Season and expected to have time and peace to consider my future. Now I have virtually the whole of my family breathing down my neck and pushing me into a marriage I don't want.'

'You don't want it!'

Her mother looked scandalised and Christabel felt stunned.

She hadn't meant to acknowledge such troublesome feelings so starkly, even to herself, let alone express them aloud. She tried to recover her composure as best she could.

'I understand my position, Mama, and I will do what is expected of me. But don't demand that I am glad.'

And with that she turned on her heel and threaded her way swiftly through the still-cluttered hall and up the stairs to her room without another word. Brother and sister, still standing amidst the clutter of baggage, looked after her in surprise.

Once in her room, Christabel flung herself down on the satin counterpane and closed her eyes. The morning had been full of shocks and she was not coping well with them. She needed to pull herself together. Sophia was an unfriendly presence that she could have done without, but nothing more. As for Benedict, he would be filling Mount Street with noise and disturbance. Maybe that would be beneficial; it would help to distract her from the reality of her life. Which was what, exactly? Marriage to a man she did not love and hatred from the man she had once loved. The near-fatal accident, her siblings' unwelcome arrival, her mother's pretence, could all be forgotten. It was Richard's undisguised hostility that stayed with her.

Early the next morning she woke to a household already on the move. She'd slept badly and wanted nothing more than to stay curled in bed. But very shortly Sophia bounced into her room, more than happy to explain the bustle.

'Mama has said that I am to go shopping and you are to accompany me,' she announced peremptorily.

Christabel blinked sleepily and reached for her cup of chocolate. 'Don't you already have enough clothes?'

'No, I don't. I shall need a completely new wardrobe to make a splash in London. *You* have a rail of exquisite dresses, so don't be selfish, Bel!' Her sister was at her most indignant.

She flounced out of the room only to be replaced by a second morning visitor.

'Bel, my darling, I know you're not happy about accompanying Sophia, but I would count it a great favour.'

'I will go, of course, Mama, but I won't be able to stop her buying the most dreadful clothes. She will listen to your advice far more readily than to mine.'

'My dear, Sophia listens to no one, as you well know. And you have such elegant taste—I'm hoping some of it will rub off on her.'

Christabel did not share that hope, but felt it only right she attempt to help. Her mother was looking unusually tired and harassed by the sudden eruption of two youthful and demanding offspring into her hitherto peaceful household.

Within the hour they were in the carriage and on their way to Lady Harriet's favourite modiste. The morning that followed was one Christabel never wished to repeat. Again and again she sought to dissuade the younger girl from unwise purchases: heliotrope was not on the whole an immensely flattering colour; a bonnet sporting six ostrich plumes and a cluster of brightly coloured gemstones might be thought a trifle vulgar; a dress of gauze worn over a transparent petticoat was unlikely to ingratiate her with the most illustrious members of the *ton*. But she was helpless against the onslaught of Sophia in full cry and could only watch in despair as the carriage gradually filled with an array of packages containing the most unsuitable attire.

The clothes had been costly and eaten up most of the very generous allowance bestowed by Lord Tallis and still they had not purchased gloves, slippers, reticules—all the myriad accessories necessary for a young lady about to embark on a social whirl. Christabel's tentative suggestion that they go to the Pantheon Bazaar where she'd heard there were bargains to be had was received with surprising enthusiasm and they drove immediately to Grafton House. Very soon they found themselves immersed in stalls displaying an abundance of coloured muslins, ornate trimmings, silk stockings, fine cambric handkerchiefs, all at astonishing prices. The bazaar was not generally visited by ladies of high fashion, but within minutes of entering the emporium Sophia was exclaiming loudly over the bargains to be had. The only drawback to the shop was its popularity for by noon it was completely full and shopping had become a tedious business of jostling elbows. Both young ladies were heartily relieved when the last piece of lace and the last pair of kid slippers had been chosen. Their relief was short-lived, however, for the increasing crowds made it necessary to wait a considerable time to pay at the final counter.

Sophia had at last reached the head of the queue when Christabel heard a voice that was faintly familiar. She turned her head and caught a glimpse of a stylishly gowned woman holding in her hand a collection of colourful loo masks.

'They will be just the thing, Aunt Loretta, if we go to Vauxhall—and you did promise!' The woman's younger companion was almost jumping with enthusiasm.

'I think you're stretching the word promise, Domino. I said we *might* go.'

But Domino had lost interest in the masks and was staring

instead at Christabel. She darted forwards eagerly and offered her hand.

'Miss Tallis, isn't it? How are you feeling? I'm so sorry about the accident yesterday—I was worried about you.'

'Thank you for your concern, but I'm perfectly well.'

'Richard said that you would be fine and he's always right. He said that you were the coolest of women and unlikely to suffer any disordered feelings. You see, I've remembered his words exactly.'

'What accident, Domino?' her aunt interjected.

'Only a small one, Aunt, a little frightening at the time, but over in a moment.'

She looked from one to the other, a pleased expression on her face. 'I must introduce you immediately. Aunt Loretta, this is Miss Christabel Tallis—I have it right?—such a difficult name for my tongue! Miss Tallis, this is my aunt, Lady Blythe.'

'How do you do,' Christabel responded in her musical voice, 'I'm very happy to meet you.'

Lady Blythe smiled anxiously as she shook hands. 'Domino said nothing to me of an accident.'

'Please don't be concerned—I have taken no harm from yesterday's adventure, as you see.' And she smiled reassuringly at aunt and niece. She had no wish to get this vivacious young girl into any further trouble.

'Is not this shop the most wonderful you've ever seen, Miss Tallis?' Domino's eyes were lit with pleasure.

She glanced around her rapturously and Christabel glimpsed a uniformed footman standing a few paces away already loaded with packages. Lady Blythe saw the direction of her glance and said wryly, 'As you see, Miss Tallis, we have had a busy morning.'

'You know you've enjoyed it as much as I,' Domino protested. 'And I did need to add to my wardrobe, didn't I? I've been invited to so many parties.'

Her aunt smiled indulgently as her niece, still prattling happily, turned to Christabel.

'I've been in London only a very short while, Miss Tallis, but already I must have been to a dozen entertainments. It's been splendid. And Richard has been a wonderful escort. He's been wonderful, hasn't he, Aunt Loretta?' and she turned impulsively to the older lady, her cheeks glowing.

'Lord Veryan has certainly been a good friend to us,' her aunt agreed.

The girl's soft brown eyes were smiling and she looked the picture of happiness. She obviously revered Richard and just as obviously knew nothing about Christabel. He had not told her of their shared history. It was as though he wished to wipe the slate clean and obliterate that part of his life. The Christabel he'd known in his youth had ceased to exist for him. Instead a callous and unfeeling woman, a woman whose emotions were never disordered, had taken her place.

She was saved from making any further conversation by Sophia, who had finally finished paying for her goods. Before Christabel knew what was happening, her sister had seized her hand and was dragging her towards the entrance of the shop without a glance at the couple standing nearby.

'Come, Bel, or we'll be late for luncheon.' Christabel had time only to execute a hasty bow before she was bundled outside.

'Really, Sophia, there is little point in buying smart dresses and clever fripperies if you lack manners to match,' she remonstrated, as they emerged into the fresh air and once more climbed into the waiting carriage.

'I had to get out of that shop. It was so hot that I thought I'd melt. And I must go home this minute and try on all my new outfits.'

Her sister demurred. 'Before we return to Mount Street I'd like to call in at Hatchards to collect the book I ordered. *Mansfield Park* is being spoken of everywhere and I'm most anxious to read it.'

'You can pick the book up tomorrow,' her sister complained. 'At this hour of the day Piccadilly will be blocked with traffic and it will take an age to get home.'

Christabel remained unmoved. 'I particularly wish to begin Miss Austen's novel today and we'll only be in the shop a few minutes. You owe me a little time after this morning, don't you think?'

Sophia looked sulky, but did not dispute further. The traffic was lighter than expected and very soon they were standing outside Hatchards's impressive bow windows. The smell of leather greeted them as Christabel trod briskly across polished wood to a large counter where a stack of volumes of different shapes and sizes was awaiting collection.

Already bored with the errand, Sophia began an immediate prowl around the lines of high-sided bookshelves in the hope of seeking out possible acquaintances. Soon she had disappeared from view so completely that when Christabel went to look for her, she was nowhere to be seen, even in the furthest recesses of the shop. A carriage full of new dresses had been too much of a temptation, Christabel thought, and Sophia must have ordered the groom to drive her home and left her sister to make her own way back. It was a nuisance, but not a disaster. Mount Street was a ten-minute walk away and she had no fear of undertaking the journey on her own.

She began to make her way to the shop entrance, zigzagging around the rows of tall shelves, and was just turning the corner of one particularly high stack of books when she looked up to find Richard Veryan barring her way. For a moment she froze. He was the last person she expected to see. He wore a drab riding cape over a tightly fitting coat of blue superfine and what looked to be a recent purchase, a cut Venetian waistcoat and the palest of fawn pantaloons. His air of elegance was subtly enhanced by the powerful muscularity of a body long hardened by physical activity.

He smiled sardonically as he swept her a bow. 'Good morning, Miss Tallis. I trust I find you well. I hope that you haven't suffered unduly from yesterday's unfortunate incident.'

For a moment she was mesmerised, unable to speak, unable to take her eyes from the figure who stood in her path. It was as though she were seeing him for the very first time. Yesterday his sudden appearance, when she'd imagined him still on the high seas, had sent her mind into disarray. She had been conscious only of those crystal-hard eyes raking her down. Now the full force of his masculine attraction hit her hard. She struggled to find words.

'I'm well, Lord Veryan, thank you, and have suffered no lasting effects,' she managed at last.

'I'm very happy to hear that. I would not have anyone injured because of my lack of foresight. But I could not have anticipated Miss de Silva's actions—it was sheer recklessness, I fear, on the part of my young companion.'

'This is her first visit to London and she can surely be excused,' Christabel returned gently. 'She would not know the regulations governing riding in Hyde Park.'

'She does now, however, and will in future follow them strictly. Then we should go on well enough. Rules are a necessary part of civilised society, don't you think? Myself, I've always placed a good deal of trust in observing them, but I imagine you must know that.'

Christabel said nothing. He was clearly intent on upsetting her.

'You're silent—perhaps you're unwilling to criticise the young lady in question? Rest assured that I've already done so. She's received a trimming she'll not forget. But she has youth on her side and youth has one great advantage, I find—it can learn from its mistakes.'

'I'm sure Miss de Silva will. No doubt you are a proficient teacher, sir,' she replied sharply.

'I trust so. I certainly should be. I was lucky enough in my own youth to have an equally proficient teacher who taught me to learn from my biggest mistake.'

His face was grim and she had an overpowering desire to flee, but he was barring her way and escape was impossible. She steadied her nerves and refused to be intimidated.

'I hardly know the young lady, of course, but she seemed well able to manage her own affairs.'

'She gives that impression to the uninitiated, but to those who know her well,' he said meaningfully, 'the case is otherwise. Her spontaneity is certainly entrancing, but is like to run away with her. She needs someone to exercise a firm control.'

'I hope she sees the situation as you do.'

'And if she does not?'

'Then she will reject that control and simply be herself,' she threw at him.

'Naturally I should have expected you to say that, Miss Tallis. But for the moment I'd forgotten that you are an arch advocate of self-expression, no matter what the cost.'

His smile was belied by the frost in his cold, grey eyes and she felt her stomach twist into knots. It seemed he'd accosted her quite deliberately in order to bait her, but she could not let him ride roughshod.

'You misunderstand me, sir. I was not encouraging Miss de Silva to break rules, simply proposing that everyone must have the freedom to make some mistakes.'

'Ah, yes, you would know a deal about such freedom. Dare I suggest that restraint is a more admirable quality?'

'Restraint and youth do not sit easily together,' she retorted.

'Yet for most they can be negotiated. Dishonour is a powerful deterrent, would you not say?'

She was weary of the cat-and-mouse game he seemed to relish and made to walk forwards. 'If you will excuse me, I am meeting my sister here and would not wish to keep her waiting.'

He made no move to allow her to pass, but instead looked around him mockingly. 'I don't see her. She is certainly nowhere in the shop. Are you sure you were supposed to meet her here?'

'Yes, indeed. She will no doubt be outside.'

'And if she is not, you will have no companion to accompany you home. May I offer my escort?'

'I thank you, but no,' she said hastily, 'I have my carriage.'

'I fear you're out of luck. There was no sign of a carriage on the road when I entered the shop. It must have left without you—but then perhaps Sir Julian Edgerton is close by to take you home?'

She shook her head.

'No? I made sure that he would be. From our meeting yesterday, he seemed a most attentive gentleman. Our untimely descent on you perhaps interrupted an important conversation. I do apologise if this was so—I wouldn't want to frighten him away. Where is he now?'

She was angered by his insinuations and also bewildered. How had he known that Sir Julian was about to propose?

'He is visiting his country estate,' she said in a ruffled tone. 'If you wish to see him, I suggest that you call at his town house in a few days' time. It is in Brook Street, I believe.'

'There you are, Bel. I've been looking for you everywhere.'

Sophia bounced suddenly into view, almost running around the adjacent bookcase and only just preventing herself from cannoning into Richard. He turned round with annoyance; the interview had just been getting interesting. He'd followed Christabel into the shop on impulse, feeling an overpowering need to confront her with the words he'd kept suppressed for so long. Even more compelling had been the need to protect himself from her, to keep her at a safe distance, by wielding ugly recriminations.

'Good gracious, are you who I think you are?'

Sophia had been just twelve when Richard quit England and had only a vague memory of her sister's former fiancé.

'Whatever are you doing *here*?' Sophie continued a trifle too bluntly.

Christabel intervened. 'Lord Veryan is newly arrived in town. We met yesterday in Hyde Park when there was a slight accident. He has been kind enough to enquire how I am, but I think it's time for us to go.'

Richard glanced at Sophia with disfavour. She had never been an appealing child with her insistence on frills and furbelows and the constant preening in every mirror she could find. To his jaundiced eye she looked very little improved. Christabel as a child had been so different—a skinny, reckless tomboy of a girl with a tangle of red hair and freckles to match. She had always been ready for adventure and just as always ready to drag him into whatever trouble she had been brewing.

Looking at her now, a slender vision in eau-de-nil silk, a matching ribbon threaded through those wonderfully fiery curls, he smiled inwardly, forgetting for the moment his purpose in accosting her. No greater contrast between past and present could there be. He remembered the day he'd returned from Oxford to find his one-time playmate transformed, a butterfly fluttering the hearts of all the local beaux. He had gazed at her in wonder, drinking in her beauty, spellbound.

His reverie came to an abrupt end as he became aware of Sophia still scowling at him from a few feet away. With a brief bow, he moved aside for the sisters to make their exit.

'Where were you? I've been an age looking for you,' Sophia scolded as she marched forcefully towards the glass-paned doors. 'The carriage was causing an obstruction and Stebbings has had to move it. We'll have to walk the whole of Picadilly now.'

Christabel made no reply, but moved swiftly along the flagged thoroughfare in deep thought. Richard had appeared in Hatchards at the very time that she'd chosen to call at the shop. It was as though he'd been shadowing her, waiting for

an opportunity to confront her. And it had been a confronta-
tion. She recalled the ice in his eyes and the anger in his voice,
as he sought to remind her of her crime.

And he'd been at pains to emphasise his new-found intimacy with Domino de Silva, while a few hours earlier the
young girl had made it clear that she admired Richard greatly
and that in her eyes he could do no wrong. Christabel didn't
blame her for that idolisation. Richard was the perfect hero for
an adolescent dream—a honed body, a handsome face alight
with intelligence and an air of innate strength, which more
than matched his elegance. And, if she were honest, he was
a hero for more than adolescent girls. When he'd appeared
so suddenly before her, polished and powerful and block-
ing her escape, she'd felt a charge of pure sexual magnetism.
But it was momentary and quickly evaporated as it became
plain that he intended only to distress her. She must not dwell
on his beautiful form and face, nor on his seeming desire to
exact some kind of retribution. Her life would soon resume
its normal peaceful rhythm. Sir Julian was returning and, she
told herself severely, she would look forward to that. By dint
of repetition she was sure she would come to believe it.

Chapter Three

'You've not forgotten that Lady Russell is to collect you at eleven o' clock?' her mother prompted the next morning, whisking through the hall on her way to consult with the housekeeper.

'Lady Russell?' Christabel grappled with the name for a moment.

'Sir Julian has arranged it, has he not? The tickets for Montagu House?'

'Ah, yes, I remember now,' she said heavily, 'He was keen that we view the Marbles that Lord Elgin has brought back from Greece.'

'A stuffy museum *and* Lady Russell all in the same morning,' interjected Sophia as she emerged from the breakfast room in one of the eye-opening ensembles she had purchased yesterday. 'Rather you than me!'

Her mother rounded on her sharply. 'You're becoming far too pert for your own good, Sophia. You must learn to keep a check on your tongue or you will fare badly in society.'

This was an important consideration for an aspiring belle and Sophia looked suitably contrite. 'I'm sorry, Mama, but, from what I hear from friends who are already out, Lady Russell is a gorgon.'

'That's as may be, but you had much better keep your opinions to yourself. And, Christabel, you must hurry. You will need to dress in something a little more demure.' Christabel glanced down at the low neckline and French trimmings of the apricot sarcenet and sighed. Her mother was right. Lady Russell was a stickler for correctness and only a simple day dress of sprigged muslin with a high neck and a matching spencer would satisfy that matriarch.

It was weeks ago that she'd agreed to the visit. At the time she'd been feeling more guilty than usual at her lack of enthusiasm for Sir Julian's company and he'd been so touchingly anxious that she become better acquainted with what small family he possessed that she'd felt forced to consent. Since then she'd acquired a genuine interest in the marble wonders that had travelled all the way from Athens and, were it not for Lady Russell, she would be looking forward to the morning's expedition with pleasure.

Sir Julian's sister was punctual to the minute, an erect figure in a heavy but serviceable barouche, awaiting Christabel outside the Mount Street house with scarcely concealed impatience. The severe grey kerseymere gown and dreary poke bonnet that she wore did nothing to lighten the atmosphere. Her greeting was perfunctory. She was not at all sure that this young woman was a suitable wife for her brother. She was altogether too beautiful, and beautiful women usually meant trouble. And there was that unfortunate business years ago when her name had been bandied around the town as a tease and a jilt by every wicked rattlejaw. Her modest behaviour

since had done much to redeem this unsatisfactory reputation, but still one never knew when old habits would surface.

You only had to look at that hair—wild to a fault. But Julian
was evidently head over heels in love with her and you could
hardly blame him. Men could be very stupid, never seeing
beyond what was in front of their eyes.

'Are you looking forward to viewing the Marbles, Miss
Tallis?' she eventually asked her companion as the barouche
rolled smoothly forwards. Her smile was one of gracious con-
descension.

'Indeed, ma'am, I am. I have been reading a good deal about
them and my interest has been greatly stirred.'

Lady Russell unbent slightly. At least the girl had some intelligence, which was all to the good. It was necessary that
Julian marry a woman who was serious enough to understand and tolerate his charity work. As far as Lady Russell
was concerned, her brother's projects for the labouring classes
remained wholly inexplicable.

'I have learned,' she remarked magisterially, 'that a special
gallery has been built for these statues at a vast cost so we
must hope that they warrant such expenditure.' The faltering
conversation was effectively closed down.

Once the carriage left Mayfair and was bowling towards
Bloomsbury, the roads became a great deal clearer and they
reached the entrance of the British Museum only a few minutes
later than expected. It did not stop her ladyship tutting loudly
at her groom, who had made the journey to Montagu House in
record time and was even now negotiating a difficult manoeu-
vre to bring the carriage exactly to the bottom of the flight of
steps which led up to the impressive panelled entrance.

A steep staircase, a spacious entrance hall and they were

upon the Marbles almost before they realised. Two long white-washed galleries had been constructed for the purpose with exhibits laid out on either side. The monumental size of many of the statues was staggering and both ladies paused on the threshold to adjust their perspective. Then they began a slow inspection of the initial gallery, first down one side and then the other, with Lady Russell insisting on reading aloud every handwritten label the curators had provided.

During this prolonged examination, the room had been gradually filling up and by the time Christabel was ready to tackle the second gallery a considerable crowd had gathered. She looked across at Lady Russell, who appeared weary and a trifle disenchanted, and was not surprised to hear her excuse herself, saying that she would await Christabel in the spacious hall beyond. The carriage, she reminded her severely, would leave promptly at one o'clock.

Christabel nodded assent, happy to be rid of the older woman's irksome presence. With a new sense of purpose she crossed into the adjoining room; almost immediately her attention was caught by the statue of a woman, a large sculpture of Iris which had once decorated the west pediment of the Parthenon.

She stood enthralled, marvelling at the precision with which the intricate folds of the goddess's dress had been carved—the marble seemed to sing out life. The harmony of the carving and the sheer exuberance of the goddess was a joy. Lost in thought as she was, the voice at her elbow startled her.

'It's so sad, isn't it, that she has lost her legs *and* her arms?'

She turned to her questioner. It was Domino, looking freshly minted in primrose-figured muslin and carrying a matching frilled parasol.

'She may not be complete,' Christabel agreed, 'but it doesn't seem to matter. She possesses such enormous vitality, don't you think?'

Domino gave a small laugh. 'What must she have been like as a whole woman, Miss Tallis!'

'Very powerful, I imagine, particularly as she enjoyed such a prominent position on the top of the Parthenon.'

'Poor thing, she must find it very cold in London.'

'No doubt.' Christabel gave an answering smile. 'But if she'd been left to bask in her native sun, we wouldn't have been able to see her today in all her glory.'

'I don't think I would have minded too much,' the younger girl divulged. 'There are so many statues to see and some of them are just fragments. I don't find them particularly inspiring.'

'You didn't wish to come to the exhibition?'

'Not really, but Aunt Loretta said I should as all of London is talking about it. She said that if I'd seen the statues I would be able to join in conversations and not sound too silly.'

'Aunt Loretta has a point.'

'I know, but to be honest I would much rather have gone to Astley's,' she confided naïvely. 'I've heard they keep troops of horses there who can re-enact scenes of war and that there are daring equestriennes who perform the most amazing acrobatics on horseback!'

'I believe so,' Christabel answered her seriously, though she was amused by the young girl's enthusiasm for the less-than-refined pleasure. 'The equestrian ballet of Astley's is famous.'

'A ballet on horseback?' Domino's eyes grew round with amazement. 'I *must* see that.'

'What must you see?'

A man's voice broke through the female weavings of their conversation. It was Richard. He bowed unsmilingly at Christabel. He was looking exceedingly handsome in a claret-coloured waistcoat and light grey pantaloons, which fitted to perfection. The folds of his snow-white cravat were precisely arranged and held in place by a single small diamond stud.

'Miss Tallis says there's an equestrian ballet performed at Astley's. Can we go, Richard?' In her eagerness Domino tugged hard at her companion's immaculate coat sleeve.

'You must ask your aunt to take you. In the meantime, where is your taste for higher culture?' and he waved his hand carelessly towards the statues on either side of them.

'Aunt Loretta will never agree to go to Astley's. It will be much too vulgar for her. Now she is even saying that she doubts we will go to the fireworks at Vauxhall.'

'Then you must be content with more refined pastimes, child.'

Christabel was disconcerted by his tone. He sounded almost like a parent. The surprise she felt must have shown on her face because almost immediately he sounded a softer, even caressing note.

'By all means put Astley's on your list, Domino, and we will make every endeavour to get there.'

She clapped her hands in pleasure watched by Richard, an indulgent expression on his face, but his words were for Christabel.

'Books yesterday, statues today, Miss Tallis. You appear to be an avid follower of cultural pursuits.'

'I partake in them only as much as any other rational woman, Lord Veryan.'

'But then how many women are as rational as you?'

She made no answer, but his eyes remained fixed on her. 'Very few, I make sure,' he continued sleekly.

'I bow to your vast experience, my lord.'

'Hardly vast, but enough—sufficient to suggest that logic and reasoning are not always becoming to a woman.'

She felt herself being forced into another confrontation and when she spoke, her tone was cold but measured. 'I cannot imagine why you should find fault with rationality. My sex is usually criticised for precisely the opposite.'

'In general it's an excellent quality for a female to possess, I agree, but taken to extremes rationality can destroy a woman's natural affections.'

'I think that unlikely,' she retorted.

'Do you? Then consider the case of a woman who decides "rationally" to prefer one man to another on the grounds that he is likely to be a bigger matrimonial prize. When logic leads, a woman's heart is prone to wither.'

Fire began to simmer within the green depths of her eyes and her whole body tensed for combat.

'By that reasoning, sir, only women who are witless can know affection.'

'That's a trifle crude, but the sentiment is not entirely without merit. I think it likely that many men, including Sir Julian Edgerton, would agree with me. By the way, does he accompany you this morning?'

'He is still out of town.'

'Dear me, he appears to spend an inordinate amount of time away from London.'

Christabel took a deep breath and replied as levelly as she could, 'Rosings is a large estate and takes a good deal of his time.'

'Of course, he *would* have to have a large estate.' His expression was sardonic, a trace of a sneer on his unyielding mouth.

Domino looked from one to the other, aware of the tension which crackled between them, but bewildered as to its cause.

'As you appear interested in the trivialities of my life, sir, you may wish to know that I am accompanied this morning by Sir Julian's sister.' Christabel's perfectly sculpted cheeks were flushed an angry pink. 'She is waiting close by so I must beg you to excuse me.'

And with a hasty bow to them both, she walked briskly towards the entrance hall, her mind seething and her form one of unexpressed anger. The frills on her muslin gown tossed as though caught in a tempest and the wayward auburn curls began to tumble out of the restraining satin bandeau she wore. It seemed she was to be followed at every opportunity and forced to submit to any taunt or goad he wished to aim. It was insufferable. She was truly reaping the whirlwind she had sowed all those years ago.

Still standing beside the figure of Iris, Domino wore a puzzled look and her tone was one of concern.

'Do you not like Miss Tallis, Richard?'

'I neither like nor dislike her.'

'I think you made her angry.'

'I would be sorry to give offence, but if she was angry, it was quite unnecessary.'

She frowned at this. 'She was offended and I don't think it was unnecessary. I think she had good reason. You seemed to want to upset her. But why?'

Richard contemplated pretending ignorance, but then said, 'It's an old story and not for your ears.'

'Then you knew her before you came to Argentina—from when you were last in England?'

'I've known her all my life.'

'How is that possible?'

'Her family's estate runs alongside mine in Cornwall. We played together as children—like brother and sister,' he ended drily.

'Then you should be friends.'

'Oh, we were, very good friends.'

'So what happened? Why are you so unhappy with each other now?'

'A betrothal.'

'A betrothal? Whose?'

'My betrothal to Miss Tallis. We were to be married.'

'You were betrothed to Christabel Tallis!' Domino gaped with surprise. 'What happened?'

'We decided that after all we did not suit each other.'

'But if you were both agreed, why are you still so unhappy with her?'

Richard sighed. 'It's complicated.'

'It doesn't seem that complicated to me,' she said with decision. He saw that he would have to tell her the full story or at least enough to satisfy her.

'I was away at Oxford for three years,' he began, 'either at the university studying or staying with friends in the holidays, so I didn't see her for a long time. When I finally returned home to Cornwall, I found her very changed. She'd always been a tomboy, a thin, gawky girl with her dresses usually torn and her hair in a tangle. But now she was this amazingly beautiful young woman. I could hardly believe my eyes the first night I saw her again. She was the toast of the

county, worshipped by Cornish manhood from Penzance to
St Austell—and that's a long way, Domino.'

He paused for a moment, remembering that evening when
he'd walked into the drawing room at Lamorna and found her
waiting, a slender vision of cream lace and gold roses. When
she'd glided forwards and laughingly put her arms around
him in welcome, she'd taken his breath away.

'I suppose I was irritated,' he continued. 'Whenever I visited Lamorna Place I tripped over some lovesick swain clutch-
ing a posy of flowers or reading her the latest bad poem he'd
written in her praise. It was comical, but also annoying. She'd
always been my particular friend and now I was supposed to
share her company with all the fops and dandies from miles
around. So I decided to woo her myself, win the prize and
delight my parents—it was what they'd been hoping for since
we were children.'

'And Miss Tallis?'

'I think she was flattered by my sudden interest. I was a
welcome diversion from the cloying attentions of her local
admirers, but only a diversion—until her come-out at the
next London Season. But she never did come out that year.
Her mother couldn't leave the younger children to travel to
London, so she deputed the task of presenting Christabel to a
relative. Then the relative became ill quite suddenly and the
plans were cancelled. Christy had to resign herself to staying
in Cornwall and it was then that she agreed to marry me.'

'So when did you find out that you had both made a mistake?'

'When she made love with another man.' Richard had not
been able to stop his bitter denunciation.

Domino looked shocked.

'His name was Joshua,' he said acridly, discarding any hope now of keeping the full story from his young admirer. 'My mother had accompanied Christabel and myself to London to buy bride clothes. Instead Christabel purchased a very different item—the attention, for I cannot call it love, of a man I'd thought a friend. She confessed that she'd fallen in love with him. Perhaps she had: he was clever and handsome and the sole heir of a very wealthy uncle. She said that she could no longer marry me. I left for Argentina shortly afterwards. The rest you know.'

Domino considered his story for some time. Christabel Tallis had not seemed the kind of woman who would treat a man so shockingly, but there was no doubt Richard had suffered hurt.

She turned impulsively to him, but her question was tentative. 'It happened such a time ago, Richard, can you not forgive her?'

'There's nothing to forgive,' he said in a breezy voice. 'It's over.'

But it wasn't, he thought, as he escorted his young companion to Gunter's for her favourite elderflower ice. It was far from over. Christabel had come back into his life and the world he'd built for himself had begun to shatter. He remembered how in those early months in Buenos Aires, he'd walked around a stunned man. He'd lost so much, not just the girl he loved, but his entire life. Early one blisteringly hot morning, he'd walked on the beach when the world was still asleep and he was alone. Looking out over the limitless ocean, he'd willed himself back to his beloved homeland. But friends and family had gradually faded from view and he'd been helpless to recall them. He'd borne the rupture calmly, stoically, never allowing a hint of trouble to show, and he'd grown to love Argentina. He'd put down new roots, made new friends, taken new lovers. So why was he allowing such furious resentment to seep into his life and destroy the pleasure of his homecoming? After his scourging from the Tallis affair, he'd become adept at sidestepping deep feeling and for the first time in years strong emotions were crowding in on him. Ever since he'd seen Christabel. His constant need to provoke her, to disturb her, was a signal that he'd never truly overcome her betrayal. He'd simply shut it away. Seeing her afresh had reawakened feelings that he'd thought dead.

His anger was directed as much at himself for still being in thrall to her. If he were to know any peace, he must exorcise that demon and do so as quickly as possible. The lawyers, he'd learned, would be ready within a fortnight and last night he'd written to his mother to expect him shortly. But how to free himself of this unwanted legacy from the past? In the heat of their first unexpected meeting, he'd entertained some wild thoughts. But were they that wild? If he could prove Christabel unchanged, prove that she was the same inconstant woman, surely that would get her from under his skin.

Instinctively he knew that she was not wholly indifferent to him. Her face might remain immobile, but her eyes gave her away. He had the power to rouse this cold and remote woman to strong feeling—anger and love were bedfellows, after all. There was a lingering tie between them, he was sure, and he'd taken every chance to play on whatever jealousy Christabel might feel towards the young girl who walked beside him. He had done so in the hazy belief that he might force her into showing her true colours. But there had to be more. He would have to entice her into his arms, tease her, goad her, until she was ready to say she loved him, ready to be disloyal. Ready to betray Sir Julian Edgerton as she'd betrayed him. The man who had taken her arm so proudly would be forced to recognise her for the jilt she was. And if he could learn the same lesson himself, her power to perturb would be over. He would be free of her—for ever.

The Tallis family ate an early supper, for Christabel and Lady Harriet were engaged to attend Almack's. Christabel felt no joy at the prospect. This morning her pleasure in viewing the Marbles had been spoiled by Richard's antagonism and an evening spent at the exclusive club was no compensation. It would be a tedious few hours although largely effortless. Several glasses of lemonade, a number of country dances, a nod or two at acquaintances and then they would be free to return home. She'd never understood what made the place exceptional, but her mother always held it to be good *ton* to attend regularly and made a point of escorting her elder daughter every week. Sir Julian, too, was a frequent visitor and Christabel derived some comfort at least in knowing that tonight he was safely lodged at Rosings many miles away and she would be free of any threat of a marriage proposal.

She had dressed with some care for the evening. After the unsettling events of the last few days she felt the need to look her best. The emerald silk gown opening to an underdress of the palest green gauze was a stunning creation, her hair flaming in contrast and the green of her eyes reflected in its deepest tones. A low bodice revealed the pale perfection of shapely breasts and shoulders as smooth as alabaster. Without immodesty, she knew from experience that she would attract the attention of most of the men there. Not Richard's, though. He would certainly not be at Almack's. Even in his youth it had been a place he'd always refused to attend, though she had often begged him to be her escort.

She looked across the table at her sister who was drinking soup with exaggerated care, intent on preserving her gown. With a start she realised that Sophia was dressed rather too elaborately for dinner at home and wondered why. The conundrum was soon solved.

'Sophia will be coming with us,' her mother announced with studied carelessness.

'To Almack's?' Christabel asked blankly.

'Yes, of course, to Almack's.'

'But what about vouchers?'

'I have managed to obtain some. Lady Jersey was kind enough to bestow them on me at short notice. She understood the position and wanted very much to make Sophia's acquaintance.'

'Nobody gets tickets for Almack's that quickly, Mama, so you must have known for some time that Sophia was coming to London.'

Her mother made no reply and the ruthless interrogation continued. 'I thought you said that you and Papa had decided only recently that she should visit—in fact, you must have been plotting it together for weeks!' The net seemed to be closing in on her ever more tightly.

Her mother's telltale blush revealed her unhappiness at the deception while Sophia's face was one of untroubled victory.

'Hardly plotting, Bel. Sophia's coming to stay was certainly not part of any grand plan. But when Sir Julian began to grow ever more particular in his attentions to you, it seemed sensible to introduce Sophia to *ton* society a little earlier than we planned. I heard only last week that your brother and sister were on their way, but said nothing. I knew you had a lot on your mind and thought it would be a delightful surprise.'

'Delightful,' Christabel offered drily. 'But do you feel that the dress is quite right for the occasion?'

'And what, pray, is wrong with my dress?' Sophia asked combatively.

Lady Tallis, who had unsuccessfully tried to direct her younger daughter to one of the more modest creations hanging in her wardrobe, interjected gently, 'Christabel has such refined taste, my dear, and she is familiar with what is most suitable for Almack's. Why don't you reconsider the magenta? The rose chiffon would become you so well.'

'The rose is boring and I have no intention of being boring.'

'You won't be that,' Benedict put in unhelpfully, 'the whole world will see you coming at fifty paces.'

'You have no notion of female dress, so hold your tongue,' she spat.

'I have no notion of going to Almack's either so I won't be the one who has to hand out the sunshades,' her unrepentant brother grinned.

'What is this, Benedict, of course you are to come with us,' his mother chided. 'You will need to put on evening dress. I assume that you brought it with you.'

'But not to do the pretty at Almack's,' he grumbled.

After a good deal more in this vein he agreed reluctantly to squire his mother and sisters. Almack's he stigmatised as being the waste of a good evening and issued a cryptic warning that he would be leaving pretty promptly as he had far more interesting prospects in view.

* * *

Almack's was always crowded even at nine o'clock in the evening. The doors shut promptly at eleven and anyone arriving after that time, no matter how important, was barred. The patronesses controlled every aspect of the club with iron fists and Lady Jersey's vouchers had been hard won. In the entrance hall Sophia stopped to preen herself in the Venetian mirror, which hung at the bottom of the red-carpeted stairs, but not for long. Her mother was soon ushering both girls upwards into the main salon, ablaze with a thousand candles hanging from crystal chandeliers and tucked into the wall sconces. People looked curiously at the small party, finding it difficult to believe that this new young woman was Christabel's sister. There could be no greater contrast, one tall, willowy, an ice maiden with flaming hair, the other shorter, rounded and an undistinguished brunette. No wonder the gown had to be magenta. It was Sophia's way of seizing some of the attention that always fell so unfairly to her sister.

In the event neither girl lacked for partners. For some Sophia's was a new face and a likely diversion while for others she promised to be the means of an introduction to the peerless Christabel. Happily she had no notion of this and smiled benignly on the world as she passed down the rows of the country dance on the arm of one partner after another. Benedict had discovered a few choice spirits who had also been coerced into escorting family members and was content for the moment to bide his time. The evening was young and he felt sure that it could only get better.

Only Christabel felt depressed. This night was one like so many others. She smiled gracefully at her partners and diligently performed each dance. Between cotillions and quadrilles she sipped lemonade and made kind conversation with those young damsels sheltering by the wall and too shy to talk to anyone else. But there was emptiness in her heart. Soon it would be time to call the carriage and return home, but for what? In two days' time Sir Julian would return and her future would be decided for ever. If she accepted him, this was one engagement that would have to stick.

A sudden flurry at the top of the stairs made her look up. A small brunette, her dark curls glistening in the candlelight, had just made it through the doors before they were locked. The girl looked around her with animation and then turned to her companion, grasping his arm and pointing out the glittering chandeliers and frescoed ceilings. Christabel drew a sharp intake of breath. It was Richard, of course. Richard, who had never before set foot in this hallowed place, now dancing attendance on the little Spaniard. She watched as though in a dream as he presented Domino first to Lady Sefton, one of the patronesses present that night, and then on to Mr Davenant, Lord and Lady Wivenhoe and the Misses Newcombe. The girl had an entrancing smile, Christabel thought, and though she beamed happily on everyone she met, it was clear that she smiled for Richard alone. *She loves him*—the thought struck her with explosive force. Her stomach began to churn sickeningly, but why she could not understand. Richard had been dead to her for six years. Why should it matter who his fancy now alighted on?

At that moment she was claimed for a country dance. Somehow she managed mechanically to perform the steps without making a mistake. Out of the corner of her eye, she saw Richard and Domino take the floor. He'd always been a graceful dancer and she noticed that in this respect he hadn't changed. Throughout he kept up a lively conversation with his partner and it was evident that he was delighted to be with her. Social rules dictated that they could not stand up together for more than two dances, but when they were not on the floor he talked to her; when she partnered other men, his gaze was never far away. And so it went on, dance after dance, while Christabel watched the clock and prayed for the carriage to arrive. She felt she could not bear to look at them a minute longer and yet her eyes were instinctively drawn in their direction. They made a handsome couple and it was clear that others thought so too. There were many admiring glances and much chatter behind opened fans.

When the orchestra struck up for a waltz she was relieved to be sitting out the dance. For some years she'd been permitted by the patronesses to waltz at Almack's, but Sophia was not in that fortunate position and she had no desire to irritate her sister any further. She had deliberately kept her dance card free so that she could keep Sophia company.

'Miss Tallis, I believe you waltz?'

Richard Veryan stood before her, immaculate in white ruffled shirt and black long-tailed coat. The crisp white folds of his silk neckcloth were tied in a perfect *trône d'amour*. Well-fitting black-satin knee breeches did nothing to disguise the muscular thighs beneath. His attire was that of the most fashionable of London gentlemen, but the lean, tanned face hinted at another story.

Christabel found herself once again struggling to maintain her composure.

His grey eyes, flecked with flint, were fixed penetratingly

on her and without speaking he held out a hand and with the other gestured to the dance floor.

'Thank you, sir,' she said, recovering her wits a little, 'but I do not care to waltz while my sister does not dance.'

Richard glanced indifferently at Sophia, who stared haughtily back at him.

'I'm sure Miss Sophia Tallis would not wish to keep you from enjoying a dance she must know you love.'

It was true. Ever since she'd learned to waltz, she'd treasured the joy of floating light as thistledown across the ballroom, her feet skimming the floor and her whole body responding to the rhythm of the music. Her sister pursed her lips angrily, but said nothing. Richard was still holding out his hand, his cold eyes seeming now to blaze with something akin to fire. Christabel could not understand his persistence, but found herself mesmerised into accepting his invitation.

A slight pressure on her waist and he had led her into the dance. His arms encircled her body lightly at first, as, twisting and pirouetting, they became familiar with each other's paces. They had always danced well together and soon they were in tune, step by step, movement by movement. The music's lush strains trembled through her limbs and she lost herself to its rhythms.

Gradually his arms tightened around her and she was acutely aware of the warmth of his body pressing her close. The heady smell of his scent enveloped her as she was held ever more nearly, his face almost bruising her cheek. Carelessly his mouth brushed the top of her hair and without thinking she melted more closely into his embrace. They were dancing now as one, their bodies a rhythmical caress which shocked those who witnessed it. Yet the power of Christabel's beauty held them spellbound. She looked magnificent, almost other-worldly in her splendour, the green silk of her dress swishing across the floor, little emerald slippers on her feet and that haze of red curls cascading downwards to meet her wonderful white skin.

Her mother, sitting on one of the small gilded chairs reserved for chaperons, looked up and caught her breath in distress. That was surely Richard Veryan!

She had no idea he had returned to England. And Christabel was dancing with him and in a fashion that could only be described as provocative! Richard's hand was curved around Christabel's waist and his face so close to hers that he could, if he'd wished, nuzzle and caress the soft skin almost touching his.

And he did wish. He felt his body hard against this woman he'd loved so well. He felt her soft pliable form fusing with his and rejoiced in the sheer physical exultation that was pulsating through him. He could have danced with her all night and then—no, he could not think like that. It was his mission to entice her and the dance must be part of that. His delight in her proximity was something he must not acknowledge.

The music stopped and for a moment they stood dazed. Then he led her back to the row of chairs, every eye in the room upon them.

'Thank you, Miss Tallis, for a most enjoyable dance,' he said formally.

'It was a pleasure, my lord,' she replied, equally formal.

'We must waltz more—I hope to see you at Almack's again very soon.'

'I fear that is unlikely. I shall not be in London long and I imagine that you will be leaving shortly yourself.'

'Why are you so sure?' and he looked over to where Domino was standing, wide-eyed and apprehensive.

'I beg your pardon, but I thought you would be returning to Cornwall to be with your mother.' Christabel sounded puzzled.

'One can return, and return again—if one has something worth coming back for,' he replied smoothly.

Once more he looked meaningfully across the room at the young girl waiting patiently for his return. Christabel was bewildered. Seemingly he wished her to understand that Domino de Silva was the woman who held his heart, yet just seconds ago he had been dancing with *her* in so intimate a manner that together they'd shocked the assembled company. They'd danced as one body, man and woman, merged in a sensual unity. She'd felt his warm breath so close she could have reached out and tasted it. And now this.

'I do believe that finally I have something to come back for,' he continued, making it impossible to mistake his meaning.

She gathered up all her reserves of dignity and faced him with a studied calm. 'You are indeed fortunate.'

'I think so, Miss Tallis. And I trust that you too will know such good fortune.'

'You are all kindness, sir.'

His answering bow was mocking. With a kiss of her hand, he turned around and walked across the room to Domino, who greeted him with a shy smile and outstretched hands.

'Well!' Sophia was at her elbow. 'You're a sly one. You seem to make a habit of meeting Richard Veryan—you must have known he would be here, but you never said a word. And to see you dancing with him! It was shameless! What would Sir Julian say?'

'It really is none of your business,' Christabel snapped.

'It will be if you disgrace the family again by breaking a second engagement,' her sister retorted.

'There is no second engagement,' she muttered though clenched teeth, 'and rest assured that you would be the last person I'd ask for advice on my conduct.'

'You could do worse. At least I haven't made myself an object of scandal.'

She had an insane desire to scream at Sophia for her spitefulness, but, constrained by the hallowed portals of Almack's, she kept silent, biting her lip so hard that she drew blood.

'What *were* you thinking of, Christabel?' Her mother was at her side, throwing more coals on a fire which was already burning brightly. 'To dance in that fashion with a man, and with Richard Veryan of all people. What would Sir Julian have said?'

Her mother's echo of the earlier taunt breached Christabel's iron control. She broke free from Lady Harriet's clasp and said in a stifled voice, 'I'll not wait for the carriage. I will walk home.'

'But you cannot…' Her mother's words were lost in the distance as she turned swiftly and made for the door.

Richard watched her go. He had been badly disturbed by their dance. It had thrilled him to take Christabel's glacial beauty in his arms and mould it to his desire. The feeling of her body against his still resonated. While they'd danced, the ardent girl of yesterday had broken through that frozen surface—and he had been the one to melt her. She was a magnificent creature and he had gloried in the moment. What was she doing contemplating a mediocre marriage with a milk-and-water nonentity? But he must think objectively, he told himself, and objectively his plan was working. He should be pleased. He had stirred the embers of passion in her and soon he would awake such a frenzy of feeling that she would be desperate to know his love. He would have proved her inconstancy and be free to walk away. That moment was a little way off, but he should be satisfied with what he'd achieved that night. He wasn't sure why the victory felt forlorn.

Chapter Four

'It's time I took you home, Domino.'

Richard's tone was decisive. Once Christabel had left, he had no inclination to remain at Almack's and was anxious to return the girl to her aunt's care. Loretta Blythe had been suffering from a chill for some days and this evening had finally succumbed to a fever and taken to her bed. It was inconvenient. He'd hoped to dispense with his escort duties before now, not least because Domino showed no sign of tiring of his company. He'd expected that once fully launched into the delights of London society she would cease to have an interest in him. Instead, the wider she spread her acquaintance, the more she seemed to cling.

Having reached Lady Blythe's house, Richard stepped into the hallway and made ready to wish Domino goodnight, but instead of taking the hand he held out, she raised herself on to her toes to reach his cheek and planted a gentle kiss. Seriously disconcerted, he remonstrated with her.

'You mustn't do that, Domino. Remember that I stand in

your aunt's place. You must think of me as a friend—an elder brother, if you will.'

'I don't see why,' she exclaimed rebelliously. 'You're by far the most attractive man I know!'

'I thank you for the compliment, but I'm not a suitable partner for you.'

She shook her head as if to block out his words. 'I don't believe that. You think me too young to love truly, but you're wrong.'

'I am eleven years older than you and my situation is not a happy one.'

'You mean that you're still in love with Christabel Tallis.'

Surprise rendered him silent.

'You see, I have her name at my fingertips. How could I not? She is a truly beautiful woman and I can't blame you for caring for her still.'

There was a sparkle of tears and her voice was that of a chastened child. He felt a deep sympathy for her.

'My relationship with Miss Tallis should not concern you,' he rebuked her gently. 'The situation I referred to was my father's death. In a very short while I must return to Cornwall. My mother needs support and I have to get to grips with the management of the estate. It's been allowed to drift since my father's death and that can't continue.'

'I understand,' she breathed eagerly. 'Of course you must go to your mother. But I can wait until you're settled. Then perhaps you'll invite me to Madron Abbey. I would love to see your home.'

'It will be a great pleasure to show both you and your aunt around. But you will come as a guest, Domino, not as a future bride.'

The girl lowered her head, a mulish expression on her face. Baffled by her obstinacy, Richard spoke more bluntly than he intended.

'I am truly sorry that you have feelings I cannot reciprocate, Domino, but you must be sensible. You're no longer a child. You have built a fantasy and started to believe in it. For your own sake, you must dismiss it from your mind. In time you will find the man that is right for you.'

'I have found him,' she said, gulping down unshed tears, 'but he is too stupid to see.'

He strode to the front door, but before he could open it, she called out to him from the marble balustrade above, 'Will I see you at Richmond Park tomorrow?'

'Richmond? Ah, yes, the Wivenhoes' alfresco lunch, otherwise known as a picnic.'

'I believe the Park is charming—such a large space of countryside and so near the city. You *are* coming?' she asked anxiously.

He didn't answer directly. 'I'm sure you'll find your aunt a great deal better in the morning and she'll be looking forward to accompanying you to Richmond.'

He felt too unsettled by their conversation to return immediately to his hotel. He had decided from the outset that he would put up at Brown's rather than opening the house in Grosvenor Square. A solitary stay amid its lonely expanses did not appeal and the few days he planned to be in London would have meant unnecessary disruption for its skeleton staff. But tonight the hotel looked just as uninviting and he needed to clear his head. He would walk a while in the evening air and then look in on one of the gentlemen's clubs that lined St James's Street.

He'd been scrupulous never to suggest that he could be more than a friend to Domino, but he still felt guilty for causing her unhappiness. It hadn't helped that he'd been her constant escort since they'd arrived in London. If he'd not spent so much time with her, what had been an incipient affection on board ship would have been nipped in the bud. But Lady Blythe had shown herself only too willing to delegate her duties whenever possible and now the wretched woman had taken to her bed. Surely she would be better in the morning.

Richard's resolve that he would no longer be Domino's escort was broken almost as soon as it was made. A loud banging at his door early the next morning woke him from a deep sleep. It seemed as though he'd hardly been to bed and his head ached from too much brandy the night before. But the hotel porter, breathing heavily in the doorway from his climb up the stairs, was waving a badly folded sheet of paper under his nose and clearly expected an answer.

'Who brought this?' Richard asked blearily.

'A groom, my lord.' The porter was disapproving.

'Whose groom?'

'That I couldn't say, my lord.' The porter held his face aloof, expressing in no uncertain manner that Brown's Hotel thought poorly of such early morning intrusions.

Richard pulled back the curtain better to read the note and groaned as the morning light flooded the room.

'Get me some coffee, for heaven's sake.'

'Certainly my lord. Shall I tell the groom to wait?'

'If he wants an answer. But get me that drink.'

He spread the crumpled note out and saw at once that it was from Domino. He knew almost without reading that it would be a plea to accompany her that morning to the Wivenhoes' picnic. It seemed that her aunt was still not feeling well enough to undertake a long drive. And Domino wanted so much to see Richmond Park. Could Richard please come and this would be the very last time she would ask, she promised. Aunt Loretta had signalled her willingness for Richard to be her escort.

I have no doubt she has, he thought savagely. He hardly knew Domino's aunt, but from his few meetings with her she seemed to be the sort of woman for whom ill health, as long as it were not too severe, was entirely beneficial.

In an hour he had washed, shaved and dressed, and presented himself in Curzon Street complete with hired curricle. Domino had evidently been watching at the window for she appeared almost immediately, tripping lightly down the front steps, her face glowing with pleasure. Her patent delight in going on the expedition almost reconciled him to the prospect of attending an event he'd hoped to escape.

For Christabel there was no escape: she would have to join the family party. She sat at the breakfast table, listlessly toying with a piece of toast and looking tired and pale in the harsh morning light. Her mother had accepted the Wivenhoes' invitation on her behalf weeks ago and at the last moment her siblings had been hurriedly included. Her heart felt leaden. She was certain that Richard would be there, squiring his new love and flaunting his happiness. She would have to endure their close proximity for hours without giving the slightest hint of discomfort. It would be necessary to put on a guise not only for her fellows, but also for her family.

Her mother was worried, she knew. Late last night after

Sophia had danced her fill at Almack's and the two had returned home to Mount Street, Lady Harriet had tiptoed into the bedroom. Christabel had pretended sleep and not answered her mother's anxious query. Instead she had lain silent and still, the tears pricking at her eyes and her heart a confusion of pain. She didn't understand what Richard was doing nor even why she felt so deeply upset by his conduct. It was evident that he'd not forgiven the broken engagement. But surely his humiliation could not still be so raw that he needed to wage a war against her. Yet that was exactly what was happening. One minute he was angrily haranguing her for past crimes, the next he was caressing her—with his smile, his voice, even his body. When last night she'd danced with him so freely, she had been careless of gossip, careless of her reputation. She had given no thought to guarding her feelings and she'd allowed herself to desire. She'd allowed him to stir emotions within her that she'd schooled herself never to feel again and now today she would have to face him once more. She would have to put on the performance of her life.

'Where's the ham?' Benedict demanded as he breezed into the breakfast room and searched the side table anxiously. He looked fresh and full of energy, despite having slept little.

'Bel, where's the ham? Sophy, you've eaten it all,' he accused as his younger sister appeared in the doorway, elaborately dressed in a bright green-velvet spencer over daffodil-yellow silk.

'I've had a great many things to do other than eating breakfast, you stupid boy. If you want ham, ring the bell for more.'

'Who's stupid? At least I don't look like a parrot,' he said, gesturing to Sophia's preferred apparel for driving in Richmond Park.

'Someone should have told you that making personal remarks is offensive.'

'Someone should have told you that dressing like a pantomime is even more offensive.'

'Do stop, both of you!' Christabel's quiet voice intervened, the steely tone surprising them into silence.

'Hoity-toity,' said Benedict half under his breath. 'By the way,' he offered as he sat down at the table, his plate groaning with devilled kidneys and a couple of eggs he'd unearthed, 'd'you know what they're saying in the clubs?'

'The rubbish that men bandy amongst themselves is of no interest to us,' Sophia said haughtily.

'It might be since it concerns a very close neighbour of ours.'

Both sisters looked at him, Christabel's face devoid of expression, but even paler than before.

'Rick Veryan, Richard. You saw him last night at Almack's?'

'Of course we saw him.' Sophia was impatient.

'He was with that pretty, dark-haired girl. She's from Argentina.'

'We know.' Sophia's tone was getting dangerous.

'Bet you didn't know that the odds are mounting on his marrying the girl within the year. Can't be any earlier—he's in mourning—bad *ton*.'

'What do you know of bad *ton*?'

'It might surprise you, Miss Superior, just how much I do know. Anyway a lot of money was changing hands last night, betting on the marriage. Lucky old Rick, eh? Comes back from some outlandish place and walks straight into a title and now a fortune.'

His sisters looked blankly at him.

'Loaded,' he said succinctly. 'That's the word. Full of juice and a good looker too. What more could a man ask? I talked to her myself last night. Introduced by the *grande dame*, Mrs Drummond-Burrell. I think she thought Domino—what a name—was in need of younger company.'

'She certainly got it with you,' Sophia said derisively.

'And she enjoyed it, may I say.' He ruminated for a while, chewing thoughtfully on the last kidney. 'Taking little thing, I thought, though she never quite mastered the steps of the cotillion.'

'And you, of course, are the supreme exponent of the dance.'

Christabel got up swiftly, unable to bear her siblings' bickering a minute longer. Benedict's words had washed away her earlier resolve. How could she possibly keep an impassive countenance when she knew for sure that Richard was planning to marry? She would make her excuses. The family must go without her.

'What's the matter, Christabel?' It was Sophia stopping her at the door. 'Can't face seeing your old beau getting wed? Why should it matter to you? After all, aren't you marrying Sir Julian?'

Benedict gaped. He knew little of the events of six years ago, having been away at school, and had not realised the effect his news might have. But it was Sophia's words that cut Christabel most deeply. In her spite, her sister had arrowed straight to the question which was causing her such agitation. Why *did* it matter so much to her that Richard was to marry? She must prove that it did not. She must prove Sophia wrong. There would be no evasions—she would go to the picnic.

It seemed that the Wivenhoes could not have chosen a better day for their alfresco party. An almost cloudless sky and an unusually warm April sun enabled their guests to view the beauty of the park from open carriages. Herds of red and fallow deer grazed undisturbed in a pastoral landscape of rolling hills, grassy slopes and woodland gardens. The fresh untouched green of springtime already clad most of the ancient trees and beneath their light shade shimmered daffodil gold. The company drove leisurely through this sylvan setting before arriving at a central pagoda where they were to be served refreshments.

Christabel, her mother and sister were soon ensconced on its terrace, sitting comfortably on a padded *chaise* and gratefully sipping tea. Servants bustled to and fro, some bringing additional cushions and blankets for the older members of the group, and others plates of dainty sandwiches and small iced cakes. Sophia made ready to plunder the dish of madeleines left temptingly on their table.

'What a beautiful place,' her mother murmured to her hostess as she passed by. 'And such a wonderful day!'

'Indeed—it seems that summer is already with us!' Lady Wivenhoe happily mingled among the knot of people gathered on the terrace.

Christabel hardly heard them. The cream muslin gown she wore, trimmed with delicate chartreuse lace, might pay homage to the season, but her spirits remained locked in winter. She felt frozen in time, yet her mind was never still, never at peace. She thought she might be going mad. For the hundredth time she tried to understand why in that faraway summer she'd acted as she had. Richard had meant so much to her and yet, with hardly a thought, it seemed, she'd returned his ring and thrown herself at a man who even then she'd suspected was not to be trusted. Why, oh, why had she done that?

Only the intoxication of first sexual awakening could explain the wilful breaking into pieces of the jigsaw of her life. But it was not quite the first awakening, was it? There was that evening in Cornwall when she and Richard had thrown themselves into the sea together. They'd been just a little crazy and the swim had sparked something deep and elemental between them, or so she'd thought. But almost immediately he'd turned away. He'd not wanted that intimate bond and she'd been left bewildered, ashamed of the physical ache that had taken hold of her. And then the trip to London with all its glamour, all its glories, had pushed everything else out of her mind. Joshua had swum into her presence, a man who was more than willing to set her body alight. She had loved him dreadfully. No, she corrected herself, she had lusted for him dreadfully. And lust had its own shameful penance. She thought she'd paid that price, but now, it seemed, she must continue to pay.

In the distance she could see Domino laughing and prattling with Richard. On occasions he responded in a similar vein, but there was a serious expression on his face which seemed at odds with the frolicking of his younger companion. At length the girl seemed to grow tired of entertaining him and turned to Benedict, who had just then emerged at her side and was making ready to reintroduce himself. When the two young people began to stroll together across the greensward towards King Henry's mound, the highest point of the park, Christabel thought that Richard looked almost relieved. How strange. But she'd probably imagined it.

Sophia, meanwhile, was maintaining a critical commentary on her fellow guests as they strolled along the intersecting pathways which met at the pagoda.

As each new costume passed beneath the balcony, it duly

received the full force of her disapproval. Her own ensemble had attracted a mixed response and she was still smarting from some of the remarks she'd overheard. Her mother, anxious to restore her to good spirits, extended a comforting arm but in doing so caught her hand in the intricate pattern of the lace tablecloth and spilled the contents of her teacup on to the disputed outfit.

'Mama, just look what you've done—how clumsy!'

'I am sorry for the accident, Sophia, but your rudeness does you no credit,' her mother reproved.

For once Sophia looked abashed. Her nerves were on end. She had dreamed of making her mark in *ton* society, but so far society had shown an entire lack of interest. This morning she had tried particularly hard with her *toilette*, but it appeared that this effort was still not enough. To add to her misery her elder sister sat next to her, seemingly serene and unruffled, but looking effortlessly lovely and attracting frequent glances of open admiration from the other guests.

'Come with me,' Lady Tallis urged, making for the small cloakroom at the rear of the pagoda, 'we must sponge your dress immediately.'

Sophia trailed miserably behind her and Christabel was left alone with her thoughts. But not for long. The sound of firm footsteps on the stairway leading to the balcony made her look up.

'I trust I see you well, Miss Tallis.'

'Thank you, Lord Veryan, I am most well,' she answered curtly.

'And how are you enjoying Richmond Park?' he pursued.

'It is very beautiful.'

'You have seen it only by carriage? It is even better viewed at close quarters.'

She nodded briefly, but said nothing, averting her glance. His shapely legs encased in well-fitting breeches and riding boots of dazzling gloss were an unnecessary distraction.

'If you would care to take a stroll, I would be happy to escort you.' He was smiling and for once the grey eyes smiled with him.

'Thank you, but I have already walked a distance around the park,' she lied.

'Then you are before me.' A slight flush crept into his lean cheek as he recognised the snub.

'It would appear so.'

He had been studying her from a distance, seen the sadness in her face and felt his determination waver. But her flagrant rejection of courtesies hardened his heart again and spurred him once more into attack.

'I'm surprised by your energy. I would have thought you had little left after last night's magnificent display of dancing.'

'I am not such a poor creature.' And the flash in the emerald eyes was unmistakable. He remembered well that indomitable spirit and once more his heart softened a little.

'You were never a poor creature, Miss Tallis,' he said quietly. 'Far from it, as I recall. I still have the scars to prove it!'

She looked at him, surprised.

'I spent my childhood following you,' he offered. 'Jumping rocks, climbing trees, hacking my way through woods. It was a tough training.'

Her face broke into the shadow of a smile, the troubles of the present for the moment cast aside.

'And were you always the follower?'

'Always. I rarely saw more than a tangle of red curls in the distance.'

Her smile broadened. 'I was always that far ahead?'

He looked quizzically at her. 'There were times when I got to see the back of two skinny brown legs, but never much more.'

'Why did you follow me if it meant suffering scars?'

'Why wouldn't I? Life was a daily adventure and the scars were simple ones. Childhood was the easy part. It was growing up that was difficult.'

Her smile vanished. 'How sad it is that we cannot stay children,' she almost blurted out.

'Unfortunately we cannot. Nor can we undo life.'

'But surely we can start again.' Their reminiscence had emboldened her and her voice now held a definite plea.

'I fear not,' he said sternly. 'We are prisoners of the life we make and we must live with that knowledge.' His face had entirely lost its earlier warmth.

'I cannot agree,' she said vehemently. 'That would be to underestimate the human spirit and its capacity for change.'

'I have never underestimated *you*, Miss Tallis.'

His words were oblique, but she knew well their meaning. Nothing had altered and she felt sick to her stomach. He was still her implacable enemy.

'Nor I you, Lord Veryan,' she managed at last.

'It seems that we are agreed on one thing at least.'

'It matters not to me whether we agree or disagree. If you will excuse me...'

And with that she rose in one fluid movement, pushed back her chair and was tripping down the steps before he realised her intention. The breeze caught her mane of red curls and tangled them wildly into a fiery haze. He felt a momentary madness to rush after her and take hold of that hair, smooth it, caress it, cover it in kisses. It deserved to be worshipped.

'Richard? I thought it must be you. I am very pleased to see you again. You were at Almack's last night, I believe, but there was no opportunity to speak to you.'

Lady Tallis had appeared from the rear of the pagoda and was now standing beside him looking, despite her words, not at all pleased. She had glimpsed the figure of Christabel in the distance walking rapidly away towards the lake and drawn her own conclusions. In her short absence the sky had begun to cloud alarmingly.

'Lady Harriet! How good to see such an old friend.' Richard felt genuine pleasure at meeting the woman who for much of his life had been a second mother to him.

'I have to admit some surprise at seeing you in London,' Lady Tallis returned. 'I had no idea you were in the country.' Her tone verged on reproof. 'But naturally I am delighted that you have returned safely. I make no doubt that the voyage was a testing one. Your mother must be overjoyed.'

He looked a little self-conscious, but felt there was no point in dissembling.

'She will have learned only recently that I landed safely.'

Lady Tallis raised her eyebrows. 'Forgive me, but should you not have apprised her of that fact immediately?'

'I've been a little delayed in London, but intend to leave for Cornwall within the week. By now she will have had my letter telling her to expect me shortly.'

'I see,' she said thoughtfully, though in truth she did not. Whatever could have kept him in London? She had heard gossip about a young woman from Buenos Aires, someone he had supposedly escorted to England, but that surely would not have prevented him making for home as soon as he was able.

She fixed him with a severe expression. 'Anne will be waiting in some anxiety for you.'

She felt strongly that he should be with his mother in Cornwall and almost as strongly that he should not be in London upsetting Christabel. Particularly not at this delicate moment when she was poised to accept Sir Julian.

A sudden clap of thunder shook the pagoda roof and in seconds shattered the gentleness of the April morning. A moment later shards of rain were beating on the woodwork and bouncing off the grass. The party on the balcony hastily decamped to the back of the pagoda for shelter, but Lady Tallis bethought herself of Christabel, under the open skies and without protection.

Richard was before her. He grabbed one of the umbrellas presciently provided by Lady Wivenhoe for her guests and ran down the steps, striding rapidly in the direction he had last seen Christabel heading. On the way he passed a furious Benedict and a joyful Domino. The rain had obliterated Benedict's carefully crafted hair style *à la* Brutus to the huge amusement of his companion. Despite being severely buffeted by the sudden tempest, her peals of laughter rang out across the park.

Richard ignored the noisy pair and hurried on. He found Christabel in minutes, standing motionless by the waters of the storm-tossed lake. She was drenched, her skin translucent and gleaming beneath the downpour, and the curves of her lithe figure apparent through the sodden muslin of the once-beautiful dress. She turned at that moment and her face wore such a look of unhappiness that he wanted to take her into his arms there and then and put a stop to the nonsense he had started. But he knew well that beyond the fragility lay pure steel. The deep-green eyes flashed anger at him and bade him keep his distance just as surely as if she had spoken.

Mutely he offered the shelter of the umbrella. Even she had to smile at that ineffectual gesture. She could not become any wetter.

'Thank you for the thought, Lord Veryan. I fear, though, that you are a little late in coming to my rescue.'

There was more meaning to her words than the social nicety she expressed. He looked at the rain-soaked figure before him, his gaze lingering unwillingly on her form. The long shapely legs and the soft swell of her breasts were clearly visible through the transparent muslin and he knew desperate desire. He moved towards her as though in a dream.

She remained where she stood, unflinching. She saw his arms slowly reaching out towards her and then her long, cold fingers were held tightly within his, sending a warmth coursing through her body until she was tingling from head to toe, from her saturated slippers to the riot of wet curls framing her face. They stood, body to body, for what seemed an age. She felt her pulse beating tumultuously and her limbs tremble as the hard planes of his body pressed against soft flesh. Wave after wave of flaming heat swirled through every small part of her, melting resistance, dissolving protest. His hands were on her waist, pulling her urgently towards him, his body even closer, even harder against hers. Now his hands were sliding upwards and over her breasts, cradling them, brushing at their fullness and sending swirls of shocked pleasure spiral-

ling through her. Onwards and his hands were cupping her
cheeks, tipping her face to meet his. She looked into his eyes
and drowned, drowned in pools of molten grey.

'Christabel,' he began, the soft whisper of his voice flowing through her and reaching to her heart. 'Christabel, I—'

'Christabel! Come quickly.' It was her mother's urgent tones.
'We must get you home immediately or you will become ill.'

Lady Tallis was hurrying towards them, waving yet another
umbrella. The moment of intimacy was at an end, diffusing
itself amid the misty rain.

Christabel's hands slipped from his and she walked away,
leaving him to curse her power and his weakness. This was
not what he intended, to be caught in the web of his own spinning. He must subdue this wretched, uncontrollable desire that
once more threatened to tear him apart. He must stay aloof
even while he continued to entice her into betraying herself.
There were only a few days left to accomplish his plan and
every one of those must count.

By now Lady Tallis had reached his side and was observing him with disapproval.

'Miss de Silva is ready to leave, Richard. I understand that
you are her escort?'

'You are right to remind me of my duties, Lady Harriet,' he
replied stiffly and began to make his way back to the pagoda.

Christabel caught his words on the air and was deeply puzzled. Could he really be speaking of his future wife when he
talked of 'duties'? And if he were promised to Domino de
Silva, why had he allowed himself just now to hold her so long,
to touch her so intimately? During their scandalous dance at
Almack's she'd imagined for a moment that he felt the same
attraction as she. But only for a moment. His hurtful rejection

had soon disabused her. This time, though, she could not be mistaken. There had been a charge so powerful between them that she was left dazed. Naked desire—that's what she'd felt. Not even the errant Joshua, in her days as a green girl, had aroused such fervour in her. And it was Richard, a man she'd once dismissed as worthy only to be a friend, who'd provoked it. Nothing made sense. Richard today must be a very different man to the one she'd once known—or maybe she'd never really known him. Perhaps she'd been too young, too inexperienced, to recognise what might have been. The irony of the situation hit her hard. It seemed that she could feel passion for this man, a passion that shook her to the very core, but only now that he was promised to another woman.

She thought back to the moment when she'd first seen Richard on his return from the university. He had grown into a dashing young man, a figure far superior to any of her local suitors and she was no longer the skinny, freckled tomboy he'd known from the past. She'd watched with amusement his stupefied expression when he'd first caught sight of her and knew instantly that she had captivated him. His jealousy of the gaggle of admirers who daily haunted Lamorna was evident and she thought guiltily of how she'd enjoyed playing one man off against another. In her defence she was hardly more than a child and the game was a heady one. The distant cousin who was to present her had fallen seriously ill and her planned come-out had not materialised. The excitement of having young men vie for her favours was a pleasing compensation. Richard's courtship had been swift. He'd capitalised on their long childhood friendship to infiltrate her life with ease, and in no time he'd succeeded in banishing his rivals and filling the centre of her world. Suddenly she was engaged and unsure of quite how it had happened. It seemed natural to be promising to spend the rest of her life with him, but also something of an anticlimax. She'd been exhilarated by the excitements of the chase and revelled in the handsome and vigorous man he'd become, yet she knew him almost too well. There were no secrets, or so it seemed, no concealed feelings, no hidden fire.

Until, that is, that one evening in the cove. In her memory she retraced their steps that night. They'd walked out together after an early dinner, escaping the last frenetic preparations for the morrow when they would travel to London in company with Lady Veryan. Christabel was to stay at the Veryans' town house and Richard's mother was to supervise her purchase of bride clothes, her own mother being unable to leave her younger siblings for any protracted period.

It had been a beautiful evening in early summer and they'd sauntered at dusk towards the sea along a lane already heavy with hawthorn. Very soon the granite rocks and soft white sand of their beloved cove came into view. The sea was flat calm and Richard had begun to skim stones along the surface of the water. She had joined in, trying to make her stones bounce further. It was an old game of their childhood. The competition between them grew fierce and he shouted with delight when he finally made an unbeatable shot. Beneath the newly polished surface, he was still not much more than a boy. With mischief in her eyes, she'd challenged him to another contest from their childhood: who could swim out the furthest without pausing for breath. He'd demurred; they were not dressed for the water and in any case it hardly seemed proper. In answer, she'd stripped off her clothes down to her chemise, leaving Richard staring in wonderment at the lithe, willowy figure standing so close to him. Then he had been seized by the same madness and was stripped and plunging into the cool water before she had time to reach the sea's edge. They had swum out until they were both exhausted and then drifted lazily back towards the shore, the waters around them silvered by the moon newly risen in a clear sky. She was floating beside him and on impulse it seemed he'd caught hold of her, encircling her waist with his arms and tangling his face in her salt-soaked curls. The feel of his hard, male body against hers took her breath away and she knew a frantic desire to hold him close to her, to meld her body to his. Her legs looped around him and their flesh met in a mutual caress. Even now she grew hot thinking of it.

But the moment was over almost as soon as it arrived, the spark extinguished, and they were scrambling up the beach and into their clothes as though pursued by the Furies, ashamed it seemed of that instant of burning connection. The next day they had left for London and a round of parties, routs, ridottos, balls, such as she'd never before encountered: a kaleidoscope of pleasure which took over her life. As an affianced woman she'd enjoyed the freedom it conferred, freedom to talk unchaperoned with other men, freedom to dance and even to flirt with them, and freedom to meet a Joshua.

A magnificent rout was to be held that evening at the Seftons' London mansion, a short distance from Mount Street. Sophia, insatiable as always for *ton* society, was greatly excited at attending such a prestigious event. It was sure to afford her a splendid hunting ground for potential partners. The torrential rain had done Christabel little harm other than a ruined dress, but she was grateful that it served as an excuse for staying home that night. She was more than happy to spend a quiet evening by herself when the alternative was the painful spectacle of Richard and Domino together. She was lying curled on her bed, flicking through back numbers of *Lady's Magazine*, when her mother slid quietly into the room.

'Have you seen these extraordinary models, Mama? They must be at least ten feet tall,' she said with an attempt at gaiety. The emaciated females depicted were so long and thin as almost to disappear off the page.

Her mother smiled slightly. 'Extraordinary indeed! They would be quite terrifying to meet in the flesh.'

She sat down on the bed and took her daughter's hand. 'I came to say, Bel, that I won't be going to the Seftons' rout tonight. There is little need for my presence: their house is within easy walking distance and Benedict can act as escort to his sister for the evening. It won't do him any harm to take on a little responsibility while he's enjoying his holiday. And it will give us the chance to have a comfortable coze.'

Christabel's heart sank; an evening spent alone with her mother was the last thing she wanted. Pressing her hand to her forehead in a gesture of pain, she hoped that she looked convincing.

'I'm so glad you're staying home, Mama, I'm not feeling at all the thing. I must have caught a chill in that downpour.'

Her mother looked suspicious and glanced pointedly at the magazines her daughter had been devouring. Christabel redoubled her efforts.

'I've been trying to distract myself with these,' she murmured, leafing through them with a weary motion, 'but without much success. I feel so hot—I think I may be developing a fever. It's best if I retire to bed early and try to sleep it off.'

Her mother's expression remained sceptical, but without another word she turned to go, quietly shutting the door behind her. It was unlikely that Lady Harriet would believe in her illness, but Christabel was beyond caring. After the day's events, her mother's gentle enquiries would be the last straw. Until Richard arrived in London, her future path had been clear, if uninviting. The time had come for her to step out of her sister's way and there had been a simple choice: wed a good man who loved her or remain a spinster without consequence or respect.

For years she'd kept at bay even the most determined of suitors. A glacial reserve had served her well, but now it had been ruptured. She had begun to feel again. The dance at Almack's, the encounter by the lake, had begun an unstoppable thaw which threatened to trigger an avalanche of feelings she must not entertain. Today by the lakeside she had known no reserve. She had responded ardently to her body's impulses, she had throbbed with desire for Richard to possess her. How truly shocking! But *his* conduct was even more shocking. He was not hers to be possessed and yet he'd sought her out, danced with her as though he could have danced her into bed—she blushed deeply at the thought— embraced her, caressed her, imprinted her with his passion. And at the very same time he'd used every possible opportunity to taunt her with his new-found love, the girl it appeared he was ready to make his wife. It had to be part of his plan to pay her back for betraying him—there was no other explanation. No matter how softly he spoke or how enamoured he appeared, he was intent on exacting a penance from her. The thought overwhelmed her. She felt as though a giant hand had descended out of nowhere and squeezed every vestige of life from her heart and her body. She was no longer the woman who had bid Sir Julian farewell just a few days ago and she dreaded meeting him again.

Sir Julian, meanwhile, was looking in vain for his beloved at the Seftons' rout. He had despatched his business at Rosings as swiftly as he could and returned to London in time to attend the evening event. He knew that Christabel had been invited and was hoping that he would have the chance to talk privately with her.

He had unfinished business and was anxious to settle it as soon as possible. He had no doubt of her answer—she had made it plain that he was her preferred suitor—and had not her sister called him Christabel's fiancé, making it clear that the Tallis family expected an imminent betrothal. But he wanted their relationship to be made firm and public. He was a man who liked an ordered life and was looking forward to planning their future together.

'How good to see you back so soon, Sir Julian!' It was Sophia, looking a little less exotic this evening in rose-pink lustring.

Sir Julian searched his memory, for he was sure he should know this young woman.

'Sophia Tallis, Christabel's sister,' she helped him out.

'Why, of course. I am very pleased to make your acquaintance again, Miss Sophia.' Sir Julian sounded genuinely glad to see her. If she were here, then Christabel would not be far away.

'And how was your visit to Rosings?'

'Busy, very busy,' Sir Julian mused, 'but nevertheless restful. I find the house has an aura of great tranquillity about it.'

'Indeed, yes,' she said encouragingly. 'I understand that its atmosphere is most mellow. I read in *Ackermann's Repository* that it is one of the oldest houses in England.'

Sir Julian's interest increased. 'I knew that certainly but I had not realised that Rosings had been featured in such a well-known journal.'

'You are too modest, Sir Julian. You must know that you own a most famous property,' Sophia cooed.

Feeling that the subject had now been exhausted, Sir Julian was eager to discover his beloved's whereabouts.

'Christabel?' Sophia responded carelessly. 'She's not here this evening.'

'How is this? Surely she was invited?'

'Naturally she was invited, but she didn't care to come.'

Sir Julian's well-bred eyebrows rose slightly and Sophia saw her chance.

'You must know that Christabel is invited everywhere, Sir Julian. She is the toast of the *ton*, I believe. She picks and chooses as she wishes.'

'I must admit I am a little disappointed. I returned from Rosings today on purpose to see her and was sure she would attend the rout.' He breathed a small sigh and looked slightly wounded.

'She probably didn't give a thought to your being here tonight. She isn't the most reliable of people.'

'Miss Tallis has always been most scrupulous about keeping appointments,' Sir Julian said a trifle sharply.

Sensing that she might have gone a little too far, Sophia carefully backtracked. 'Ah, now I recall—she was not feeling too well earlier this evening. She must have thought it best to stay at home.'

'Not well? How is this? She was perfectly well when I last saw her.'

'There's nothing to worry about, I assure you. The family attended a picnic today in Richmond Park and we were all caught in the rain. It meant nothing to me, of course, I'm built of stronger stuff, but Christabel is a little fragile.'

'Yes, indeed, almost ethereal, I sometimes think.'

This was not the effect that Sophia had hoped for, but she recovered quickly. 'I'm sure her decision to stay home was right. She would not have wanted to attend with blotched cheeks and a red nose.'

Sir Julian looked aghast at this unimaginable picture of his loved one and sought reassurance. 'I trust that Miss Tallis is not seriously unwell.'

'She will be greatly improved in the morning, I'm sure. She is some years older than me, you know, and needs a little time to recover her spirits. And if she had come tonight, I doubt she would have had the energy to dance,' Sophia finished pointedly as the orchestra struck up for a country dance.

The Seftons had decided that though refreshments and conversation were normally deemed sufficient for a rout, their guests would be treated to a little informal dancing if they so wished. Sir Julian, mindful of his duties as a gentleman, immediately begged Sophia to grant him the favour of a dance. She accepted primly and only spoilt the effect by scowling at her brother who was leading Domino de Silva down the opposite line of country dancers.

'Is that not your brother I see, Miss Sophia?'

'Yes', she admitted in a bored voice, 'he's supposed to be my escort though he chooses rather to dance attendance on some foreigner.'

* * *

The foreigner was putting on a good show of enjoying herself despite an aching heart. Ever since the evening at Almack's, when Richard's lack of interest had been made so brutally clear, her happy spirits had been slowly and surely evaporating. The dance came to an end and Benedict, tired of having his feet crushed by an inattentive partner, said hopefully, 'You don't want to dance any more, do you?'

She shook her head and looked around the room in search of her aunt. Even her chaperon appeared to have deserted her.

Sensing her dejection, Benedict tried a diversion. 'Have you ever gambled?'

She opened her eyes wide. 'My father used to gamble sometimes in Buenos Aires, but he said the clubs were not fit for young girls.'

'There are clubs like that in London too—' Benedict grinned '—but you don't have to go to them to gamble. There's usually the chance at most parties.'

'Really? You can gamble here?' She was genuinely taken aback. To be offered gambling in what seemed the wealthiest and noblest of settings was curious.

'Let's find out. I think they've set up a hazard table or maybe faro in the next room. Would you like to watch the game?'

It was a distraction. She would go and watch until her aunt found her. They strolled into the adjoining card room and saw that a game of faro was in full swing. The bank had already amassed what looked like a fortune in rouleaus and the expressions on the players' faces ranged from boredom through irritation to downright vexation. It took little time for Domino to understand the simple rules with Benedict as her willing tutor. As she watched card after card emerging from the spring-loaded faro box, heard the click of tokens changing hands and felt the building tension as losses and wins followed in quick succession, she began to forget about the interview with Richard. Gambling, it seemed, was the perfect antidote for a broken heart.

'I want to play too,' she whispered.

Looking into her glowing face, Benedict stifled any misgivings and deftly inserted her into the circle. Very soon she was in the thick of the play. Her flushed face and sparkling eyes spoke of pleasure, but Benedict began to feel uncomfortable. She had taken to the game rather too enthusiastically, he thought, and now, looking around the table at their fellows, he didn't like what he saw. To Domino they appeared unexceptional. The women perhaps were showing too much *décolletée*, but they were sumptuously and fashionably dressed and hardly differed from their sisters dancing just a few yards away; the gentlemen were very correctly attired in evening dress and treated each other with a jokey politeness that spoke of long-term intimacy. But from Benedict's limited knowledge some of those gathered around the table were hardened gamesters and whispers of compromised virtue swirled around a number of the women. There was at least one wholly disreputable rake in the room.

Lord Moncaster lazed at the head of the table in charge of the faro bank. It was customary for the wealthiest of patrons to take turns in running the bank and Leo Moncaster enjoyed riches enough to run a hundred faro banks and still have plenty left to indulge his every whim. At that moment his whim was turning to Domino. His weary eyes rested gratefully on her, savouring her youthful beauty and unsophisticated delight

in this novel entertainment. As his eyes ran over her assess-
ingly, she looked up from the table and caught his glance. She
wasn't sure what to think of him. He certainly made a splendid figure, looking as though he could have stepped straight
out of one of Byron's poems, but there was something in his
glittering gaze that disconcerted her and she looked quickly
away. Benedict had seen that gaze too.

'Let's go back to the salon and find a cold drink,' he suggested.

'Not yet, Benedict. Just one more wager. Next time I'm
bound to win.'

'That's what everyone thinks, and you won't.'

'How do you know that? Just because you always lose.'

'I don't always lose—well, not all of the time,' he finished
lamely.

'There you are, then. It's my turn to win.'

'I should take you back to the salon. Your aunt will murder
me if she knows I've brought you in here.'

'If you're afraid of my aunt, you'd better go.'

He was getting heartily bored with this recalcitrant girl.
Perhaps if he upped and left she would follow. 'I'm going,
then, and if you're wise you'll come too,' he whispered rather
too loudly.

Lord Moncaster raised a quizzical eyebrow, causing
Benedict to flush with annoyance and make haste to leave.
Once out of the room, he shrugged off any qualms at desert-
ing the girl. She wasn't his responsibility and he wanted to
enjoy the rest of his evening.

Chapter Five

Christabel came down to breakfast the next morning still looking pale, but unruffled. She'd spent a difficult night, unable to sleep with any ease. Her mind had for hours refused to stop its constant churning of the past week's events, but finally she had found some repose. Her decision was made. She had allowed herself to be manipulated, to be too easily swayed by feelings she should never entertain. From now on she must ignore Richard's behaviour and concentrate on her own. With great severity she reminded herself that she was the only person responsible for her actions. If she could hold to that determination, she would cope with what lay ahead. Sophia's chatter had alerted her to Sir Julian's return to town and she knew that it would not be long before he renewed his proposal. She must be ready.

She saw that her mother had taken note of her pallor and was looking at her with gentle concern. 'Bel, are you well enough to pay that morning call on Lady Blythe?'

'I feel a good deal better, thank you, Mama, and I will be happy to go.'

It was a lie, for Domino was likely to be present and the

thought of meeting the girl so soon after the disasters of the picnic troubled her. But she needed to appear unconcerned and calm in the face of any suspicions her mother might harbour.

Lady Harriet looked relieved. Her daughter seemed not to have been so badly affected by yesterday's events as she had feared. And she had a mountainous collection of letters awaiting her attention. Christabel's offer to attend on Loretta Blythe was most welcome.

'Perhaps Sophia would care to accompany you?' her mother suggested tentatively.

But Sophia instantly forestalled that notion; she was far too busy this morning organising her steadily increasing wardrobe. Christabel was more than happy to go attended only by her maid, and a walk to Curzon Street would be a pleasant escape from the house. The rain clouds, which yesterday had appeared out of nowhere, had vanished entirely and in their place was the deepest blue covering and a spring sun already climbing the sky and warming the world it shone on.

She sauntered slowly along the tree-lined pavements with Rosa by her side. The slightest of breezes washed over her, catching at the primrose ribbons in her hair and twisting them in and out of the soft tendrils of auburn that framed her face. With each step on this glorious day she felt herself walking away from discord and entering a place of deep calm. The night had brought counsel. Whatever the truth of Richard's relationship with Domino, it was their affair, not hers. It was immaterial, too, whether the passion he'd poured on her was genuine or simply feigned as part of his plan to punish. Certainly those moments by the lakeside, moments scorched into her consciousness, had not appeared feigned. He had seemed as fevered, as impassioned, as she.

'Curzon Street is the third turning on the right, Miss Christabel,' her maid reminded her. 'What number is Lady Blythe's?'

'Number Twelve, I believe,' she answered absently.

No, it wasn't important whether or not he'd meant the caresses he'd lavished on her—what was important was how she reacted to them. And so far her reactions had been far from laudable. Twice in the last few days she'd been overcome by desire for a man who should mean nothing to her. The old Christabel, rebellious and passionate, had risen again and exploded into the ardour of yesterday's embrace. But she was no longer the girl she'd been and instead must be true to her new life. How could she have allowed herself to behave in that fashion when she was as good as promised to another man? And such an upright man who would never give her cause for concern. *He* would never find himself locked in a fervent embrace with a lover from his past! The unlikely image made her smile.

'This day is meant for smiling, is it not?'

A male voice cleaved through her thoughts. Richard was there, in front of her, doffing his curly-brimmed beaver, grey eyes smiling and flecked by the sun's rays. As always his Hessians were polished to a blinding finish, complementing a pair of immaculate, close-fitting cream pantaloons clearly designed to display his legs to advantage. She forced herself to remember the vows of just a few minutes ago.

'It is a most beautiful morning,' she agreed, trying to keep her voice steady and her gaze neutral. Trying very hard not to think of their last encounter, their last few minutes together.

A difficult silence began to develop.

'At least we can be certain that today we won't receive a soaking,' he said mildly in an attempt to break it. 'I trust you suffered no ill effects from yesterday's downpour.'

'Indeed, no,' she responded quickly, relieved at this unexceptional topic of conversation, 'though I felt very sorry for the Wivenhoes. They had taken so much trouble over the arrangements only to see their plans ruined.'

'Forces of nature can't be gainsaid.'

His remark had been lightly meant, but it was not the most felicitous, he thought. A force of nature had destroyed the icy reserve which for years had defended Christabel, and he was responsible. He was not proud of that. In the night watches he'd argued himself into never-ending circles. It was essential that he prove her base, yet she was the woman who warmed him, excited him, entranced him. His plan was a clever strategy, he told himself, yet he felt shame in its tawdriness.

The image of Christabel's abject unhappiness haunted him, knowing that he was its architect. It turned out that her unhappiness was his also. Yesterday by the lakeside he'd wanted to take her into his arms and kiss the tears away one by one. And he *had* taken her in his arms. More than that, he'd felt every beautiful curve of her and his heart had sung. When he'd caressed her, she'd responded as ardently as he could ever wish. He could have taken her there and then, he was sure—hotly, urgently, beneath the sheeting rain. What was that but inconstancy! He had surely proved what he'd set out to, proved that she was incapable of being true. By rights he should feel free, released from her spell, so why did he not?

In truth, in the deepest recesses of his heart, he could not believe her a false woman. She had been disloyal once, in a lifetime of loyalty. So why had she behaved so much out of character and to such devastating result? During the endless night, watching the shadows darken into unrelieved blackness, watching the dewy light of dawn creep gradually into the four corners of his room, he too had come to a decision. He had to know why she'd betrayed him. He had to hear it from her lips. If he could understand that, then he was certain that he would finally be able to lay the past to rest.

Silence stretched between them once more and again he was the one to break it.

'Are you on your way anywhere in particular? May I escort you?'

'Thank you, but I'm very close to my destination. I am to pay a morning call on Lady Blythe.'

'Then let me offer you my arm,' he said briskly, nodding dismissal to Rosa. 'You may return home, your mistress will not need you.'

Before Christabel could protest, her maid had begun retracing her steps to Mount Street.

She did not take his arm, but stood facing him on the narrow pavement.

'That was high-handed, Lord Veryan. It is my prerogative to dismiss my maid.'

'I'm sorry if you disapprove. I have no wish to quarrel with you.'

'That would certainly be a change,' she returned acidly. His arrogance had helped her regain her poise.

'I hoped that I might speak with you alone.' His tone was level, giving no hint of what he might be feeling. And for a moment he appeared unwilling to go on, unable to find the words he needed to broach the topic burning so brightly in his mind.

'Shall we walk on?' The movement seemed to act as a release. 'After yesterday, you see, I've done some thinking,' he continued quietly. 'In fact, a good deal of thinking.'

He paused again and Christabel waited, her composure once more in danger of slipping away. What was he about to say? That he loved her after all? That after their impassioned lovemaking, he still cared deeply for her and could no longer consider marrying Domino de Silva? What traitorous thoughts, what stupid thoughts, she chastised herself.

'I wanted to apologise,' he began again. 'I wanted to tell you how deeply sorry I am for any upset I've caused since my return to London.'

'Any upset? You must know that you deliberately set out to distress me.'

'I won't deny it, but I am still sorry.'

He was looking contrite, unusually so, and she felt emboldened to question him.

'I cannot understand why you have been so intent on hurting me. Why?'

He shook his head. 'I'm afraid I can't answer with any truth. I don't know myself. When I disembarked at Southampton, I thought the past was dead and buried for me.'

'But it wasn't,' she said flatly.

'No, it wasn't.' He paused and then said with deliberation, 'I've behaved foolishly, I'm willing to admit, but if I could understand the past, then I think it would finally die for me.'

She wore a puzzled expression and he turned towards her, looking at her directly, his gaze searching and serious. 'If I knew, if I could understand, why you did what you did.'

She gave a small, uncertain laugh. 'I could echo your own words. I can't answer with any truth, I don't know myself.'

They rounded the corner of Curzon Street and, with an effort, she tried again. He deserved that at least.

'Put it down to naïvety, youthful stupidity, if you will. When you are young and untried, it's easy to be dazzled by surfaces. I was living in a world I'd never known before, a world heady with excitement.'

'But to be taken in by a creature such as Joshua,' he protested.

'You were equally taken in,' she reminded him sharply. 'He was your friend.'

'And that surely makes it worse. It makes me more stupid and you more venal.'

She flinched at the word. 'He made me feel special,' she said defensively.

'And I didn't?'

'I was just part...' and she strove to find the phrase which would adequately convey her sense of his indifference '...I was just part of the furniture of your world.'

'Never!' He felt stunned. He had been drowning in love for her and she hadn't noticed! 'How could you not know—?' He broke off, biting back the words of passion he'd been about to utter.

But Christabel, deep in that distant past, had hardly noticed. 'Joshua made me feel that I mattered to him, really mattered. I know now that I was a fool.' Her voice was barely more than a murmur and she glanced down at the delicate kid sandals she wore, as though hoping she might be absorbed into the pavement. 'In fact, I knew that almost immediately.'

'You parted very soon? I never knew.'

'Why would you? I can't imagine you wanted to hear any news from home.'

He grimaced at the truth of the observation.

'It was never going to work.' She sighed. 'Joshua was charm itself, but he was an opportunist.'

'A here and thereian?' It was doing Richard good to hear how miserably the affair had ended.

'If you like.'

'But someone who wreaked destruction wherever he went,' he pursued, his tone now one of quiet sympathy.

'I won't make him an excuse,' she said robustly. 'I caused damage to everyone who cared for me. I recognise that. But as you were happy to remind me just yesterday, I can't undo it. Any of it.'

'But you don't need to compound it.'

'What do you mean?'

'Don't make another bad choice.'

She bridled. 'And how might I do that?'

'I'm hardly the right person to give advice, but you must know that the future you're proposing is wrong—for you, for everyone. You've earned your freedom, so live free.'

'You're quite correct,' she responded tartly, 'you *are* hardly the right person.'

They had reached the door of Number Twelve and with this parting shot, she climbed the front steps. His face, as he raised his hat in farewell, was blank of all expression. He turned around and walked away down the road and Christabel was left bewildered. He'd shown himself sorry for his conduct, sorry for the distress he'd caused. He'd conversed seriously, dared to talk about the past with her, and amid the barbs of resentment there had been sympathy. It seemed that he'd had a change of heart. But why? And what did he mean, that she should live free? How dared he presume to tell her how to shape her life? It was well enough for a man to say 'live free'. He had the luxury of choice but, as a woman, she did not.

The door opened and she was ushered into Loretta Blythe's drawing room. She knew most of the faces gathered there and it was an easy matter to smile sweetly and murmur the necessary vacuous compliments. But while she observed the social niceties, her mind was roving through every detail of the recent encounter. Was it just luck that she'd met Richard where and when she had? She thought not. It was clear to her that he'd been visiting at Curzon Street. And he would have come, not to sit drinking tea with Lady Blythe and her intimates, but to see Domino. He'd been visiting Domino, the girl he intended to marry. Naturally they would have wedding plans to discuss for when his period of mourning was at an end, even now perhaps arrangements to make for the girl to visit Madron. Christabel quailed at the thought, but that was something she must grow accustomed to. It was possible that his forthcoming marriage had contributed to a new generosity of spirit, his willingness finally to forgive and forget the past. She should feel grateful for that, she supposed.

That night she slept better than she had for days. Whether it was sheer exhaustion or the fact that she and Richard were no longer enemies, she didn't know. But his interference in her life appeared to be at an end. So did his interest, another voice whispered unkindly. But that voice was swiftly squashed. She must bury the past as Richard was doing, bury it and move on to a new and different existence. That evening she'd had plenty of time for reflection, the family for once spending it by their own fireside, and by the time she'd crawled into bed, she was ready to fall into a deep and dreamless sleep. Not even Benedict's noisy return with the dawn had the power to waken her.

Benedict's mission to enjoy himself to the full had been so successful that when the next day, bleary eyed and slumped over the breakfast table, his mother reminded him that he'd agreed to escort his sisters to St James's Park, his only answer was a heartrending groan.

'We really don't need him, Mama,' Sophia chirped. She was in fine form, still bubbling from the two long dances she'd managed to extract from Sir Julian at the Seftons' party. To add to her pleasure, Christabel appeared of late to have lost her usual bloom.

'Stebbings will be with us and that will be sufficient. In fact, Bel can stay home too. She still doesn't look at all the thing,' she added solicitously.

'What nonsense. You cannot possibly go driving with just a groom for company.' Lady Harriet looked anxiously across the table at her elder daughter, 'You will go with Sophia this morning, I trust?'

'Yes, of course, Mama, it's arranged that we meet the Misses Banham at eleven.'

She couldn't remember exactly why she'd agreed to drive with two sisters she privately considered bird-witted in the extreme, but managed to finish brightly, 'It's another beautiful day for a drive in St James's.'

She went quickly upstairs after breakfast to complete her *toilette*. Sophia was already arrayed in midnight blue and she had no wish to challenge her sister's colourful palette. Instead she donned a robe of figured cream lace over an underdress of soft amber silk. Her hair was brushed into shining auburn curls and threaded through with a simple cream ribbon. She felt instinctively that this was an important day and she wanted to look her best in meeting it head on. A newly discovered sense of purpose had brought back colour to her face and the porcelain cheeks now sported a delicate glow. She looked as fresh and as young as the spring morning into which the sisters now ventured.

Sophia glared at her in annoyance. A resurgent Christabel was not what she wanted. Sir Julian had mentioned at the rout that though he must give immediate attention to business brought back from Rosings, he would be riding in the park this morning and hoped to see both herself and her sister there. Sophia was under no illusions as to whose company he really sought and had hoped to intercept him before Christabel once more entered his orbit. She was anxious to exploit their friendship of two nights ago in any way she could and her sister's radiant presence would hardly further her plan.

Once out of the house Benedict suddenly remembered a prior engagement and swiftly excused himself. He had made a casual promise to Domino to ride with her this morning and this was likely to be more entertaining than plodding dutifully after his sisters' carriage. He was also feeling a little guilty at having abandoned the girl so cavalierly at the Seftons'.

Sophia was pleased to see him go. If she could only think of a pretext to lose Christabel too, she would be free to seek out Sir Julian and fascinate him as she knew she could. But Christabel was going to be difficult to evade; her sister had opted to take the reins, the groom by her side, and further frustration swiftly followed when they encountered the Misses Banham waiting for them at the north gate of the park. Annoyingly they had remembered the arrangement to meet and while Christabel held the horses steady, they were soon clambering noisily into the carriage. They were arrayed in matching dresses of sprig muslin and each carried a frilled parasol in a contrasting colour. They positioned themselves on either side of Sophia, like two chattering bookends. Laughing and giggling their way into the park, they exclaimed at Christabel's skill at driving the carriage through such busy thoroughfares and asserted with loud squeals their complete confidence that she could be trusted to tool them around the park without mishap. Most of what passed for conversation between them—the latest scurrilous *on dits* circulating in town—went unanswered, but since they needed no audience but each other, they were not disconcerted by their hosts' silence.

When they'd finally exhausted current gossip, they turned their attention to their companions. They complimented the Tallis sisters on their looks, their dresses, their carriage. Everything that could be praised, was praised. Unusually for Sophia she seemed not to notice their flattering remarks even when they were particularly lavish in their admiration of her blue satin. Christabel thought she seemed disturbed, almost excited, looking nervously from right to left and then behind, sometimes even hanging over the side of the carriage to gain a better view. It hardly seemed likely, but was it possible that Sophia had made an assignation with someone?

'There's Lucy,' the elder Miss Banham suddenly shrieked. 'And with Petronella!'

'Our cousins,' the younger sister explained to the startled

Tallises. 'Miss Tallis, Miss Sophia, would you mind awfully if we were to get down? It's an age since we've seen our cousins and there's so much to tell!'

The Tallis sisters readily assented. They were both heartily weary of the clamour that had accompanied their drive around the park. Sophia's face became intent. She had now only to free herself from her sister's company and she could at last seek Sir Julian alone. But nothing happened to aid her plan and just a few minutes later they saw him riding towards them.

He hailed them with pleasure, reining in his horse by the carriage to greet Christabel for the first time in nearly a week. For a while he sat silently gazing at her. He had forgotten just how beautiful she was and was suffused with eagerness to make his declaration and possess her as his wife. Belatedly he remembered her sister's presence.

'Good morning, Miss Sophia. I trust you suffered no ill from your exertions at the rout?'

Sophia smiled a little sourly. Sir Julian seemed not to notice and immediately turned his attention back to Christabel.

'I was most sorry to hear of your indisposition, Miss Tallis, but I see from your looks that you are now fully recovered. I had hoped to see you at the rout but in your absence your little sister kept me on my toes.'

'So I understand, Sir Julian.' Christabel smiled, her green eyes warm and welcoming. 'And how did your business at Rosings prosper?'

'It went well, plenty to do, you know, as always, but also plenty of time to plan.' He looked suddenly serious. 'I am most pleased to find you here this morning. There is something particular I wish to discuss with you. I wonder if you would do me the honour of walking a short way with me?'

She knew that this was the moment that had threatened for so long. Now that it had finally come, she felt calm and resigned. This was something she must do for herself and her family. It was no good thinking that a dashing white knight was going to ride to her rescue. Those were the foolish daydreams of an immature girl. This was the reality—a comfortable life with a comfortable husband. She allowed Sir Julian to hand her down from the carriage and stood waiting for him. He was about to join her when Sophia indicated that she also wished to alight. Sir Julian was surprised by this lack of tact, but, polite as always, he carefully handed the younger girl down and they began walking together over the luxuriant carpet of grass from which the dew had only just disappeared.

At that moment Benedict and Domino were manoeuvring their horses through the busy West End traffic. Pedlars, carts, every kind of carriage thronged the roads leading to St James's and all their attention was taken up with gaining a safe passage through the maelstrom of noise and bustle. Twenty long minutes later they finally reached the safety of the park and trotted smartly through its eastern entrance. Benedict glanced briefly at his companion. He was not the most acute observer, but she seemed unusually subdued. At first he had put it down to the late nights and this morning's early rising, but as they rode, he became increasingly aware of tension within the slight figure alongside him. After a few abortive attempts at conversation he gave up talking and they rode in silence.

The air was still and cool and shafts of sunlight filtered

through the newly leafing trees overhead. As they pushed their way further into this small island of nature, Domino decided to make her confession. Her frustration at Richard's continued blindness had been replaced at the rout party by a new fascination. In that hot, enclosed little room she had been captivated by the ebb and flow of changing fortunes, the excitement of placing her stake, the rush of adrenaline as the cards sped from the faro box and the thrill of delight when the pile of rouleaus in front of her began to grow.

Not so delighted, though, when they began to disappear. But then Lord Moncaster had come to her rescue, had advanced her some of his own rouleaus for no more payment than her handkerchief. In the thrill of the game it had seemed perfectly normal for her to hand over this small personal possession. But the sly looks the other players exchanged alerted her to the fact that his lordship's offer was hardly usual. He'd behaved impeccably, though, even advancing more tokens without demanding anything further from her. At least for the moment. He'd said that he would think of some way she could repay him, but that she wasn't to worry her pretty head. He was a rich man, a few losses meant nothing to him. At these last comments Domino's immediate neighbour, apparently so correct and punctilious, had smirked knowingly. She caught both his grimace and Leo Moncaster's answering smile and a vague discomfort became a pressing anxiety to leave.

'What do you know of Lord Moncaster?' she asked suddenly.

Benedict looked at her cautiously, trying to gauge how much he should say. 'Not a lot,' was his unhelpful reply.

He saw her biting her lip and relented a little, 'Why do you ask?'

'Only that I'm interested in the people I met at the Seftons'. I understand it was Lord Moncaster who held the faro bank.'

'He often does. He's a very rich man.'

'Is he married?'

Where was this leading? thought Benedict. 'No, not married.'

'Yet he's quite old.'

'He's not that old and he doesn't exactly lead the kind of life that goes with being married,' he added bravely.

'What kind of life?' came the inevitable question.

'Pretty rackety.' Better to be brutal to be kind if the girl had any idea of snaring Moncaster.

'Benedict, I lost money to him,' she disclosed in a sudden rush of words.

'We all lost money to him.'

'I mean, I lost more—after you left.'

'You couldn't have lost much more. You only had enough rouleaus left for one more stake.'

'I borrowed more.'

'Borrowed? From him?' He whistled under his breath.

'It was not a good idea?'

'Definitely not. What did you pledge?'

'Pledge?'

'What did he ask for?' Benedict was getting seriously alarmed.

'My handkerchief, first, but then he gave me rouleaus for free.'

'He never gives anything for free.'

'That's what I'm thinking now,' she said miserably. 'What will he do, do you think?'

Benedict hardly liked to put his thoughts into words. The

vague feelings of guilt that had previously visited him found vent in scolding.

'Whatever made you do such an idiotic thing?'

'I didn't realise it was wrong until later. You were not there to advise me,' she accused him.

'It shouldn't be me advising you. It should be your aunt. You must tell her what you've done and she must repay Lord Moncaster his debt.'

'I can't do that. She will be so angry with me and despatch me immediately to Spain.'

'I wouldn't blame her. You're too much of a responsibility. Anyway, you're leaving for Spain at the end of the Season, so why not now?'

'I have my reasons,' she said gravely, the image of Richard hovering close. Then, following her train of thought, she asked in a falsely bright voice, 'Is Miss Tallis riding here today?'

'She's out driving with my sister. I'm supposed to be with them, but Sophia's screeching sends me insane. I thought you were the better bet!' He grinned.

She ignored the witticism. 'Is she here right now? Perhaps we should go and find her.'

'We won't have to look too far.' He raised his arm to point ahead. 'She's there, just to the right of that clump of trees.'

They reined in their horses. A carriage had been drawn up beneath the trees and to one side they saw Sir Julian Edgerton talking animatedly to Christabel. He had her hand raised to his lips and then, as they watched, slipped what looked like a ring on her finger.

'Perhaps not the right time to interrupt,' Benedict commented drily.

Domino felt considerable surprise, but also a warm pleasure. If Christabel were pledged to another man, it might mean Richard would look more kindly on her. 'They are to be married?'

'My mother's been waiting an age for this—Bel must have finally decided to put the man out of his misery.'

'It's a very happy day, then. Let's go and congratulate them.'

'I don't think I will right now,' he prevaricated. 'Just look at Sophia!'

They looked across from the betrothed couple and saw a figure in bright blue satin some distance from the carriage, standing rigidly with averted head.

'Like I said, perhaps not the best time to interrupt.' He gave a mischievous smile. 'Come on, let's have a gallop. No one's around to tell tales.'

'I must not, Benedict. I'm already in trouble for that.'

He set himself to persuade his companion that a gallop was just the thing to blow away her megrims when a large black stallion cut across their path and Richard Veryan was hailing them with a smile.

'Good morning to you both. I'm very glad to see you, Domino, though I must admit I didn't expect to meet you so early in the morning.'

'It's such a beautiful day that I couldn't lie abed. Did you particularly want to see me, Richard?' Her tone was eager, almost breathless.

'I was worried that I might miss you, knowing what a crowded social calendar you have,' he teased. 'I wanted to tell you that I'm leaving for Cornwall very shortly.'

'Cornwall? But why now?' Her dismay rang out clearly.

'Why not now?' he said bracingly. 'I've tarried too long in

London—my mother deserves better. I should be at her side, don't you think?'

'Yes', she stuttered, 'of course, but it seems a sudden decision.'

'Hardly sudden. It's taken time to organise my affairs, but everything is now in a fair way to being settled. There's no need for me to remain in London any longer.'

Benedict saw her face and knew instantly that his supposition over Moncaster was false. But this relationship didn't look much more promising. There was an awkward silence and he felt it incumbent to oil the social wheels.

'I'll be returning to Cornwall myself pretty soon, Rick. We must make sure to ride out together—if you can spare the time.'

The other man smiled his assent. 'There's always time for a decent gallop.'

Domino had been following her own thoughts and blurted out abruptly, 'But won't you stay for the Vauxhall spectacle, Richard? It's only a few days away.'

'I think not, but you're sure to enjoy yourself. I remember seeing the fireworks for the first time when I was about your age and they were truly spectacular.'

Domino dug her nails into her hands and screamed inwardly. Wanting to hit out, she said as casually as she could, 'If you're leaving so soon, you'd better make haste to congratulate Miss Tallis. She is close by, I believe.'

Benedict looked at her with surprise, wondering what her game was. Not for the first time he felt completely out of his depth in trying to fathom females.

'Congratulate Miss Tallis?' Richard was questioning.

'We've just seen her with Sir Julian Edgerton in a most

romantic situation, haven't we, Benedict?' Her companion looked suitably revolted. 'Benedict tells me that the betrothal between Sir Julian and his sister is something the whole family has been expecting, and it looks as though today it's finally happened,' she added helpfully.

Richard was far too self-controlled to betray his feelings, but his face grew austere and the light went out of the smiling grey eyes.

'I had better do as you suggest, then, and seek Miss Tallis out.'

He wheeled his horse sharply around and rode away. His face might be an impassive mask, but inside he was incandescent. She was going to marry the man! How could she even consider it? Just a few days ago she had kissed him, caressed *him*, laid herself open to *his* lovemaking. The thought almost tore the breath from his body. Only yesterday in Curzon Street he'd felt certain that he could leave behind the old history at last. He'd been shocked to discover that Christabel had never known the depths of his youthful love and begun to understand just how easy it had been for Joshua to mislead her. The familiar, nagging hurt hadn't disappeared completely, but he'd felt better able to contemplate the past with some serenity. Now, though, the wound had opened again and lacerantingly. Yet another man was to smile into those startling emerald eyes, to run his hands over that beautiful, lithe body, to laugh and tease and fun with her. No, *that* he wouldn't do. Sir Julian Edgerton was not a man made for fun. Nor was he a man made for love, not the kind that she needed at least. If *he* were still in love with her... But he wasn't, was he? Her betrayal might have been an act of youthful folly, but she had damaged him too badly for him to trust her again. And now she was to marry this dull do-gooder and be lost to him for ever. How could she? The question thrummed blindly through every particle of his flesh.

Behind a veil of tears, Domino watched his figure as it grew slowly smaller in the distance. Riding alongside, Benedict maintained a discreet silence. He trusted that he would not be called upon to become a confidant and waited for her to recover herself. With a great effort, she turned to him with a show of enthusiasm.

'That was exciting, wasn't it, but can we return to my problem? I need to win back the money that I lost to Lord Moncaster. Will you help me do that?'

'You want me to win it?'

'Of course not, I want to win it. It's my debt. But I need you to introduce me to a place where I can do that.'

'You're asking me to take you to a gambling den?'

'Yes.'

'I won't,' he said flatly.

'Why not? If you're scared we might be recognised, I could go in disguise.'

'It gets worse.'

'No, it doesn't, I can disguise myself very well as a boy and go as your friend.'

He looked at her slim figure appraisingly. 'I'm sure you can, but I'm not taking you to any gaming hell.'

'I don't want to go to a hell, just a place where I can win back the money.'

'That's a gaming hell.'

'Please, Benedict.'

'No, no and definitely no.'

'Then you won't help me.'

'I've told you what to do. Go to your aunt and confess. The worst she can do is to pack you off to Spain. Would that matter so much now?'

She flushed at the implication, but knew that he was right. She supposed that she must find the right opportunity to tell Lady Blythe what had happened. But then her aunt would be sure to tell her Spanish relatives of her disgrace and from the moment she arrived in Madrid, they would be watching her every movement. She wished she'd never left Argentina.

In the distance Richard had ridden up to the small group standing beneath the trees. Sophia had joined her sister and Sir Julian near the carriage, as anxious now to leave as she had been earlier to find him. She scowled even more ferociously as she recognised the man seated astride the glossy black horse picking its way towards them.

Richard Veryan slid from the saddle as Christabel turned. He came forward and bowed just a little too deeply.

'I understand from your brother that felicitations are in order.' His voice was harsh, slightly disdainful. 'May I take the opportunity, Miss Tallis, to congratulate you and Sir Julian, on your forthcoming marriage,' and here he bowed extravagantly towards the other man. 'I wish you both all the happiness you are capable of.'

Christabel flushed, knowing the double edge of those words, but executed a dignified bow in response. Her fiancé smiled happily and without guile.

'Thank you, Lord Veryan. Your good wishes are most welcome. I consider myself to be blessed indeed to have won this remarkable lady for my future wife, a gift beyond anything I deserve.'

Richard's expression was sardonic. 'You must not sell yourself short, Sir Julian. I'm sure Miss Tallis would be the first to agree that your honesty and loyalty are qualities to aspire to.'

Sir Julian blinked at this sentiment, but his smile broadened even further. He felt supremely happy and nothing was going to spoil this wonderful day for him. Sophia stood close by, an interested observer. Richard's comments appeared to be coming from between gritted teeth and offered a small hope. She might yet salvage something from the plans that had gone so badly awry.

Pinning on her most enticing smile, she turned to the happy lover. 'I believe, Sir Julian, that you were involved in plans for the canal which has been constructed to feed the lake. I would love to see it and understand exactly how it works. Would you be good enough to take me?'

If Sir Julian felt this was a strange request coming at the very moment of his betrothal and from a girl who had hitherto not shown the slightest interest in engineering, he was far too polite to show it. Willing to do anything for anybody on this glorious morning, particularly a close relative of his beloved, he immediately agreed.

'It appears we must leave you, sir,' and he bowed his farewell. 'Thank you again for your good wishes.'

He began to walk towards the Chinese bridge with Sophia in tow, already beginning a complicated discourse on his understanding of the water-management system. Equally bewildered by her sister's request, Christabel turned to follow them, but was stopped in her tracks by Richard roughly grabbing her arm. He hardly waited for the others to be out of earshot before grinding out, 'You can't really mean to marry that man!'

'I beg your pardon!' She was genuinely shocked.

'I think you understand me, but, just in case, I was questioning your sanity in agreeing to marry Julian Edgerton.'

'How dare you presume to question whom I marry!'

'I dare to presume because I seem to know you better than you know yourself. But even you must be aware of how unsuited you are to each other.'

The red cascade of curls trembled with anger. 'You are insulting, sir!'

'I would call it honest rather than insulting, but it's better to be insulting than concur in this charade.'

'You are misinformed, my lord. There is no charade. Sir Julian and I have known each other for many months and have agreed that we will suit admirably.'

She wondered why she was defending her choice of husband to Richard of all men but she felt compelled to continue and found herself declaring, 'Sir Julian is a man of the highest honour and integrity.'

'I'm sure he is. He's also a gudgeon if he thinks he can control you.'

'No man controls me and Sir Julian is far too wise to wish to do so.'

'But not wise enough to refrain from marrying you,' he retaliated.

She glared furiously at the tall, elegant figure in front of her and responded in a voice crackling with ice, 'This is mere ranting and I will listen no more. I bid you good day, sir.'

Her cream skirts swished to one side as she made to walk

away. But Richard would not concede. Ignoring her cold fury and the summary nature of his dismissal, he called out, 'If you value his happiness as much as your own, don't do it.'

She retraced her steps and stood looking directly up into his eyes, now dark and glittering.

'If we are to give each other marital advice, I would suggest that wedding a child fresh from the nursery is unlikely to guarantee success. I, at least, intend to marry a man of my own age and one I have known for many months.'

Brushing aside his supposed alliance with Domino, he coldly countered her logic. 'But how much of a guarantee is that? You once agreed to marry another man of your own age and one you had known a *very* long time, but that alliance wasn't too permanent, was it?'

He smiled derisively at her. 'At the moment Sir Julian is living in his own little paradise, but how long do you give him? He would be well advised to grow steel armour in the very near future, say three weeks from his wedding day.'

'You have been as offensive as it is possible to be, Lord Veryan, but nothing you say can touch our happiness.'

He grimaced. 'How charming! And how strange that there was a day when I felt that too. I looked deep into your green eyes, touched your luminous skin, tangled my hands in that wild red hair—and what a premonition that was—and believed that I was as happy as it was possible to be, that nothing could ever touch that happiness. How wrongly can a man judge!'

Christabel swallowed hard. 'Yesterday you assured me that you considered the past dead. Can you not accept that we made a mistake and forget?'

'*You* made a mistake, Miss Tallis. For myself, the past is

nothing. But I find it difficult to forget those others for whom the pain still lives. But then you never cared too much about them—friends, parents, all could be sacrificed. All that mattered was that you had your desire, a desire, it seems, which died almost as soon as it flickered into life.'

He was being unjust, deliberately stoking his anger against her, but he found himself powerless to stop.

'You are unfair to accuse me of not caring for the pain I caused. You must know otherwise. It has been an open wound for all these years.' Her voice faltered and unshed tears stung her eyelids. She steadied herself and tried for a calm she was far from feeling.

'In my youth I made a mistaken attachment—I have freely confessed it—and I have paid for that mistake. If you once cared anything for me, can you not find it in your heart, if not to wish me well, at least not to wish me ill.'

For a moment he felt an overpowering weariness. Had he not made the decision just hours ago to put this anguish behind him? So why was he continuing to haunt this woman, to pile hurt upon hurt? She saw the trouble in his shadowed eyes and the frown that appeared between the dark brows and pushed her advantage.

'Because *our* betrothal did not succeed, that is no reason to suppose that my marriage to another will not.'

'If so, that other will need to be a very different man from the one you have chosen. He will need to be a man who matches you in strength of character and depth of feeling. For all his honour and integrity, Sir Julian is not that man.'

He spoke the words slowly and deliberately, his fierce gaze searching, seeking, tugging at her soul. For a moment she forgot they were antagonists engaged in cruel conflict and flamed beneath his regard. For what seemed an age they devoured each other with their eyes, neither speaking. Then recovering a frigid poise, she snapped back her response.

'And who would you suggest, Lord Veryan? Where is this model of manhood I must aspire to? Surely not yourself?'

'I would never again willingly endure such an ordeal.' His tone held a bitter intensity. 'You say *you* have suffered. I hope so indeed, for my years have been every bit as painful.'

His voice sliced through her skin like a scalpel. She could only murmur, 'I know nothing of your life in Argentina, but I cannot imagine it was devoid of all pleasure.'

'Argentina?' he questioned bleakly. 'I refer not to life there, but to the constant pain of living with betrayal.' And then in a searing aside, 'Naturally you would know nothing of that.'

'On the contrary, I am no stranger to betrayal,' she said in a low voice, 'though you would judge it well deserved.'

She found herself moving towards him, drawn by the warmth of his body and a strange need to offer comfort. She resisted the urge to take his hand but could not stop herself pleading, 'I thought we had agreed, Richard, to put injuries aside. I wish you well in the alliance you are doubtless about to make. Can you not wish the same for me?'

His eyes found hers and for an instant there was an answering warmth. The taut lines of his face relaxed and his mouth softened in the way she remembered so well, a prelude to his kiss. She waited, hardly daring to breathe. But then his whole body visibly tightened and his face resumed its hardened expression. When he spoke, it was clear that anger had reasserted itself.

'My relationship with Miss de Silva has nothing to say in

the matter,' he ground out. 'The truth remains that the man you propose to marry is not worthy of you.'

She took a step back as though he had slapped her in the face, and observing her shock, his anger flared again. 'Good grief, can you not see what a travesty this marriage is? Have we suffered so much for so little?!'

His wrath was answered by a newly awakened fury in her. 'Allow me to tell you, sir, that I find your sentiments abhorrent and your conduct highly improper.'

They stood facing each other so close they could taste one another's breath. Both had been shaken by the intensity of their anger. Both had felt the familiar throb of desire, which neither could acknowledge. Christabel drew her slim figure erect and confronted him with eyes which glinted like green glass.

'I have borne much in this interview, sir, but will not do so again.' Her voice was brittle with feeling. 'Leave me now, please, and ensure that you never again approach me.'

His face expressionless, Richard turned on his heels and scooped up the reins of his mount grazing quietly nearby. Without a backward glance, he flung himself into the saddle and dug his heels into the flanks of the startled beast. Christabel remained where she stood as the horse bounded forwards, her face equally impassive, but her heart beating tumultuously.

Sir Julian, having by this time exhausted his knowledge of canal engineering, was in time to see Richard ride furiously away. Clearly there had been an altercation.

'Let us make haste, Miss Sophia,' he said in a worried tone, 'I fear all may not be well with your sister. That man—Lord Veryan—appeared extremely angry and I am concerned that she may have suffered some mischief from him.'

'That man has known Christabel all her life, Sir Julian, and is hardly like to prove a threat. In fact, he knows her so well...' and here Sophia produced her trump card with a fitting display of naïve innocence '...that they were once promised to each other.'

'Betrothed?' Sir Julian looked bewildered. 'How is this?'

'Oh, I do beg your pardon. You didn't know? How stupid of me. I assumed that Christabel would have told you or that you would have heard mention of it—it was the town's biggest *on dit* for many weeks. But perhaps you were away from London at the time?'

'What happened exactly?' he asked weakly.

Sophia was admirably succinct. 'She jilted him three weeks before the wedding.'

'Good gracious,' was all he could utter before Christabel joined them. He managed to smile solicitously down at the lovely face, trying to blot out Sophia's last words.

'My dear...' he patted her hand ineffectually '...I do hope all is well.'

Still reeling from the encounter with Richard, she withdrew her hand with a little shrug of impatience. 'Naturally, Sir Julian. What could be wrong?'

'Then shall we continue our stroll in the park? The weather looks as though it will hold for some hours.'

His face was hopeful, but she longed for solitude and the latter won. 'Will you forgive me if I cut our walk a little short today? There are things awaiting my attention at home.' It was a feeble excuse, but it would have to do.

'Sophia, are you coming?' Christabel was already climbing into the waiting carriage.

Her sister was equally quick with her response. She would

return to Mount Street on foot and Sir Julian would escort her. 'For I don't doubt that he could do with some company,' she said repressively.

Christabel stared hard at her sister, but the bland face gave nothing away. Beside her Sir Julian stood looking dazed, even shocked. She knew that she could no longer bear to be in his company. Richard's strictures rang ceaselessly in her ears and she had to get away. She gave a sign to Stebbings that she wished him to take the reins and in a moment the carriage had jolted forwards.

The journey to Mount Street was accomplished in less than a quarter of an hour, but she hardly noticed. She should be used to Richard's animosity by now. From the moment they'd literally bumped into one another in Hyde Park, it had been plain there was to be no truce between them. Yesterday's interlude was simply a pause in hostilities. His conduct had swung between indifference, discourtesy, even aggression, intermingled with moments of rekindled desire. But whatever extremes he'd loosed upon her, they seemed always to proceed from a deep-seated antagonism, a fierce desire to make her regret what she'd done.

Yet even when she was thinking the worst of him, she'd sensed a kindness that he couldn't quite suppress, some feeling for her from the past that he couldn't quite dismiss. And today he'd confessed that she had hurt him badly. That must mean that he'd loved her once, not as a sop to parental wishes, nor as a trophy, but deeply and heartfelt. If that were true, she had judged him very wrongly. If that were true, it would explain why he could not overcome his anger, why he was still her enemy.

And now his love was no more: he'd made that plain. He didn't want her for himself, but he had no intention of letting her go quietly into a new life. He was seeking to destroy even that solace. Until this morning she had never truly grasped the power of his ill will. This morning he'd made a mockery of her wish to consign the past to oblivion. It would always be with her. Despite the warmth of the sun that flooded through the open carriage, the thought made her hands shake and her teeth start to chatter as though she suffered a severe chill.

At home she climbed to her room with a bone-weariness, her feet dragging from stair to stair. Once in the safety of her chamber, she flung herself on the bed and lay there in a state of utter fatigue. The day's events—Richard, Julian, even Sophia—rushed past her unseeing eyes in a chaotic blur. Even Sophia! Her sister's behaviour was not the least odd thing that had happened. She wondered what ailed the younger woman.

An hour later the front door slammed and purposeful steps sounded outside her room. Sophia jerked her head around the door, looking unbecomingly flushed, but with a smug expression on her face.

'I'm sure you'll be pleased to know that I more than compensated for your absence,' she taunted.

Christabel stared at her uncomprehendingly. Her head had begun to ache. 'What are you talking about, Sophia?'

'I'm talking about your fiancé. Well, I presume he still *is* your fiancé. I've just returned with Sir Julian and it's clear to me that he's deeply upset by your behaviour. I've tried to smooth things over but I can't be sure how successful I've been.'

Christabel sat up swiftly, her indignation banishing the incipient headache.

'I don't understand what right you think you have to speak to me in this fashion or indeed to discuss me with Sir Julian, but be very sure that I have given you none.'

Sophia remained in the doorway, her arms crossed in defiance. 'I know nothing about rights,' she declared truthfully, 'and of course I don't possess your rather obvious enticements, but I think I know a little better how to treat a man. And it's not with the contempt you deal out.'

'What nonsense you talk.'

She laid her weary head back on the pillow once more. There was a grain of truth in Sophia's pronouncement, but only a grain. And why was her sister so exercised on Sir Julian's behalf?

'Contempt!' Sophia reiterated ringingly. 'You become engaged to an honourable man and immediately begin consorting with your old lover. You accept Sir Julian's ring and then refuse to spend time with him.'

Christabel no longer seemed to be listening, but this did not deter her sister. Sophia was becoming ever more agitated, her face working furiously.

'How do you think that makes him feel?' she harangued, taking angry strides into the room and pointing dramatically at her guilty sister. 'You don't deserve his love!'

'And you do?' Christabel suddenly understood the drift of her sister's conversation. It made sense of her earlier conduct. She had evidently been on the look-out for Sir Julian, hoping to meet him alone in the park.

'More than you at any rate,' Sophia snapped back. '*I'm* not made of ice!'

And with that she banged the bedroom door behind her, leaving Christabel to wrestle with this new and unwelcome development.

Chapter Six

Sir Julian had made elaborate preparations for an evening's visit to Vauxhall. It was not a venue he would ordinarily have patronised—the Gardens had a reputation for encouraging wanton behaviour—but the Prince Regent himself was to sponsor a fête there and nothing else had been talked of among the *ton* for days but the magnificent firework display to be mounted in his honour. So it was that Sir Julian planned with great care every detail of the evening's entertainment. His carriage was to call at Mount Street at seven o'clock and take up Christabel and her siblings. Lady Harriet had cried off at the last moment, citing the burden of preparations for Sophia's ball. The party would drive to Westminster Pier and from there take a boat over the Thames, approaching the Gardens by the water entrance. Sir Julian had already hired one of the hundred supper boxes available in the central amphitheatre and looked forward to serving his guests the wafer-thin ham for which Vauxhall was famous, washed down with the very best champagne. A fifty-strong orchestra would entertain them throughout the meal, but their box was sited far enough away for conversation not to be unduly disturbed. Reserved places at the fireworks arena were also secured. Nothing had been left to chance; he was determined to make the evening a fitting celebration of his recent engagement.

To his dismay the expedition got off to an uncomfortable start. Christabel was already waiting in the hall when he arrived at Mount Street, looking voluptuous in a low-cut silk robe of the deepest gold worn over a flimsy underslip of ivory gauze. He had never before seen her dressed so seductively and after his initial surprise, felt himself falling ever deeper under her spell, the perplexities of their last encounter well and truly forgotten. His enchantment, though, was soon fractured by the sounds of a stormy dispute above.

'You foolish boy, look what you've done!'

It was Sophia, thumping down the main staircase in an unladylike fury. Hardly able to speak, she glared at the two of them patiently waiting and pointed a trembling finger at the hem of her dress.

'Do you see that? It's torn beyond repair! And all because he can't keep his clumsy feet to himself. He's not content to stand all over my dress, oh, no, he has to tear it to shreds.'

'If you hadn't got into such a temper and pulled against my foot, it would never have torn.' Benedict arrived down the stairs two at a time, looking as cross as his sister.

'I didn't pull it, idiot. I was trying to free it. Why did you stand on it in the first place?'

'Why does the sun shine? Why do you wear ridiculous frocks? There's no answer.'

She was just about to loose another tirade at him when Christabel intervened, 'You could change into your lilac silk, Sophia. It will be perfect for the Gardens and then tomorrow you can ask your woman to restitch the hem.'

'How can she mend such a huge tear? And why should I wear the lilac? It's completely insipid and I hate it. I shan't go to Vauxhall and it will be your fault.' She rounded angrily on her brother.

Sir Julian, ever more aware of the advancing hour, thought it time to try his own hand at peacemaking. 'Miss Sophia, you have a wardrobe of beautiful dresses from which to choose. Please do so and favour us with your company this evening.'

Benedict snorted derisively, but his sister allowed herself a glimmer of a smile in Julian's direction before she retraced her steps to the bedroom. Sophia's infatuation was still in place, Christabel noted. Her sister's passions had a tendency to disappear almost as quickly as they erupted and she hoped that this would prove to be the case with Julian. If she made sure that Sophia knew their engagement to be happy and secure, she was hopeful that her sister would shortly transfer her affections elsewhere.

They had been late for the boat and Sir Julian had had to pay a hefty waiting charge, but was relieved simply to have got all of them to the Gardens. Sophia and Benedict kept up a low-level sniping for most of the journey but Christabel blocked her ears to their wrangling. She was determined to make the evening a success, to make amends for her earlier dudgeon and show Julian that she appreciated the considerable thought he'd expended on the evening. And she was enjoying herself. She had never before visited Vauxhall, even though it was a popular pleasure haunt of the *ton* between April and June, and when they stepped from the boat and began to make their way along the Grand Walk, she was entranced. Tree-lined promenades and gravelled pathways led

off from the main route and everywhere fountains, statues and
even artificial ruins dotted the landscape. The evening light
had by this time darkened and they walked in a fairyland of
thousands of lanterns hanging in festoons from the trees and
between the cast-iron pillars of the vaulted colonnade which
ran alongside the Grand Walk.

'What a magical place!' she breathed, her eyes in the shadowy light deep pools of turquoise, 'and how good of you to
think of this excursion.'

Sir Julian, suffused with happiness, smiled benignly and
tucked her arm tightly into his. Benedict had disappeared
almost as soon as they'd reached dry land, and although Sophia
maintained a forbidding frown, a degree of peace was restored.
Lavish praise of a particularly fetching loo mask that she had
bought for the occasion mollified her sufficiently to consent
to explore the Gardens with her sister and future brother-in-
law.

For an hour or so the three of them strolled along the walk-
ways, listening to the bands of Pandean minstrels which played
on platforms scattered around the Gardens. Even Sophia was
intrigued at some of the innovations that had been placed to
interest visitors, marvelling for some time at the mechanical
Cascade which played endlessly at the centre of the South
Walk, another stately avenue spanned by three triumphal
arches. Eventually they made their way to the two central
semi-circles around which supper boxes provided places to
eat, to listen to the orchestra or simply to watch the strolling
crowds.

Sir Julian, all attention, made his two guests comfortable.
A shawl here, a cushion there, and a hovering waiter des-

patched to fetch the supper he had previously ordered. Dozens of waiters ran from box to box, bringing platters of chicken or ham with salads for the guests to mix themselves and bowls for them to brew their own very potent arrack-punch. This was already having some effect in a few of the supper boxes, their inhabitants masked and feeling free to conduct themselves with abandon. The masqueraders were laughing immoderately at their own jokes or cavorting to the music which played nearby. A few of the women were already looking a little dishevelled. Their own box was slightly set back from the majority and Sir Julian felt relieved that the ladies under his charge would not be incommoded by such improper behaviour.

'What curious murals!' Christabel pointed to the rear wall, hazily illuminated by the globe of light hanging from the roof and covered with paintings.

'I believe they were done by a Francis Hayman in the last century,' Sir Julian intoned, 'but they have to be constantly repaired because so many people examine them a little too closely!'

'I do believe you've been researching this information for us,' she teased.

He smiled and admitted as much while Sophia scowled and ostentatiously yawned with boredom. It was fortunate that a distraction soon materialised in the form of supper and with it Benedict, who appeared out of nowhere to eat his share. He didn't stay long, however. As soon as the chicken and ham had been despatched he excused himself with the words that he thought he might try a little jaunt around the dance floor. At this Sophia scowled even more ferociously and began pointedly to tap her feet. Christabel was by now wholly out of pa-

tience with her sister though she knew well the cause of her
bad temper.

But Sir Julian, blissfully ignorant of the tension, offered
his arm to the younger girl, saying genially, 'I think it must
be time for us to repeat our efforts of the other evening, Miss
Sophia—that is, if your sister has no objection.'

Christabel was only too pleased to be left in peace. There
was now quite a crowd of people dancing to the infectious
music of the orchestra and she enjoyed watching them twirl-
ing and spinning beneath the trees, the lanterns dusting the
moving figures with sprinkles of light. A carnival spirit was
abroad, many of the dancers dressed in full disguise. She
thought she saw Domino and her aunt among the crowd of
harlequins, cavaliers, jesters and shepherdesses. She could
have been mistaken, but it was possible that Lady Blythe had
been persuaded after all to bring her charge to this den of in-
iquity. If so, it was strange that Richard was not with them.
She fell to wondering why she and Richard had never visited
Vauxhall when they were a betrothed couple. But those had
been awkward weeks in London when her decision to marry
had begun to seem hideously wrong. The growing influence
of Joshua had seen to that. He, of course, would have leapt at
the chance of meeting her at Vauxhall. Masked and disguised,
it would have been a perfect opportunity for the kind of underhand lovemaking he was so good at. But Richard would
have shrunk from it. He was too upright, too conscious of
what was deemed proper conduct. Or had been, she amended.
The Richard she'd encountered in the past few weeks was
anything but proper. He was unpredictable and passionate
and his tirade in the park just a few days ago had gone well
beyond the bounds of correctness. Had he really changed so

much and Argentina made him literally into a new man? Or had that streak of dissent, of recklessness, of fervour, always been there just waiting to be lit? Six years ago she had chosen not to apply the flame, but instead had turned away to Joshua. It was a sobering thought.

'All alone, sweetheart?'

She looked up, startled. A man dressed in a scarlet domino had suddenly appeared at her side. She had been so deep in thought that he must have leapt over the wooden barrier without her hearing a thing.

'We can't have that, can we, not on a night made for merrymaking?'

The man let out a harsh guffaw and breathed fumes in her face. Repulsed, she rose from her seat, thinking to escape down the staircase at the side of the box, but he was too quick for her. Grabbing her arm, he pulled her close and began to rub his face against her cheek. With a mighty wrench she snatched herself away and desperately made for the stairs, but her flimsy slipper caught in the table leg and he was on her again almost immediately. His arms encircled her waist and dragged her into a clumsy embrace. She shrank back against the wall of the box as his fleshy mouth hovered over her lips. Then a hand alighted on the man's shoulder and jerked him roughly backwards. He let go in surprise and turned to face the cause of this intrusion. Dark grey eyes gleamed behind a black velvet mask and a steely voice commanded him to leave immediately. Christabel knew the voice and the figure instantly.

'Who d'you think you are to tell me what to do?' the man in scarlet protested.

The grim figure stood tensed. 'You'll find out soon enough unless you leave now.'

The man put up his arms in readiness for a brawl. Dreading the scene to come, she looked wildly around for Sir Julian and her sister. Even Benedict might be of use in this situation. Then quite suddenly it was over. The intruder had been picked up bodily and tossed over the barrier he had earlier jumped. At the first sounds of the quarrel people had begun to emerge from the neighbouring supper boxes to see what was amiss and now a small crowd gathered around the prostrate man. Those revellers who had imbibed most seemed to think the whole thing a drama put on for their entertainment and were loud in their praise of the acting. But the more sober were plainly concerned with this breach of the peace and began to mutter ominously amongst themselves.

In response the black-masked figure grabbed Christabel's hand and propelled her swiftly down the stairs and out of the box. He carved a ruthless path for them through the now restive crowd, always holding to her tightly, and a few minutes later she found herself running with him up the Dark Walk. No lanterns hung here and the only light was that of a crescent moon filtered through the rags of lowering clouds. The air was heavy with the scent of lilacs now in full bloom, their abundant foliage casting inky shadows on the gravelled pathway. She could hardly see a foot in front of her, but her rescuer's firm hand kept her from stumbling. The crowds gradually dwindled and the sounds of music faded into the distance. Breathless, they came to a halt outside a small rustic shelter cleverly hidden within a clearing in the mass of surrounding trees. It was invisible, except to those standing immediately outside. Richard pulled her into its sanctuary, hardly allowing her to catch her breath before he began to berate her.

'Where the hell is your fiancé?' he uttered explosively.

She bridled immediately. 'How dare you use such language in my presence?'

He ran his hand through his already dishevelled hair and attempted to gain control of his rage.

'I apologise for my intemperate speech, but I repeat—where is your supposed fiancé?'

'He is not supposed, he *is* my fiancé,' she retorted icily.

'Then why isn't he taking care of you?'

'Sir Julian has taken every care of me. He was absent for a short time only while he danced with my sister.'

'And while he placates that bad-tempered little vixen, he leaves you exposed to the attentions of any rake on the cut.'

'You exaggerate. The man was a nuisance, no more.'

There was silence while they glared furiously at each other. Then in a challenging voice she said, 'I thought I'd made it clear that I never wished to speak to you again.'

'And I'm most happy to concur, but what am I to do when I see a woman, any woman, menaced by a scoundrel?'

'You make too much of the incident—there was no cause to intervene.'

'Really? Then why were you cowering in fear?'

'I was not cowering, nor did I wish to become embroiled in an unseemly wrangle. Did you have to be quite so brutal?'

'Would you have preferred to be ravished?'

'That was hardly likely. The man was clearly drunk.'

'But sober enough to see the prize he was winning.'

She said nothing and again a long, tense silence filled the air between them. The moment of danger had passed and they were both acutely aware of their isolation from the crowd and their proximity to one another. He could not resist looking at her, his gaze growing rapt as the seconds passed. He longed to unpin her curls and bring the burnished curtain cascading down. The sensuality she radiated was engulfing him and the soft contours of her body seemed to cry out for his touch. Exerting all his self-control, he expunged the expression from his face and when he spoke his voice was heavy with irony.

'Evidently I misjudged the situation. The man was no threat to you and I have done him ill. I'll leave you to convey my apologies to our unfortunate friend,' and he gestured back the way they had come. 'You'll doubtless make a better job of it than I.'

She followed the direction of his hand and looked quickly behind her. 'Has he come after us?'

He shook his head. 'There's no one there.' He knew he should leave it at that and walk away, but his frustration impelled him to carry on the fight.

'You can relax, you're quite safe,' he jeered, 'but then you always have been with me, haven't you? A little too safe.'

He looked down at her with a cynical smile. 'For someone who despises the familiar, it's strange how little you enjoy excitement when it comes knocking!'

The energy drained from her. It wasn't enough that she'd been forced to brave the unwanted attentions of a stranger; now she must rekindle her strength for yet another battle with Richard. The knowledge caused her to shiver in the warm night air.

He saw and said tauntingly, 'Perhaps you should have worn just a little more this evening. Or was this a special treat for Sir Julian?'

She ignored the gibe, but a growing anger rippled through her body.

'Or perhaps,' he continued to harass, 'this is just the old Christabel resurfacing, the one that likes to give everyone a special treat!'

The blood whipped her cheeks pink and she turned savagely towards him, her hand raised. She hardly knew what she was doing. This was more than justified fury; all her suppressed desire fuelled the flight of her hand. He caught her arm mid-air and pulled her towards himself.

'What happened to the ice maiden?' he goaded, his eyes dark and brooding.

Then his hands were in her hair, tangling the wild red curls in his fingers and kissing them fervently. Unresisting, she allowed him to liberate her carefully fashioned locks until they tumbled across the smooth swelling of her breasts.

She knew that she was a lost woman. She wrapped her arms around his neck and offered her face to his. Hungrily her lips sought his mouth. She needed his touch with a desperation she had not thought possible. His mouth fastened on hers and she took in the full taste of him. His lips grazed her cheeks, her neck, and glided downwards to the smooth whiteness of her breasts.

Then his fingers were undoing the tight bodice, slowly exposing the yielding flesh of her bosom, slowly but firmly stroking her into ecstasy.

Cupping her breasts in both hands, he brought his mouth to them, one after another. Slowly and expertly he savoured her, until her whole body was swept by a coruscating fire.

She moaned with the intensity of her pleasure and he pushed her against the warm wood of the shelter, fitting himself to her body, moving against her until she felt her legs would collapse beneath her. She tore at his shirt, burying her face in his bare throat. She wanted only to feel his naked skin, to feel the hardness of his body against her. Neither heard the footsteps running up the Dark Walk.

'Christabel? Christabel?' Sir Julian's plaintive cry echoed along the deserted path.

Then Sophia's impatient tones. 'She will hardly have walked here alone in the dark.'

'She may have fled this way. I shall never forgive myself if anything has happened to her.'

'Nothing will have happened, Sir Julian. My sister is well able to take care of herself.'

'We should not have left her alone. I had no idea of such a dreadful event occurring.'

'How could you? You must not blame yourself. She was alone for only a few minutes and we were dancing close by.'

'But not close enough. We should have waited until Benedict returned to the box.'

'Benedict!' she snorted. 'We would have been waiting until the Gardens closed.'

The two stood motionless in the dim shadows of the shelter, their pulses racing and their breathing irregular. She was the first to emerge from the sultry haze, fumbling with the ties of her bodice and desperately trying to smooth the creases of her skirt. She made a monumental effort to regain her calm. Richard was still gazing down at her with a look that turned her knees to water but she gave him an agitated push towards the entrance and with a last, lingering glance, he gathered up his loo mask and slipped out of the shelter into the darkness beyond.

'Christabel!' They were still calling as she stepped out on to the Walk.

'I'm here, don't worry. I'm safe.'

Sir Julian almost ran to her side. In his agitation his cravat had become untied and his carefully styled hair was ruffled beyond repair. He clasped her hands tightly. 'Thank goodness, my dear. Thank goodness we've found you. I have been out of my mind with worry.'

'I'm sorry to have caused you such concern, but I had to leave the supper box unexpectedly.' There was hardly a tremor to her musical tones.

Sir Julian still wore a worried expression. 'You gave us a serious fright, my dear. When we returned to the box, it was upside down—plates broken, tablecloth askew and chairs strewn everywhere. And you had vanished. Whatever happened?'

'Just a little unwanted notice from someone who'd drunk too much punch, but a passing gentleman intervened. I've come to no harm so let us forget about it.'

'But why did you choose the Dark Walk?' Sophia asked curiously. 'It's so gloomy and there's no one around.'

'I didn't choose the Dark Walk, Sophia,' she replied with a touch of asperity, 'I wasn't thinking where I was going. I was trying to escape.'

'Of course,' Sir Julian soothed. 'And thank heaven you were able to. This unfortunate business has been entirely my fault. I was most remiss in leaving you without an escort.'

'Are you all right, Miss Tallis?' Lady Blythe and Domino were hurrying up the gravelled pathway to join them. 'We heard Sir Julian and your sister searching for you and thought we should help.'

'How kind you all are. There was a slight incident, but nothing too troublesome.'

'What a relief! I told you that these Gardens were not at all the thing, Domino. I hope you will believe me now.'

Domino hardly heard her aunt. She was looking around her uncertainly. 'Are you sure everything is well, Miss Tallis? I thought I saw a figure among the trees just now.'

'I don't think you can have. I'm certain that I outran the man who was pestering me.'

'If he's lurking nearby, I will find the blaggard.' Sir Julian was feeling a lot stouter now that his beloved was safe.

'There's nobody here except myself. I expect you saw the shadow of a tree, Domino. There's so little light.'

The girl looked unconvinced, but remained silent. The firework display was imminent and she wanted to find Benedict and speak to him urgently under cover of all the noise. Another bruising encounter with Lord Moncaster that evening had made it urgent that she exact help from her only friend.

Sophia, too, was anxious not to miss the pyrotechnics and said grumpily, 'I think we've spent long enough in this miserable spot. For goodness' sake, let's find our places for the display.'

She had enjoyed two whole dances with Sir Julian before he remembered that they'd left Christabel alone. Surely that proved his love was weak. He might be enthralled by her sister's beauty—men could be unbelievably stupid—but he didn't truly love his fiancée, Sophia was sure. It was only a sense of duty that had prompted him to return to the supper box.

Christabel took her place in one of the front rows of chairs. Her heart was still hammering and the promised spectacle held little appeal after the tumult of the last hour. She noticed

Domino seated a little to the right. The girl must have seen Richard as he made his way back through the wood; she was attuned to him and must know his form by heart. How truly dreadful! How could Richard, how dared he, make such abandoned love to her even as his betrothed was walking close by. And after all her promises to herself, she had succumbed without an instant's hesitation. They had both behaved disgracefully.

She would never have come if she'd known he was to be here this evening. And surely he should have escorted Domino and Lady Blythe. Instead he'd chosen to come alone and in disguise, and there could only be one reason. His motive had to be the freedom it gave him to act badly, the chance to continue her punishment. His fury at her betrothal was still fresh in her mind and it would be easy for him to find an opportunity to torment under cover of darkness. Not that he'd had to search very hard. She'd offered herself, all of herself, without restraint. Willingly, eagerly. She could still see the deep grey of his eyes, glowing and intense in the shadows, the strong curves of his face sculpted out of the dark by the silvery haze and then the feel of his skin on hers, the feel of his touch as he skilfully explored her body for the first time. But in the warm darkness he had seemed as caught up in the moment as she, in thrall to this intoxicating passion that had flamed between them. Even so she knew this could not be. She lived in daily expectation of reading the notice of his forthcoming marriage. Once he had confessed this new love to Lady Anne, he would publish it to the world.

A few seats away Domino had already forgotten that shadowy figure in the Dark Walk. She had more pressing matters

on her mind. As soon as the first cluster of fireworks was tracing its multi-coloured path through the sky she slipped quietly away, leaving her aunt looking skywards. Benedict wasn't
hard to find. He was on the outer circle of people, laughing
and talking with some choice spirits he'd managed to befriend
during the evening. She recognised his slim, rangy figure immediately. He hardly need have bothered to don his loo mask.

The touch of Leo Moncaster's hands earlier that evening
was still on her and she felt slightly sick. She knew that she'd
brought this trouble on herself. She'd set out to win back the
favour that Moncaster possessed and free herself of his presence for ever. Instead she'd ended up in even deeper debt and
he now held her vowels for a sum of money she could never
hope to repay.

Tonight when he'd tracked her down and skilfully detached
her from her aunt, she'd been forced to submit to his caresses.
Under cover of darkness and in the midst of the boisterous
crowd, he'd taken liberties that Domino was desperate to blot
from her mind. It was a piece of great good fortune that at
that moment Sir Julian had raised the alarm. Moncaster had
melted away and she'd been reunited with Lady Blythe.

But not before he'd whispered his very clear threats in her
ear. A handkerchief was but a poor return for the friendship
he'd extended. She owed him money and he would be paid
one way or another. The time for settlement had come, but
this was by far too public a place. His house would prove a
much cosier love nest. They were both bid to Sophia Tallis's
come-out ball on Friday. He would see her there and when
the dancing was at its height would send a signal to her to slip
away and meet him outside. A carriage would be waiting to
take them to his town mansion for an intimate dinner *à deux*

followed by…well, he would no doubt think of something. He would deliver her back to the ball in time for Aunt Loretta to take her home and no one would be the wiser.

Domino was in despair. When she'd first met Leo Moncaster he'd seemed a dashing, handsome, experienced man of the world whom she'd managed to attract despite being little more than a schoolgirl. But very soon she'd been forced to confront the frightening reality that she was at the mercy of a predator with a perverted taste in young girls. She knew herself to be too naïve and inexperienced to deal with the situation alone and she could only hope that Benedict would prove her saviour.

'You must come away with me at the ball,' she announced to him, hardly waiting to exchange the customary pleasantries.

He gaped. 'Come away with you! What are you talking about?'

'At your sister's ball! I'll be there and so will Moncaster. You must take me away or I'll be forced to go with him.'

'Are you crazy? Have the fireworks fried your brains?'

'I'm serious. He'll make me go with him if I don't escape.'

'Don't be so bird-witted. He can't force you to do anything if you don't wish it.'

'He has my handkerchief—you know that—and now he has my IOUs too.'

'What!'

She hung her head, not daring to meet his gaze. 'You wouldn't help me and I tried to win back the handkerchief and lost even more money. If I don't do as he says, he will go to my aunt with my vowels and tell her how dreadfully I've behaved.'

He shook his head in disbelief. 'Then speak to her yourself before he can. I told you before that your best hope is to be honest with her—throw yourself on her mercy.'

'But now it's worse. It's not just the money—she'll suspect that I've behaved, well…not very properly,' she finished lamely.

'Of course you haven't behaved properly,' Benedict exploded. 'But she must know what kind of fellow Moncaster is and she won't judge you too harshly, I'm sure.'

'She'll send me to Spain immediately and I'll be travelling there in disgrace. When I arrive, they'll say I've brought shame on the family. They might even lock me up!'

'And how will going away with me be less shameful?'

'I won't really go away with you, or at least not far, but I need you to make arrangements for me. A carriage to Dover and then a passage across the Channel.'

'You can't travel all that way alone, a chit of a girl like you.'

'I'm not a chit.'

'You're seventeen and the biggest wet goose I've ever met.'

The conversation was not turning out the way she'd hoped and Domino could see her chance of securing his help fading away.

'Benedict, please, please, help me. If you don't think I should travel alone, come with me as far as Paris. My father has friends there and I could stay with them. They'll help me travel on to Spain.'

The pleading in her soft brown eyes was having its effect, but he still couldn't understand what she would gain from her plan.

'But don't you see,' she said trying hard to remain patient, 'I can leave a note for Aunt Loretta saying that I've left London because I'm so unhappy. Someone I met has hurt me.' That at least was true. 'I'll ask her to keep my confidence and not discuss with anyone why I've left. She won't know about the debts and neither will my relatives in Spain. They'll just think that I've arrived a little earlier than they expected.'

'And when Lord Moncaster knocks at your aunt's door with your IOUs after you've left?'

'Do you think he will?' A scared look had returned to her face and Benedict relented.

'Probably not. It's you he wants, not the money. Once you've fled, there won't be much point in trying to harass Lady Blythe.'

'There, you see, I'm right. All we have to do is to get to Paris and then everyone will be happy.'

'Oh yes, everyone,' he said acidly. 'And how do you propose that we get to Paris? Hiring a carriage to Dover costs money and if you think I'm travelling with you on the common stage, you can think again. And when we get to the port, there'll be money needed for a boat ticket and you might not get a berth straight away. That will mean laying down more blunt to pay for accommodation.'

'I don't think I'll stay overnight in Dover,' she said hurriedly.

There would be little point in rescuing her reputation from Leo Moncaster's clutches only to have it shredded by another man.

'We'll go on board straight away.'

Benedict wasn't at all sure that would be possible; he imagined that berths on ships crossing the Channel had to be booked some time in advance, but Domino seemed to know what she was talking about. He'd never travelled beyond

England before and the girl's assurances that she still had a large sum of her father's money intact and that she spoke passable French finally convinced him. He was still feeling guilty that her troubles had begun when he'd introduced her to gambling. He cursed that evening heartily. If he'd had a clue what she would do, he would have kept dancing that night until his feet dropped off. Wearily he agreed to ride with her the next day and make their detailed plans for her escape on Friday evening.

Christabel heard her brother coming in a few hours later. He made no attempt to be quiet, banging the front door behind him and thudding loudly up the stairs to his room. Presumably his night at Vauxhall had gone little better than hers. Her evening had been ruined. Not by the drunken intruder, for her fear of him had been fleeting; almost as soon as she'd realised that he could be a real danger, Richard had knocked the man down and thrown him over the barrier. Then in swift succession their escape from the crowd, the breathless journey up the Dark Walk and finally those moments of sweet delight. Once again he'd set her body alight and left her yearning and confused. Once again she had known no caution. Consumed by raw desire for him, she'd matched him kiss for kiss, caress for caress. The soaring pleasure she'd felt as their naked skins fused still had the power to set her heart pounding all these hours later. Surely she must believe she was loved.

But, no, he was playing with her—his affections lay elsewhere. He was simply intent on proving her unfaithful, especially now that he so abhorred the marriage she was about to make. He wished to expose her as a woman who accepted one man while making impassioned love with another. Her betrothal should have protected her from folly, but once again she had betrayed Sir Julian. While he was frantically searching for her, she was being caressed into ecstasy by another. She had wanted Richard as badly as she would ever want a man and had shown him just as plainly. If they'd not been interrupted, she knew she would have given herself to him completely. He had proved her forthcoming marriage was nothing more than a sham, proved she was the inconstant woman he'd always thought her. He had won their battle of wills.

Chapter Seven

If Christabel wondered why her old lover had chosen to roam the gardens of Vauxhall alone, masked and in disguise, Richard was asking himself much the same question. He'd refused Domino's invitation to escort her to the fête and with good reason. Accompanying her to a masked revelry was unlikely to wean her from her infatuation and he'd already been at pains to bid her goodbye. The legal papers he'd tarried for were now signed and stamped and while Domino was enjoying the party, he was supposed to be well on his way to Cornwall. Yet last night he'd lurked in the shadows, eager to avoid detection, his cloak and loo mask a flimsy disguise. Why on earth had he done so?

The news of Christabel's betrothal had fallen on him like a bludgeoning hammer. He'd felt himself disintegrating from the force of his anger and had needed immediate action, immediate distraction, to free himself from the fury that had him in its grip and was literally shaking him. He'd ridden swiftly from St James's to the livery stables, then marched straight to Jackson's Boxing Saloon where half-a-dozen rounds with the Gentleman himself had left him physically bruised and battered, but feeling a good deal better. At least for a while. But then the old haunting refrain began once more and a fervent need to see her swept over him. She'd been adamant that he stay away and he dared not risk another open confrontation. The temptation to grab her there and then and show her just why she shouldn't marry Sir Julian would be irresistible. Yet the need to see her was like a drug. It had him in its grip and would not let go. The fireworks at Vauxhall had been talked about for weeks and he knew she would be there.

In the event he'd been reduced to watching her from afar. He'd seen her take her place in the supper box with her irritating sister and that stuffed shirt Edgerton. She had looked magnificent—her wayward curls framing a pellucid skin had seemed almost alive and ready to spill into a cascade of fire. And the fall of her gown, its rich, gold silk, had transformed her slender figure into voluptuous beauty. He'd stood transfixed, desire touching every one of his senses and almost sweeping them away. He'd felt himself galvanised into action, urged forwards to leap the barrier and pull her into his arms. Almost, but not quite. Self-discipline had somehow prevailed and he'd continued to watch from the shadows.

But when the intruder had suddenly appeared and threatened her, caution had been thrown to the winds. There'd been immense satisfaction in taking out his frustration on the miserable unfortunate who had dared to frighten this goddess. And then the whirlwind run with her up the Dark Walk to elude the attentions of the gathering crowd. Looking back, he recognised their flight had been more than a response to menace. It was an attempt to escape with her, to run away and leave behind the mess they had jointly made and just simply be together. The memories of their tryst were still with him: the soft rustle of foliage, the sweet odour of lilacs and her body inviting and responsive beneath his hands. He was her prisoner and the ferocious desire she aroused in him was causing as much suffering as he'd ever inflicted.

For she belonged to another man. She could not break the engagement she had entered—the label of jilt would not be so easily shrugged off this time. She would have to marry Sir Julian. Already she was progressing steadily towards the altar, preparing herself for a calm and uneventful life with a calm and uneventful man. That was the choice she'd made and, for her sake, he must stand back and let her follow it. Wasn't true love selfless?

Somehow the injuries he'd suffered had dissolved to nothing. She'd failed him, yes, but he was sure that her heart had been honest and true. She'd been the victim of a master seducer against whom her inexperience was no match. And he was partly to blame. He'd been her betrothed, her lover, but he'd not shown her the love she had craved. He'd been stiff, awkward, shy almost. She hadn't guessed, maybe couldn't guess, the depths of his feelings for her. He saw her now in his mind's eye, a young, vital girl, saw her at the very moment that she'd agreed to marry him. They'd stood on the cliff top, the waves thundering beneath, random spray misting the very air between them. She'd gazed up at him, her face warm with happiness, and said yes. Then she'd reached for his hand and tugged him along the path to the cove, her smile urging him on, her eyes laughing with pleasure. She had been honest and true, he was sure.

After years in which he'd kept the past under lock and key, meeting her again had released a great dam of emotion. He'd thought he would never feel so deeply again, but he'd been wrong. And why was that? He could pretend no longer. Without a doubt, he knew that he loved her. It seemed that he'd always loved her from the days of callow youth through the years of exile to this very moment. His clumsy plan to teach her a lesson and free himself from her power was simply hurt love. He longed for her, burned for her, but he must subdue those feelings. Tomorrow there would be a ball at Mount Street in honour of her tiresome sister and he had been invited. He would bid her farewell in a crowded room and bow out of her life as gracefully as he could. His luggage would be packed and waiting for him at the inn. Early the next morning he would be on his way to Cornwall.

Number Six Mount Street was a house in upheaval and if Christabel were tempted to dwell on her transgressions at Vauxhall, the preparations for the ball effectively banished all such remorse. For days the housemaids had been dusting and sweeping every corner of the house, shining silver and polishing chandeliers. Every spare glass had been unearthed and washed until it sparkled.

The house was a modest size and to hold a ball for up to fifty people, though small by the Season's standards, was an immense undertaking. The two first-floor salons were to be made into one and act as the ballroom by the simple expedient of sliding back the wooden partitioning.

'We must roll up the carpets,' Lady Harriet instructed three panting footmen, early on the Friday morning. 'They will have to be taken to the cellar, I fear, but the parquet floor will be excellent for dancing.' The men, perspiring down three flights of stairs, did not appear overly impressed by this information.

'Bel,' her mother called urgently to her from the drawing

room, 'do you think the quartet we've hired could be stationed at one end of this room?' She indicated the window enclave.

'That would mean that we can't open the windows behind them, Mama,' Christabel warned, 'and it looks likely to be a very warm day.'

Her mother's brow wrinkled. 'The room is already uncomfortably stuffy, I admit, but I cannot see where else to put the musicians.' She sighed. 'It will have to do.'

'It might not matter,' her daughter comforted. 'We can fling the windows wide at the far end of the other room and if people get too overheated, they can step out on to the balcony to refresh themselves.'

'Not too many people,' her mother said wryly. The ironwork balcony which overlooked the gardens to the rear of the house was no more than six feet wide.

As the day wore on, Christabel became aware of her mother's increasing anxiety. The evening's event had been planned as a modest introduction of Sophia to the *ton*, but somehow it had escalated. More invitations had been issued than Lady Harriet had bargained for and some of these to the most fêted in society. Refreshments had been ordered from Gunter's in addition to those being produced in the kitchen by Cook and her willing helpers, and the best champagne had been ordered at a ruinous cost.

What should have been a simple occasion had been transformed into a major undertaking. Lady Harriet could not decide just how this had happened, although Christabel could have enlightened her. She knew her sister had been busy. Sophia had not been content with what she'd described privately as a paltry affair and refused to be put off with the promise of a much grander ball in her honour the follow-ing year. She was partaking of London society now and she wanted her official launch to be talked of for weeks to come. She had been unable to persuade her mother to hire a more prestigious venue but she was determined that everything that could be done to make the party memorable would be done. It was she who had chosen the champagne and ordered the ad-ditional delicacies and she who had ensured that invitations had gone out to the very highest of the *ton*.

That was her sole contribution to the evening's success. Her day was spent in her room preparing for her grand appear-ance. The dress she had originally chosen for this momentous occasion was deemed that morning to be commonplace and she was engaged in a frantic and increasingly bad-tempered search for the perfect ensemble. It was left to Christabel to assist her flurried parent in the hundred-and-one tasks that had to be accomplished. Had the flowers arrived and how were they to be arranged? Was there going to be sufficient room for the musicians in the window enclosure and what should the order of music be? Where were the dance cards ordered at least three weeks ago and why had the ices been delivered so early that they were bound to melt well before they could be served? So it went on as the hours of the day ticked by, Christabel and her mother scurrying from ballroom to dining room to kitchen to hall, solving problems, settling disputes, until they were both so fatigued that all they wanted was to retire to bed and let everyone else dance the night away.

In the confusion that permeated the house, they hardly no-ticed Benedict. He had quickly been pronounced useless in preparing for the ball and advised to lose himself for the day. That suited him perfectly. He had plenty to do if he were to carry off Domino early the next morning and his family's abstraction meant that his constant comings and goings went unremarked. It struck Christabel that he looked unusually serious, but she was too busy to enquire further. Meanwhile upstairs Sophia continued to drive her maidservant to distraction until finally she had decided on the outfit which would eclipse all others and the entire house breathed a sigh of relief.

At nine o'clock Sophia, primped and pampered, took up her place in the entrance hall at the head of the family, waiting to greet her guests. Christabel, standing slightly behind her, hoped that her own appearance was not too disordered. She had completed her *toilette* with only a few minutes to go, scrambling into her dress as the first of the carriage wheels were heard rumbling across the cobblestones outside. She need not have worried for her beauty was undiminished. In the short time available Rosa had given up any idea of achieving the latest elaborate style known as *à la Méduse* and decided on a simple arrangement of soft curls around the face with the rest of her mistress's unruly hair pulled back into an orderly chignon. Diamond clips on either side softened any severity and matching diamonds sparkled from her ears and nestled in the curves of her bosom. The Pomona-green gauze she wore over a paler underdress accentuated the emerald of her eyes and the small diamond fastenings to her bodice made her seem alive with light whenever she moved. She had made little attempt to appear anything other than acceptable, yet she easily outshone every other woman in the room. Those daring young damsels who had worn gauze dresses over damped and transparent petticoats in order to attract attention looked frankly tawdry in the face of such transcendent beauty. Fortunately

Sophia was so immersed in her own absorbing bubble of pleasure that she had no eyes for any of her family, least of all the sister she hoped to supplant.

Domino and Lady Blythe were among the first to arrive and Christabel noticed how very pale and quiet the young girl was. Something ails her, she thought, but what? Leo Moncaster followed close behind, suave and debonair as ever, but exuding a sense of threat, subtle and unexpressed. She was at a loss to understand why he'd come since he was not a particular friend of the family, but seeing Sophia's blush as she curtsied to him, she knew immediately who had pushed for his invitation. Lord Moncaster's attendance at one's coming-out ball was a fine prize to win. She had little time to contemplate the oddities of the guest list before Sir Julian was before her, splendid in black satin knee-breeches and long-tailed coat, and reverently taking her hand.

'How good to see you, my dear. And looking breathtaking as always! I seem hardly to have managed a word with you of late.'

She looked guiltily up at him. 'I'm sorry. This week has simply sped by—there's been so much to do for Sophia's come-out and Mama is without my father's help.'

'I know how busy you must have been, my dear Christabel, and that is only right. Your mother needs your support and I would expect nothing else from such a loving daughter. But when this evening is over, I hope we will have the chance to spend time together.'

'We will, of course,' she reassured him hastily.

'I am very much looking forward to taking you to Rosings as soon as ever it is convenient with you—and your mother, of course. I'm sure that you will both enjoy the country air and I hope it's not too boastful to say that you will be well pleased with the home that you find there. Every member of my staff is ready and eager to welcome the new Lady Edgerton.'

She brushed aside this reference to their marriage, but tried to sound enthusiastic about the forthcoming visit.

'I'm looking forward to seeing Rosings as much as you are to showing it to me.' This was only half a lie at least. 'But until Sophia and Benedict return to Cornwall, you must see that it is impossible.'

Sophia, who had moved towards Sir Julian as soon as she saw him enter the room, caught the tail end of the conversation and looked thunderous. Only the arrival of a new dance partner prevented an outburst. Instead she smiled extravagantly at the young man who stood before her and made a play of ticking off his name on her dance card. With a withering look at her sister, she allowed herself to be swept back on to the ballroom floor.

It was halfway through the evening before Sir Julian caught up with his beloved again. Her duties had not stopped with the arrival of guests; she and Lady Harriet had constantly to mingle, to introduce, to smooth the social waters. He finally ran her to ground just as she had finished giving instructions to one of the footmen to begin opening the final crate of champagne.

'Christabel—' he pounced '—this dance must be mine!' The musicians were just tuning up for the first quadrille of the evening.

She found herself having to apologise yet again. 'I regret I cannot, Julian—there are a hundred-and-one things I should check before I can think of dancing.'

His face fell and she glanced wildly around. 'I see Sophia is temporarily without a partner. It would be most kind of you to ask her to join the quadrille.'

Sir Julian gave a resigned smile. 'If you wish it, my dear. It's well that your sister dances so creditably.'

He moved obediently to where Sophia stood disconsolate. The name on her card had failed her and she was without a partner at her very own party, but Sir Julian's arrival transformed the miserable situation. Seeing the genuine smile of warmth directed at him, he felt that his sacrifice had not been in vain. They were soon dancing easily together, chatting almost as old friends, Christabel noted. She was satisfied. The better Sophia knew Julian, the less likely she was to continue to weave fantasies around him.

By eleven o'clock the ball was in full swing. Almost every guest who had been bidden to the party had arrived and those who were planning to go on to other and grander events had not yet left. The dance floor was crowded, a kaleidoscope of jewelled shades as the women twirled and pirouetted in interweaving patterns of colour. If the musicians felt stifled in their embrasure, they did not show it, playing without pause for the eager dancers. The temperature of the room had been rising all the time and the copious banks of flowers which decked the walls on either side were beginning to wilt. The starched shirt points of the gentlemen showed a definite tendency to limpness and even the most elegant of the women had recourse to their fans as the evening wore on. The call to partake of refreshments when it came was greeted with some relief.

Supper was a sociable event. The Tallises' dining room

had been cleared of furniture and in its stead trestle tables set up, covered in starched white linen and furnished with white porcelain and silver cutlery. Small crystal bowls of deep pink roses dotted the length of the buffet and a splendid centrepiece of mauve-and-white lilies towered majestically over the whole. The table groaned with every conceivable dainty that the combined efforts of Cook and Gunter's could produce. It was an intimate space and people gathered in groups around the table or arranged the few chairs still remaining in small clusters. The flushed, happy faces and the buzz of chatter was evidence that the event was deemed a success and Christabel could relax.

At last she had leisure to look around her. Sophia was in high gig, sitting with Sir Julian and two of her female confidantes. She was evidently pleased to have netted the man she clearly considered the beau of the evening. Benedict hovered in the background, a jumpy look on his face. Christabel watched him for a while, feeling concerned, but unsure why. She saw that he was staring rather too fixedly at Domino, who seemed to be involved in some kind of altercation with Lord Moncaster. How extraordinary! Leo Moncaster rose from his seat at that moment and made for the door. Immediately she sped to the hall to bid him goodbye, her brain teeming.

'Are you leaving us already, Lord Moncaster?' she said lightly.

He turned, smooth as always, his face giving no inkling of his thoughts.

'I regret, Miss Tallis, that I have business elsewhere. Do accept my thanks for a most enjoyable evening.'

His tone was genial, but there was a metallic ring to his voice and his smile was tight and controlled. What could have upset him so much that he would risk gossip from an angry dispute and an early departure? She noticed that his antagonist, too, was making her way to the door. Domino, still pale faced, must have persuaded her aunt to leave betimes.

The musicians struck up again and the ballroom filled with couples still determined to enjoy the evening. Christabel had just decided that this might be an opportune moment to offer Julian the dance he desired when a tall and striking figure was ushered through the door. The man wore the black satin knee breeches of the gentleman of fashion and a black tailcoat which fitted him to perfection. A white frilled shirt set off the lean, tanned face and a single diamond stud held in place a neck-cloth tied in the intricate Oriental style. It was Richard and he looked superb. She could hardly believe her eyes. Richard! Who on earth could have invited him? Her sister's cunning smile told the story. Of course, Sophia would hope to cause trouble if she could and this was her master stroke. Well, she would not succeed.

'Good evening, Lord Veryan.'

Christabel's voice strove to remain unhurried and calm. The remembrance of their last encounter came rushing back; her eyes were held captive by the figure before her, lingering on the seductive picture he presented. She gave herself a mental shake; she could not afford to show any sign of the feelings he aroused in her.

'Good evening, Miss Tallis, I hope I see you well?' His tone was crisp and businesslike. It helped to steady her.

'Yes, my lord, very well,' she responded formally.

They stood, unable to continue the conversation, unable to stop their eyes from feasting on each other. He was the first to recover.

'I'll not be staying long. I came only to say goodbye.'

'Goodbye? You are leaving London?'

'I've always had the intention of returning to Cornwall as soon as I could, but circumstances have made it difficult.'

'Really?' There was a challenge in her voice. 'I imagine Lady Anne must be very glad that *circumstances* now allow you to return home.'

He bowed his head, acknowledging her hit. She looked at him again. His eyes held a wistfulness that she did not remember before and the intensity of his gaze made her limbs begin to weaken, her strength dissolving as she stood there.

'Won't you stay to dance a little while?' she managed. 'Unfortunately Miss de Silva has just left—she could not have known you were attending—but there are many others who would be delighted to partner you.'

He blinked at the mention of Domino's name but then recalled that Christabel still believed in the fiction of their relationship, a fiction he had been at pains to foster.

'I need no other partner, but if *you* will dance with me, I would be delighted. A waltz is just beginning.'

Mindful of having refused Sir Julian earlier in the evening, Christabel demurred. If she accepted, he would feel justifiably offended and she had no wish to snub the man she was soon to marry. More truthfully, she knew that dancing with Richard was likely to unleash a tumult that would crack open the social façade she wore.

'I am not dancing this evening, Lord Veryan.'

'Come—a few steps only and then I'll leave.'

She hesitated; the temptation to find herself in his arms again and for the last time seemed overwhelming. But she must not succumb to this insistent longing; such feelings were inadmissible and must be put behind her for good. Her hand was trembling as he took it and raised it to his lips.

'A few minutes of the waltz should not take up too much of your time.'

As if in a dream she allowed herself to be swept on to the dance floor. He held her tightly, his form fitting hers, two halves making a whole. Swaying sinuously to the strains of the music, they moved as one. They heard and saw nothing other than themselves: two bodies locked in hot intimacy. Their fever mounted inexorably, licking them with its flames, consuming them with its ardour. They could not bear to keep dancing. And so it was that as they neared the far window, Richard pulled the curtain swiftly to one side and danced her on to the balcony.

She gasped. 'Whatever are you doing?'

His eyes glittered in the moonlight which lapped the ornamental balustrade; when he spoke, his voice was rough with desire.

'I came to say goodbye, Christabel, but I find I can only do so in private, just you and I alone together for a few moments.'

The soft evening air washed over them, the smell of Albertine roses on the wall below drowning them in a sweet perfume. A slight breeze flicked her curls across her cheek and his hand went automatically to brush them back. He stopped himself.

'I came to say goodbye,' he repeated, 'and to wish you well for the future.'

The sincerity in his voice was unmistakable. His anger had gone. He had accepted her betrothal and whatever schemes he'd been devising were finished. This was the outcome she'd craved during the past days of misery. Yet she was filled with the greatest sorrow—in just a few minutes she must watch him walk from the room and out of her life for ever.

As if reading her mind, he said gently, 'You deserve to live happily. I should not have hurt you, you of all people.'

She could see this sentiment came from deep within his heart and wondered what other feelings might lie beneath that calm, elegant exterior. It took her a while to answer and when she did, her voice sounded barely above a whisper.

'As we both know, my own past has not been free of blame.'

'We were young and foolish, and there I should have left it. But when I saw you again…' He shrugged his shoulders expressively. 'It was all up with me. The old grievances began to live once more and I seemed powerless to slay my demons.'

'And now?'

'I haven't exactly slain them, but they're back under lock and key.'

His smile was awry, his face shadowed despite his best efforts. She had a crazy urge to take him in her arms and kiss him back into happiness. The shocking thought rendered her silent for a moment.

'You need fear no more intrusions from me,' he said, thinking she required reassurance. 'You will have a splendid future, I'm sure, and I wish you all the happiness that is possible.'

'You were always a generous spirit, Richard,' she whispered.

'And you were always a loving girl, as I'm sure Sir Julian will find. He once said that he considered himself blessed to have won you for his wife and he was right to think so.'

His face moved closer to hers, his eyes hungrily devouring her delicate beauty. She felt herself tremble and move instinctively closer to him. His fingers touched her hand lightly and trailed their way up her bare arm. Then they were in her hair winding, stroking, caressing the fiery curls. Both hands moved to cup her face and he gazed intently into her eyes, absorbed in their emerald depths.

'One last kiss,' he whispered.

She raised her face to his, her mouth soft and yielding beneath the hard pressure of his lips. His arms were round her pulling her body into his, moulding her to himself.

'Christy,' he groaned, 'what have we done?'

His use of her pet name demolished any remaining resistance. His mouth once more fastened on hers, his lips insistent, and then his tongue was gently pressing her lips apart, delicately exploring her mouth until she wanted nothing more than to feel him, all of him, close to her and for ever. For long minutes they were oblivious to everything. They did not see the curtain being quietly lifted and two pairs of eyes staring at them, Sir Julian's in horror and Sophia's in jubilation. When they emerged from the enclave, shaken from their encounter, neither observer was to be seen. Sir Julian had taken a hasty leave of Lady Tallis and Sophia, the picture of innocence, had joined a new set for the country dance which was just then striking up.

For the few hours that remained of the ball, Christabel was glad to have plenty to do. There were still refreshments to be ordered from the kitchen, damsels to partner, coats to be retrieved and farewells to say; almost anything would do to keep at bay the deep throb of pain which threatened to crush her. Richard had gone. Those words danced blackly in her mind's eye and had constantly to be repressed. It was only when the last person had been escorted to the last carriage that she could no longer hide from her grief: Richard was gone and his leaving was for ever.

There was no sign of Benedict, but her mother and sister were in the hall, looking tired from their individual exertions, but both pleased with the evening's success.

'Thank you, Bel, for all your hard work today.' Lady Harriet clasped her hand warmly. 'Without you things would not have gone so smoothly. I'm sure Sophia is most grateful,' and she looked meaningfully at her younger daughter.

Sophia did not respond and there was an uncomfortable silence.

'What happened to Sir Julian, Mama?' Christabel asked lightly. 'He seemed to disappear in a puff of smoke.'

Her joke fell lamely on the air, but her mother smiled and said mildly, 'He left shortly after supper, my dear. I'm not entirely sure why. He said something about another engagement. It seemed rather odd to me, but I thought you might know.'

'No, indeed, I understood he would be present for the whole evening. How very strange!'

'He seemed a little distressed,' Lady Harriet said thoughtfully, 'but I could be wrong.'

'You're not wrong, Mama. He *was* distressed.' Sophia had come instantly to life and was ready for the kill.

'Why, whatever has happened?' her sister queried in astonishment.

'I don't know how you have the nerve to stand there and ask that!' Sophia was almost jumping with fury.

Her mother looked questioningly at a bemused Christabel, but no help was forthcoming.

'Explain yourself, Sophia,' Lady Harriet commanded crossly.

'If you really want me to I will, but I would think Bel should be the one to do the explaining. She's the one who's engaged to Sir Julian, but can't seem to stop kissing other men.'

'What!' Christabel and her mother exclaimed in unison.

But it was Christabel who turned pale. Sir Julian must have seen her kissing Richard and naturally it was Sophia who had led him to that window and ensured her disgrace. Her sister must have been watching them all the time and seized her golden opportunity the minute it came.

'What is this, Bel?' her mother was demanding.

'Richard came to say goodbye, Mama,' she began calmly. 'He was bidding me farewell.'

'Hmph!' Sophia interrupted crudely. 'Some farewell! You were in his arms and he was kissing you in a quite scandalous way.'

'Christabel, is this true?'

She did not answer her mother, but turned away and began to climb the stairs in silence. She was sick at heart and there was nothing she could say in her defence.

At eleven o'clock the next morning Sir Julian Edgerton presented himself at Mount Street and asked to speak to the eldest daughter of the house. He was in a chastened mood, but also determined. He had sat up late into the night, thinking through his predicament, and had come to a decision. He must see Christabel Tallis immediately before he changed his mind. He only hoped that meeting her again would not throw him off track.

When the maidservant scratched at Christabel's door with Sir Julian's name on her lips, she braced herself for what she knew would be a distressing interview. She had been up and dressed for many hours; in fact, she'd hardly slept, going over the events of the previous evening in her mind and preparing herself for the likely outcome. Now the moment had arrived. She walked slowly down the stairs, her serene expression and graceful carriage masking her discomfort. Sir Julian, looking towards the staircase, saw a vision of the palest pink tulle descending towards him. He drew himself up resolutely.

'Good morning, Miss Tallis.' No Christabel now, she reflected.

'Good morning, Sir Julian,' she responded equally formally. 'You wished to speak privately with me?' He was grateful that she had come straight to the point.

'Would that be possible?' He cleared his throat nervously.

She led the way into the library, a room normally deserted for most of the day. The servants had already cleaned and they were unlikely to be disturbed. In any case she imagined the discussion would not take very long.

'Miss Tallis,' Sir Julian began, clearing his throat again. 'We have known each other for many months now and you must be aware that I have grown to esteem you highly…and to love you.' He almost mumbled these last few words. Christabel inclined her head slightly.

'I had hoped,' Sir Julian began again with difficulty, 'that we were well enough suited to contemplate making our future lives together. When you accepted my proposal, I was the happiest man alive. However…' and he appeared to be choosing his words carefully '…it would seem that you were not of the same mind.'

She bowed her head. She must say something to this honourable man who was clearly struggling to make sense of a world turned upside down. The future he had so blithely anticipated lay now in ruins.

'Sir Julian, please believe me when I say that I also shared that hope.'

'Then I do not understand what has occurred.' His face lost its fixed expression and collapsed into a bewildered sadness; he looked hopelessly out of his depth and Christabel's heart smote her.

'I fear it will be no comfort for you to learn that I am as confused,' she offered. 'However, you should know that the painful situation that has arisen is no reflection on you. You have been wholly generous in your conduct. This is entirely my fault.'

'You are most kind, Miss Tallis, and it relieves me to know that I could not have done anything more to make our betrothal a success. But it leaves us with a problem.'

'There is no problem, Sir Julian. In the circumstances it is impossible for us to marry and I imagine you came here today to tell me so. The notice of our betrothal has not yet been sent to the papers and only a few people know of our plans.'

Sir Julian looked pained. 'I regret that you are right in your surmise. After what has occurred I feel that neither of us could give ourselves wholeheartedly to a marriage. But what shall we say to those people who have been told we are to wed?'

'We will simply say that we found that after all we were not suited to each other.'

Sir Julian turned this over in his mind and then smiled faintly. 'That sounds pleasantly vague. And people can pick it over at will and make what they wish of it.'

'Exactly.'

'As always, Miss Tallis, you have the perfect touch.' He looked regretfully at the beautiful woman who stood before him.

'Not always, Sir Julian,' she reminded him gently.

'Quite so,' he said and hurriedly turned towards the door.

The interview was at an end. They had survived it and without permanent scars on either side. Christabel breathed a sigh of relief. Now that it was done, a burden seemed to have been lifted from her. Her future life would be difficult, but she was no longer living a lie.

She followed him out into the hall and almost fell over the figure of Sophia, who had clearly been loitering outside the library door, agog to see what had happened and ready with sympathy for Sir Julian.

'Miss Sophia, good morning,' he said without much enthusiasm. The strident tones of violet silk hit him in the eyes and he winced. He had been hoping to escape from the house without having to encounter any other of the family.

'How nice to see you, Sir Julian,' Sophia chirruped gaily as if nothing of any import had happened. 'Are you intending to walk in the park? It's such wonderful weather again, it's a waste to spend it indoors.'

He had been planning to return to his own home and lose himself in paperwork. He needed to obliterate this most painful meeting of his entire life. But Sophia was smiling encouragingly at him and shafts of sunlight flooded the hall from the transom over the door. Perhaps after all a walk in the park with a congenial companion might be beneficial. Sophia had shown great enthusiasm for his latest project, the foundation of an orphanage in Shoreditch, and her opinion on a number of pressing issues which had emerged since their last discussion might be valuable.

'If you would care to accompany me to Hyde Park, I would be delighted, Miss Sophia,' he responded obligingly.

She snatched up her bonnet from the chair and was at his

side in an instant. It was clear that she was well prepared for this moment and Sir Julian was flattered that she had planned to devote herself to keeping him company. At least one of the Tallis sisters held him in esteem. He reflected on how much time he had spent with Sophia lately when Christabel had been unable or unwilling to be by his side. In hindsight those frequent absences were significant. And he had grown to like the younger girl. Admittedly her taste in dress was a little unusual, but she seemed willing to listen to whatever small suggestions he made. Above all he felt flattered by her interest in his affairs: she always gave him her full attention. There was merit attached to a girl who was not the most sought-after belle in society. And merit, a small whispering voice added, to a girl who was not prone to sexual flirtation.

Lady Harriet had come into the hall as the pair left. She looked questioningly at Christabel still standing with her hand on the library door.

'Mama, I have to tell you that Sir Julian and I have decided that we do not after all suit.' The phrase ran glibly off her tongue.

'Do not suit!' her mother parroted. 'What can you mean?'

'Just that. The betrothal is over.'

Lady Harriet sighed heavily. 'After what occurred last night, I suppose that Sir Julian could do little else.'

'It was a mutual decision.'

'Precipitated by your reckless conduct! Whatever were you thinking?'

She ignored the reference to her encounter with Richard and said soothingly, 'It's for the best, Mama.'

Lady Harriet looked bewildered. 'But why in heaven's

name, Christabel? Everything seemed to be going so well between you.'

'"Seemed" is the right word. We were never really suited. I fear that for a short time I persuaded myself otherwise.'

'And now you have a second broken engagement to your name. I hope you realise what that signifies in the eyes of society.'

'If you mean that I have no earthly chance of ever finding a husband now, yes, I do realise. But believe me, Mama, there are worse things in life.'

Lady Harriet groaned and twisted her hands. Her beloved daughter had committed social suicide and there was nothing she could do to rescue her.

'Don't be too upset—' Christabel warmed to the task of rallying her mother '—you might just catch Sir Julian for another Tallis!'

Lady Harriet's expression was fiercely indignant and it was well for her daughter that a servant appeared at that moment with a note in her hand. The maid was unable to read, but was clearly agitated by having found the paper prominently displayed on Lady Harriet's small writing desk. Irritated, her mistress snatched the note and dismissed the maidservant. She scanned the brief message and her face drained of all colour; she looked as though she were about to crumble to the floor. Christabel stepped swiftly forwards.

'Mama, what is it?'

Chapter Eight

She took the note from her mother's trembling hand and read it quickly. 'I don't understand. He's gone to Paris? Benedict?'

'How could he?' her mother wailed. 'What more will befall us?'

'But what is this about Domino?'

'It's evident, isn't it? They've eloped.'

'Forgive me, Mama, but that has to be a nonsense. Benedict eloping? He's never shown the slightest interest in females.'

'I am not at all sure that's so. He seems to have spent a great deal of time with this girl lately.'

Christabel thought back over the last few weeks and had to agree: Benedict meeting Domino at Almack's, laughing with her at the picnic, the regular rides in the park and then last night at Sophia's ball, his fixed concentration on the girl. But her lover? That still appeared unlikely.

She said as much to her mother, but Lady Harriet refused to be comforted.

'If he is not her lover, then what is he doing going to Paris with her? It's clear to me that they are eloping.'

'Mama, even if they wished to marry each other, why would

they elope? Wouldn't it be more rational for Benedict simply to ask Domino's guardian for permission to wed her?'

'That's just it!' her mother produced triumphantly. 'He must know there would be little chance of obtaining permission to marry. The girl is only seventeen and, I understand, a great heiress. Benedict hardly figures as the most eligible suitor.' A sudden dreadful thought struck. 'Do you think that he's eloping for her money?'

'How can that be? Benedict has lacked for nothing in his life.'

Her mother did not reply immediately, but began an agitated walk up and down the hall, her mind beset by this new enormity.

'I haven't said anything to you, Bel,' she began finally in a faltering voice, 'but I've become worried over some of his activities. I suspect that he has begun to gamble more seriously than we know. What if he's plunged himself into debt, huge debt, and hasn't wanted to tell us?' She shook her head in despair at the thought and her tears began to gather.

'Not even Benedict would be foolish enough to think he could elope with an under-age girl and then make free with her inheritance!'

Her mother appeared deaf to these rousing words. She sank into the large leather chesterfield that stood against the wall and stared blindly into space. When her daughter bent down and tried to hug her, she began to rock backwards and forwards, keening quietly; she seemed to have disappeared into a nightmare world of her own conjecture. Christabel was alarmed. Her mother's self-possession was renowned and had survived countless family troubles. But this new tragedy to strike Mount Street, coming so quickly after the events of the previous evening, had clearly overwhelmed her.

She came to a decision. 'Mama, I'm going to see Lady Blythe. She may know more than us.'

'No!' Galvanised by these words, her mother sat bolt upright. 'We cannot allow this news to be made public.'

'It won't be. Lady Blythe will be just as eager as us to hush things up. Together she and I may be able to put together a rescue plan.'

'Rescue? How can you rescue them? Benedict left the house before dawn. They could be anywhere by now.'

'We have the advantage of knowing where they're headed. If we could reach them within the next few hours, nobody except ourselves need know a thing.'

Particularly Richard, she thought. For his sake, if for no one else's, she must do her utmost to rescue Domino from this foolish journey.

'And who is to follow them?' her mother was saying querulously. 'Your father is hundreds of miles away in Cornwall and you have managed to alienate the fiancé who might have lent us his support.'

Before her mother could renew this still-raw grievance, she rang for Lady Harriet's dresser.

'Her ladyship is feeling unwell, Mitford. She needs to rest. Could you ensure that she is made comfortable and then bring her some sweet tea?'

Once her mother had been safely despatched to her room, Christabel donned her bonnet and walked swiftly to Curzon Street. She had dismissed her mother's suggestion that Benedict had eloped because of money troubles, but the thought that he might have become seriously infatuated with

Domino could not be so easily lost. It was true that he had hitherto shown little interest in women, but she could not deny that
he had been dancing attendance on the young girl in recent
weeks in a way that was quite foreign to him. What if Domino
returned his feelings? Where would that leave Richard? Her
heart ached for him that he should be treated so shabbily by
the two women he had asked to marry.

The moment she was ushered into Lady Blythe's presence,
she saw that the older woman, too, had received an unwelcome missive. Her face was unnaturally pale and she seemed
to have difficulty rising from her seat. She came towards
her fair young visitor and offered an unsteady hand. Once
they were alone, she silently passed a single sheet of paper to
Christabel. The note her niece had left proved much longer
and far more informative than Benedict's. The errant pair, it
appeared, were on their way to Dover and from there they
hoped to take a boat across the Channel and make their way
to Paris. Domino was sorry to upset her aunt who had been
so kind to her, but the situation in London had become intolerable and she had to escape. Benedict was to escort her on
her journey to the French capital so her aunt must not worry!

'Miss Tallis, what are we to do?' Lady Blythe questioned
in a broken voice as Christabel finished reading the note. Her
hands moved restlessly in her lap. 'I had no idea, no idea.'

'No idea of what, Lady Blythe?'

'That Domino was in love with your brother, of course.'

'She does not say that in her message,' Christabel cautioned.

'Not in so many words, but why else would she have
embarked on this scandalous journey with him? I should

never have allowed them to ride together with only a groom as chaperon.'

'She says that her life here has become intolerable. Have you any idea what she might mean, ma'am?'

'I can only imagine that she has been carrying on this clandestine relationship for some time and has become frustrated with the secrecy involved. She knows well that her father would never agree to such a match, but if she had only confided in me...' Loretta Blythe blinked back the tears. 'We have all been seventeen and convinced that our romance would last for ever.'

Christabel scrutinised the letter again. It was hardly a message from someone about to elope with the love of her life: no impassioned declarations, no pages blotched by tears. On the other hand, the intolerable situation in London sounded ominous. Could that be, as Lady Blythe surmised, her love for Benedict, which she was unable to acknowledge?

She looked at the older woman, sunk deep in her chair, an expression of quiet despair on her face, the mirror image of her own mother, and cursed Benedict. Someone had to try to put things right, restore their peace of mind and ensure that Richard never discovered this new injury to his name. It would have to be her—there was no one else.

The decision made, she rose briskly from her chair. 'Please don't upset yourself, ma'am, the situation is not irretrievable. We know where they've gone and when they left. It should be possible to catch them before they can board a packet to Calais. Fortunately the weather has turned inclement and sailings are bound to be disrupted. We have a very real chance, you know, of finding them still waiting on the quay side.'

'We? But who can go? My health is not as good as it used

to be, my dear. I cannot possibly contemplate such a journey. And Domino's father is thousands of miles across the sea.'

At the thought of Alfredo and what he would say at this latest turn of events, her face lost even the little colour it still possessed and she plunged her head in her hands, weeping copiously.

Christabel thought it prudent to take her leave at this juncture. '*I* will go,' she said quietly. 'I'll be away a day or so, I dare say, but I hope to have good news for you when I return.'

Her companion looked up wonderingly, 'You cannot possibly go yourself! My dear, think of it, you cannot travel alone, without an escort.'

'I'll take my groom. Stebbings has been with our family all my life and is completely trustworthy.'

'A servant?'

Christabel was by now losing patience. 'If you can think of someone else who could undertake this mission, then please tell me. Otherwise I'll do what I'm able.'

The older woman's voice quavered, 'Lord Veryan? I was wondering whether we might venture to call on Lord Veryan's help. What do you think?'

But before her visitor could reply, the slight glimmer of hope had faded from her face. 'But, no, I recollect now, he is on his way to Cornwall, I believe.'

Christabel had reached the door and turned in surprise, 'Surely he would be the last person you would want to know about this escapade,' she murmured as she slipped out of the room, leaving behind her a puzzled woman.

Once back in Mount Street, she hastily threw a few overnight essentials into a small valise and gave orders for the travelling carriage to be brought round to the front of the house as soon as possible. While she waited, tracing and re-tracing her steps in the hall, her mother emerged unexpect-edly from the drawing room. She'd imagined Lady Tallis to be laid down on her bed and had left a brief message of ex-planation with Mitford. She'd hoped to avoid the confronta-tion that now looked likely.

'Why are you dressed for travelling, Bel?' was Lady Harriet's immediate question.

She decided to meet trouble head on and said straitly, 'I'm going to Dover. Benedict and Domino are headed to that port, prior to crossing to France. I think if I leave now I may be able to catch them before they embark.'

'To Dover? On your own? You cannot do such a thing!' Her mother's shocked face was testament to the serious impropri-ety of her plan.

'I'm sorry if it distresses you, Mama, but I can and I must.'

'But why? What good will it do other than besmirch your name even further!'

'The weather has been stormy since they left and it's more than likely they'll be delayed. I'm hopeful that I'll be able to prevent them leaving England.'

'And if you do not, is it your intention to continue this insane pursuit across the Continent?'

She allowed herself a small smile at the image her mother had conjured, but said as soothingly as she could, 'If they've already sailed, then I will return immediately, you have my word.'

Still plainly very agitated, her mother tried another tack. 'But you will never get to Dover and back in a day.'

She indicated the valise at her feet. 'As you see, I'm prepared.'

Lady Harriet's face registered even greater shock at such brazen conduct and her daughter was forced to redouble her persuasion.

'If we must stay the night at Dover, it's surely better that I accompany Domino.' She looked directly into her mother's troubled eyes. 'As you've already pointed out, Mama, I'm now beyond any consideration of marriage so what better role to assume than that of chaperon.'

'Why are you doing this, Christabel?'

'I've just explained.'

'But not very convincingly. Your chance of success is slight. The packet boats sail in all kinds of atrocious weather, as you must know, and you will be stranded in Dover—a young woman, putting up in an inn alone—and for what precisely?'

'I have at least to try to undo the harm that has been done.' She looked steadily at her mother. 'If Domino continues with this journey, it will be because of my brother's thoughtlessness in aiding her. It will ruin her reputation and make it impossible for her to marry where she wishes.'

'But surely she wishes to marry Benedict?'

'I don't think so. Benedict is her escort. He may be in love with her, although I doubt it, but *she* is in love with Richard Veryan.'

Her mother paused. This certainly accorded with other gossip she had heard. It was more than likely, but why was Bel becoming so involved? Out loud she repeated, 'Richard?'

'I believe they are to make a match of it. No doubt he is waiting until the year's mourning is over before making an official announcement, but I think it clear that they plan to be together. I imagine some silly quarrel must have sprung up between them and would have petered out to nothing if Benedict had not become embroiled.'

Her mother remained silent, still wondering at the intensity of her daughter's concern.

'You must see that I owe it to Richard,' Christabel broke out. 'We have been an unlucky family for him: I broke his first engagement and now Benedict will be responsible for destroying the second. Unless, that is, I do something now and attempt to rescue Domino from her own foolishness.'

'You owe nothing to Richard Veryan, Bel,' her mother said quietly. 'Yes, you broke the engagement and no doubt it was very painful for him, but you have long expiated that sin. And after his behaviour last night, it is he who is in debt to you.'

'That's not so.'

'I think it is. He has cost you your betrothal; more than that, he has made quite sure that you will have little chance of any future marriage. I would say that his flagrant disregard of any acceptable code of conduct has more than balanced the books.'

'I have to help him, Mama.'

'He has ruined you, Bel!'

'I have ruined myself. I tried to follow a path which wasn't mine. For a while I convinced myself that I was doing the right thing, but all the time I was being untrue to the person I really am.'

'You will have plenty of time now to be true to yourself,' her mother remarked tartly, 'and while you're doing that you can enjoy watching your sister snare Sir Julian for herself.'

It was past one o'clock before the carriage arrived at the front door and Christabel was able to begin the journey to

Dover. It would take at least seven hours to reach the town and she made herself as comfortable as she could, nestling into the velvet seat coverings and pulling a cashmere blanket over her legs to shield her from draughts. Outside on the box, his face disapproving, Stebbings set the horses in motion. He had promised Lady Tallis that he would not leave Miss Christabel's side until they were back in Mount Street and this he was grimly determined to do.

They were soon rumbling over Blackfriars Bridge, its elegant Portland stone glinting in the afternoon sunlight. Immediately south of the river paved roads gave way to dirt tracks with cramped and ramshackle buildings huddled on either side. Vast numbers of the poor were crowded into these tenements and everywhere squalor and despair disclosed a very different London to the one Christabel knew. Garbage was strewn at random and open tidal sewers dotted the landscape. She felt a guilty relief once the carriage had left behind these desperate areas and was trundling through the quieter suburbs where market gardening and pasturage for cows still interspersed the dark of London's brick.

It was two hours into their journey before at last they reached the Kent countryside. A panorama of fields and trees passed lazily by and Christabel had ample leisure to think. The more she considered the matter, the more she found it difficult to believe this was an elopement. Benedict's demeanour had never approached that of a lover and Domino had treated him in the same carefree fashion. It was clear that Domino was the moving force behind this crazy journey. Could she have quarrelled with Richard over some trifle—perchance he'd not been giving her the attention she expected—and decided that running away was a means of teaching him a lesson? She was young enough and foolish enough.

The continual shaking and jolting of the carriage felt to Christabel as though she had been travelling for months rather than hours. After the recent spate of bad weather, the road was potholed and dangerous, with immense muddy banks on either side, and in some places reducing almost to a track. Unable to sleep, she made plans for when they reached Dover.

As long as the delinquents were still in the town, she would find them. She must convince Domino that any fears she had over Richard's indifference were groundless and that if this flight was indeed a stupid gamble to regain his interest, the girl was in grave danger of losing him. He would never allow himself to be mired once again in a scandal not of his making. She would do what she could to bring an end to this reckless journey and protect Richard from any knowledge of it.

This cheerful thought had relaxed her a little and she was at last able to fall into a fitful doze as the coach slowly made its cumbersome way towards the Channel coast. She did not awake fully until she felt the horses moving sharply downhill. Leaning forwards to peer through the window, she could see in the distance a strip of water streaking the horizon. They were descending a steep and winding hill leading to the town and gradually houses began to spring up on either side of the road and the gradient to even out. She would bespeak a room at the Ship Inn, which she knew to be the best hostelry in Dover, her father having stayed there when he made the Grand Tour as a young man. Once settled, Stebbings could make discreet enquiries of the smaller establishments. Hopefully it would

not take too long to run them to ground since Dover was not
a large town.

The wind had hardly abated from the time they left London,
but here on the coast it blew with an added ferocity. As the
carriage swung around the last corner and reached the promenade, she got her first clear view of the sea. A sheet of gun-
metal water heaved and tossed alarmingly, foaming white
flecks of waves splintering the grey. Even from some distance
she could hear the thunder of surf crashing against the harbour wall, spray after spray of icy water breaching the top of
the wharf ready to drench anyone foolish enough to be walking on this stormy May evening. Her heart warmed; surely
no one would put to sea in such weather. She lowered the carriage window and her hat was almost snatched from her head.
The titian curls blew wildly in the wind as she attempted to
give her groom directions.

'Stebbings,' she had to shout to make herself heard, 'please
make for the Ship Inn. I hope to bespeak a room there.'

'That's where I was going,' he replied grimly. 'Nowhere
else suitable for you, Miss Christabel, though heaven knows
it's a bad day when a young lady has to venture alone to any
inn.'

He left her shortly afterwards to find lodgings for himself
in the cheaper part of town, but promised that once this was
accomplished he would begin immediately to make a round of
the smaller hotels and guest houses that lined the promenade
and the streets behind. It was probable that if the runaways
were still in Dover, they would be discovered in one of these.
And so it proved.

* * *

Within an hour of arriving in the town, she was entering the tap room of the Pelican and encountering two pairs of startled eyes.

'Miss Tallis!'

Domino had been sitting by the window, gloomily watching the tossing waters, but at Christabel's entrance she sprang from her chair and stood like a statue, a stricken expression on her face. Benedict, too, had jumped to his feet, advancing on his sister impetuously.

'Bel! What on earth are you doing here?'

'Good evening, Benedict. I would think that question better belongs to me.'

She glanced around her at the soiled furnishings of the dismal room, her eyebrows raised and a quizzical look on her face.

'So what *are* you both doing here?'

Domino found her voice. 'I'm on my way to Paris,' she said tremulously, 'and Benedict is escorting me.'

'Escorting you?'

'There was no one else I could ask.' Domino's shoulders drooped in despair guessing that this sudden intrusion by Benedict's sister might mean the end of her plans.

Her escort scowled at her words. 'Thanks,' he said indignantly, 'and after all I've done—planning your escape, paying for the carriage, finding us somewhere to shelter!'

'I don't mean I'm not grateful to you, Benedict, just that you were my last resort.'

'Thanks again.' His face was red with annoyance.

It was evident that both parties to this escapade were so

tightly wound that they needed only a small excuse to explode. It would be wise to intervene while she was still likely to get a sensible answer.

'So you're not eloping?'

Both of them looked astounded for an instant and then both burst into laughter. It broke the tension of the moment.

'Miss Tallis, how could you think such a thing?'

'Quite easily. You left a note for your aunt saying that you had to slip away from London because your life had become intolerable and that Benedict was travelling with you. What else was there to think but that you were escaping because you imagined—correctly—that you would both be deemed far too young to marry.'

'Too right,' Benedict exclaimed. 'I'm certainly not in the petticoat stakes and never likely to be. I only came on this stupid journey because she mopped and mowed around me until I was driven frantic. I agreed just to keep her quiet.'

'I did not mop and mow! And you could have refused, but you liked the idea of journeying to France—admit it!'

'Not with you, that's for sure. We've been stuck in this inn nigh on six hours and watched boat after boat set sail. But could I persuade her on to any of them?' he appealed to his sister. 'No, of course not. We have to wait until the sea is dead calm, would you believe.'

'I, for one, am delighted that you decided the weather was too rough to cross the Channel.' She turned towards the young girl, who was now near to tears.

'Domino,' she said gently, 'if it wasn't love for Benedict that drove you out of London, what was it?'

The girl looked frightened and said nothing.

'Come, my dear, there must be a very pressing reason

for you to take such drastic action. And your aunt will have to know. So if you don't choose to tell me, at least prepare yourself to confide the whole story to Lady Blythe when we return.'

'Return?! I cannot do that, Miss Tallis.' Domino shrank even further into her chair, her hands twisting the already crumpled muslin of her dress.

'You must. You cannot think to continue your journey now and I am here to take you home.'

'But I must go on. I'm so sorry that you've been put to the trouble of following us and I understand that you will wish to return with Benedict, but *I* must continue.'

Christabel rose and went to the young girl, taking her hands in hers and holding them in a warm clasp.

'I cannot allow you to do so, Domino, your reputation would be ruined. I've found you in time to prevent that disaster. Until we get back to London, I shall act as your chaperon. We can say that we've been travelling together from the outset and that will quash any rumours. I'm sure we can find a distant relative who lives nearby who has suddenly become very sick.'

She began to warm to her invention. 'You promised Lady Blythe that you would pay them a last visit. Yes, that's it. Naturally your aunt's health is not strong enough for such a long journey, so I offered to accompany you. We can forget the part Benedict has played. For the purposes of our story, he never left London.'

'That's fine, write me out of the script,' he complained bitterly.

His sister wheeled on him and said sharply, 'As someone whose conduct has been grossly irresponsible, you should be glad to be written out.'

She turned again to Domino. 'I'm staying at the Ship and have ordered rooms for both of us. You must pack your valise now and return with me there. Benedict can remain at the Pelican and in that way we should be able to counter any possible gossip that might seep out. First thing in the morning Stebbings will bring the carriage round to the Ship and we will all three travel back to London together.'

The girl looked defiant. 'You don't understand. I have to get to Spain. Paris is only the first stage of my journey.'

'You're going to Spain?' Christabel looked astonished.

'I was to visit my relatives in Madrid later this summer, but I intend now to arrive a little earlier.'

'Does Lady Blythe know of this visit?'

'Of course, my father has discussed plans with her.'

'Then surely she is the person to arrange your travel and accompany you on the journey.'

'That's still weeks ahead. I cannot stay in London—I need to leave now.'

'Why is it so important for you to leave town immediately?' Christabel asked wonderingly.

The girl looked scared. 'Tell her,' Benedict advised. 'She knows nearly everything anyway.'

In a small and halting voice Domino made her confession that she was badly indebted to Lord Moncaster and that he was intent on receiving payment in one form or another.

'Threatened her, Bel,' Benedict put in. 'Tried to force her to go to his house on the night of Sophia's ball. That's his notion of her paying the debt.'

The tears began to course down Domino's face as she remembered the terror she had felt at Lord Moncaster's threats.

Christabel crossed swiftly to the sobbing girl and put her arms around her.

'He's a scoundrel, my dear, but he has no power over you,' she soothed. 'You're a minor and not responsible for gambling debts. There's nothing he can do to reclaim the money and he knows that well.'

Domino abruptly stopped crying and gaped at her. 'You mean that all this time I was in no danger.'

'None. But you have not acted well.'

The reproof in her voice made the girl wince and she hung her head again. 'I know,' she managed to whisper.

'Lord Veryan would be very disturbed if he knew of your conduct.'

Domino was puzzled at the introduction of Richard's name, but said again, 'I know.'

'We will say nothing to him. He need never know what has occurred, but you must tell your aunt and beg her pardon, not just for such foolish behaviour, but for worrying her so much with this flight of yours.'

'Is Aunt Loretta very angry?' the girl ventured.

'Not angry, just sick with worry. You haven't been thinking very clearly. If you had told Lady Blythe the true situation, she would doubtless have rung a peal over you and been displeased for a while, but she would also have applauded your honesty and forgiven you very quickly. She would have paid Lord Moncaster what he's owed and that would have been an end to it.'

'Told you so, didn't I?' Benedict smirked. 'Now perhaps you'll give me credit for some sense.'

Domino was just about to cross swords again when Christabel decided that she'd had enough. She was very tired from the journey and the thought of having to repeat it on the morrow with two squabbling children in tow was not a happy one. Nor was she anticipating with any pleasure her mother's and Lady Blythe's likely welcome to this wayward little party.

'You will accompany me back to the Ship, Domino,' she said firmly. 'We will order a late supper and you are invited to eat with us, Benedict, if you wish.

'Otherwise, we will see you outside the inn at nine o'clock tomorrow morning. If you're late, you will have to find your own way back to town.'

'No need to get on your high ropes.' He sniffed. He had never before known his elder sister to be so severe.

The image of Richard, never far from her thoughts, fuelled the anger she felt towards her brother and she lashed him with her tongue.

'Your behaviour has been as reprehensible as Domino's—more so, for you are older than she and have been on the town longer. No doubt Mama will have something to say to you when we reach Mount Street.'

He found this to be only too true. Mama had more than something to say and Benedict received the dressing down of his life from his usually mild-mannered parent. He was barely through the front door when his mother pounced, dragging him into the library and subjecting him to a lengthy and irate scolding. Lady Harriet had decided that her son had enjoyed more than sufficient holiday in the capital. He was to start on the long journey back to Cornwall in two days' time and Stebbings would not be driving him. The groom had already been forced to undertake an unnecessary and fatiguing journey beyond his normal duties and Benedict could make his own way to Lamorna Place by stage and then carrier. His mother derived a degree of pleasure in relaying this information; it went some little way to recompensing her for the worry and fright she'd suffered.

Lady Harriet followed him out into the hall where Christabel was waiting, pale but composed, ready to suffer her share of parental wrath. She had directly disobeyed her mother in going alone to Dover, but she could not be sorry for it. Domino was returned safely to Lady Blythe's care and no one else was the wiser. Certainly not Richard. He was at Madron and blissfully unaware of the drama that had been enacted.

Her mother turned back to the library and beckoned her to follow. Although it was early May, a fire burned brightly in the grate in an effort to conquer the wind and rain which battered at the windows. The unseasonable weather matched the gloom of the occasion, but her mother's scolding appeared light.

'I am delighted, Bel, that you are returned safely and that silly young girl is back with her aunt. But I cannot think it right that you involved yourself.'

'I couldn't let her plunge herself into a scandal.' Her voice was as quiet as her mother's and devoid of expression. 'Of all people, I know how dreadful it is to face down gossip and innuendo. And it was Benedict who would have been largely responsible. Surely you would not have had that happen.'

'Benedict is to return to Cornwall,' her mother said, not answering her directly. 'But what of you?'

'What do you mean, Mama?'

'You say that you travelled to Dover to protect the family's honour and to save Domino from herself—that is understandable, given your own painful experience as a girl—but why else?'

'Isn't that enough?' she challenged, hoping to steer the conversation in another direction.

'For most people, perhaps. But your emotions run deep, Christabel. You told me that you did not wish Richard Veryan to suffer another broken engagement. Why was that so important to you?'

A tell-tale blush suffused Christabel's cheeks and she said hastily, 'I believe him to deserve better. He is an honourable man and capable of true feeling.'

'Ah!' Her mother sighed. 'As I thought. You are in love with him. What a perverse creature you are. Why could you not have loved him when you had the chance?'

The reproach went unanswered and Lady Harriet continued, 'You are in love with him and he is betrothed, you say, to this green girl?'

She shook her head in disbelief, but, seeing her daughter's wounded face, moved swiftly across the room and took her hands in a tender clasp.

'Bel, what have you done? What will become of you?'

'Whatever do you mean, Mama?' The anguish in her mother's voice made her step back in surprise.

'I mean, my dear, that both the men who have figured so large in your life are now promised to others.'

She looked bewildered. 'Both men?'

'Both,' her mother repeated heavily. 'Sir Julian has asked permission to pay his addresses to Sophia.'

Chapter Nine

Richard rode along the headland. On one side of the twisting pathway stretched a patchwork of small fields, ancient granite walls and, in the distance, gently rolling hills. On the other and immediately below him the ocean thundered benignly, the sun glistening on the rocks and the spray thrusting ever higher up the cliff face. It was a glorious morning; for a short while, as he relaxed into the rhythm of the trotting horse, his mind was free of care. It had been an emotional homecoming. He'd arrived amid a torrential downpour but Lady Veryan had come running from the doorway as soon as she heard the noise of wheels on gravel. He'd hardly clambered down the carriage steps before she'd flung her arms around his neck, trembling with a mixture of happiness and sorrow. His father's absence had hovered between them. Until that moment he'd not fully realised how frail she was and how desperate to see him. Guilt at delaying his homecoming had cast a large shadow over his arrival.

But this morning after five days at the Abbey and many hours together, life seemed a good deal brighter. He was home now and home for good. Lady Anne need worry no longer

over the upkeep of house and land. Already he'd had several
sessions with his father's bailiff and acquainted himself with
many of the problems and a few of the pleasures of a landed
estate. This was surely one of its most agreeable delights: a
solitary ride in the early morning sun, king and master of all
he surveyed.

The seclusion was needed. His final farewell to Christabel
had been torture. So many things left unsaid between them,
so many feelings unexpressed. He'd intended a brief farewell,
a mere clasp of the hand and a friendly smile, enough to tell
her that she was free of him, free to make the life she wanted
with Sir Julian. But all his judicious intentions had vanished
like dew in a sunlit haze and the prudent words he'd prepared
had died unregretted on his lips. She had looked magnificent,
her beautiful form encased in a floating cloud of diaphanous
gauze, her every movement sparkling in the light of diamonds.
When the musicians had struck up for the waltz, he'd been
unable to resist one last dance with her. It hadn't lasted long.
Once his arms were round her, he was again a lost man. The
intended farewell had been abandoned and in its place that
long, lingering kiss. He'd wanted it to go on for ever. Now,
looking back, he wondered grimly how he'd ever torn himself away.

But he had and he was home and this morning was a gift
from heaven. The physical ache of losing her must one day
disappear. He'd lived without her for six years and would do
so again. His old defence of suppressing all feeling was now
forfeit, but surely he would cease to think of her so often once
he knew her to be married.

'Hey, there! Richard? Is that you?'

A faint voice calling in the distance penetrated his thoughts and he turned his head to see another rider beating his way up the headland towards him. The figure was familiar and for a moment his heart skipped a beat. Surely the Tallises had not come home already?

'Ricky, it *is* you. I thought so.' Benedict arrived in a pelter at his side. 'A bang-up morning, hey? Hope you don't mind my trespassing.'

Since the two families had always treated each other's lands as their own, this was by way of being a pleasantry.

'It's good to see you, Benedict, if surprising. Why so far from London?'

'I thought it was time I came home,' Benedict began awkwardly. 'I've been away a fair while and the old man was getting a bit Friday-faced. Started to demand that his son and heir return to the fold.'

'I see. I imagined you were fixed in London for the Season.'

'That was never the plan,' the boy rejoined quickly. 'I was only ever going to stay a few weeks. I'd had enough of town anyway—couldn't wait to get back!'

Richard looked sceptically at his young companion, but said nothing and they rode on together in silence. Thinking that some further explanation was due, Benedict found himself continuing, 'To tell you the truth, there was a spot of bother and London got too hot for me.' He grinned engagingly.

'That sounds a little more likely.' Richard returned his smile. 'What was it? Boxing the watch, gambling debts, a ladybird?'

Benedict flushed with annoyance. 'She was hardly one of the muslin company, if that's what you mean. Far too respectable, a chit of a girl, and I'm banished to Lamorna because of her.' His earlier carefree air left him as he remembered his grievances against Domino.

'I never thought of you as being in the petticoat line,' Richard remarked smilingly.

'I'm not! Most definitely I'm not. All I did was to try to help someone and look what happened.'

'And dare I ask who it was that you tried to help?'

Benedict flushed again and realised he'd said too much, but it was too late to withdraw. 'Actually you know her pretty well,' he muttered. 'It's Domino de Silva.'

'Domino! What trouble has she got herself in, for heaven's sake? I thought her aunt well able to take care of her.'

'There'd have to be a hundred aunts to keep *her* out of trouble. I can't tell you what bother she was in, but believe me, it was stupid. Still, I'd better keep mum, lady's honour, and all that rot.'

'But why are *you* exiled from the pleasures of London?'

The younger man scowled at the thought of what he was missing. 'The silly chit took it into her head to leave town on the quiet. She wanted an escort and guess who was witless enough to agree.'

Richard's face was inscrutable. 'And where were you to escort her?'

'Supposedly Paris and from there she was going to travel on to Spain, but we never got any further than Dover.'

His companion looked at him enquiringly.

'You wouldn't believe her! Said she couldn't cope with the sea unless it was dead calm. We must have seen half-a-dozen packet boats come and go and she couldn't bring herself to board any of them. I told the silly goose that the weather wasn't likely to improve and if she didn't want to be caught in Dover, she should just close her eyes and walk. But would she listen? Huh!'

'And did you get caught?'

'Oh, yes, and a right shenanigan that was. My sister turned up and gave us a real bear-garden jaw. Then she took Domino back to her aunt and the long and the short of it was that I was ordered to pack my traps and leave London immediately.'

'Sophia?'

'Sophia?'

'Your sister who discovered you in Dover.'

'Of course not Sophia. Can you imagine?'

'Miss Tallis, then?' Richard looked bewildered. 'Why would Miss Tallis come after you?'

'God knows. She's not usually interfering. She seemed very anxious about preventing a scandal.'

'But Miss de Silva is hardly her concern.'

'I suppose she thought *I* was her concern,' he said carelessly, 'although she seemed more worried about your reaction.'

'To Domino's flight?'

'Yes, didn't make much sense to me. I couldn't work out why Bel was so upset. Or why she thought *you'd* be upset if you knew Domino had cut loose. There's been a lot of chatter in the clubs, but I never thought you had any real interest there.'

Benedict looked interrogatively at the rider beside him, but Richard made no answer. His mind was busy reviewing the hints he'd been at pains to drop over the last few weeks. He might not have lied outright, but he had led Christabel to believe that he and Domino might be engaged. She would see Domino's flight as a threat to their betrothal. She had intervened, but was that for the girl's sake or for his? Whatever the case, it was based on a false premise.

'Did your sister travel all the way to Dover just to put an end to this journey?' he continued his train of thought aloud.

'Like I said. Brought Stebbings with her, too. He gave me a jobation as well. That's the trouble with servants who've known you all your life.'

'So Miss Tallis travelled a long distance, alone apart from her groom, to find you both and bring Domino back.'

Richard was slowly trying to make sense of what had happened. If Christabel *had* braved that journey for him, it meant that she'd wanted to protect him, wanted to save him from the hurt of another betrayal. She must still care for him! Beyond the physical hunger he'd deliberately set out to nurture and with a deep and tender love. He knew himself to be wholly undeserving, but the idea flooded him with its spreading warmth.

Conscious of Benedict eyeing him askance, he blocked these dangerous thoughts and made every effort to continue the conversation.

'I would say you were extremely lucky that your sister intervened when she did. You might well have found yourself in difficulties once you were the other side of the Channel and without friendly help to hand.'

'To tell you the truth, I'm glad to be out of it. I was a bit blue devilled at first, but not any more. I miss the fun of being in London, but not the family's constant carping. And now all this fuss over Sophia's wedding—that's beyond enough. The more I think about it, the better I'm pleased to be at Lamorna.'

Richard stared at him. 'Sophia is getting married? But surely…'

'Turn up for the books, eh? Sir Julian decided that she was a safer bet! He must want his head examined.'

'Are you saying that Christy is no longer to marry him?'

He felt the world shifting beneath his feet and inadvertently used his pet name for her.

'That's right. Bethrothal off. Then betrothal on—but different sister.'

Surely Sir Julian could not have taken such serious exception to his fiancée's rescue mission. It had after all been an attempt to avoid scandal in the family. His conduct was inexplicable.

'Do you know why the engagement to Miss Tallis was called off?' he asked cautiously.

'They're puffing it off that they no longer feel suited to one another, whatever that means. Never thought they did suit, if you ask me. But no one ever does—ask me, I mean.'

'It seems to have taken them both some time to come to that conclusion.'

'Between you and me, Rick, and I know you won't spread this around, there's more to it than that. Bel was crazy enough to kiss another man and Julian saw her. That was enough to send him fleeing to the hills. Very straight, very proper, Sir Julian.'

Richard felt an iron bar descend on his chest. Without a doubt he was that other man. Sir Julian Edgerton had seen him kiss Christabel on the balcony and decided that she was not a fit wife for him. The popinjay! The self-righteous popinjay, to reject a woman like Christabel and to turn instead to that screeching harridan of a sister! He was pretty sure that Sophia was responsible in some way for Christabel's downfall; the girl was by nature underhand. Sir Julian would soon realise his ghastly mistake, and there would be no going back on this one. He deserved everything he got, Richard thought bitterly.

They rode on in silence, Benedict aware that somehow he'd

upset his companion, but unsure just what he'd said that had been so disturbing. At the old mill post Richard broke the unnatural calm to bid him goodbye.

'I have an appointment with my bailiff, Benedict,' he said with a faint smile, 'and regret I must leave you here. Enjoy the rest of your ride.'

'I will. Perhaps we can ride out tomorrow,' he said eagerly, hoping to put right whatever ill he'd unwittingly committed.

'Perhaps,' Richard said vaguely. 'But there is a great deal of work to be done in the estate office and I can't afford to play truant too often.'

'Surely you can spare an hour or two,' the younger man protested.

'I would hope so, but I fear that my business affairs are likely to take me away again very soon.'

And with that he wheeled his horse around and cantered off towards the Abbey, leaving Benedict puzzled and slightly alarmed at this sudden turn of events.

Richard did not fulfil his promise to go to the estate office, but instead left the stable lad to rub down his sweating horse while he strode towards his study. Flinging his gloves to one side, he wrenched off his boots and sat down in an easy chair to consider what he'd just learned. If Benedict's news was correct, and he could see no reason why the boy would make up such a story, then Christabel was now a free woman. How was she feeling? How deeply would Sir Julian's rejection bite? He'd never been convinced that she loved the man, but in the end he'd accepted that she had the right to find happiness with him if she could. But now? Her whole life had been overturned and his kiss had been the catalyst. Marriage to Sir Julian was no longer on offer and as a woman who'd provoked two broken engagements, she was perilously close to social ruin.

And how must she feel losing the man to that sister of hers? What was wrong with Edgerton! How could he prefer Sophia, an ill-dressed, ill-tempered young woman? Christabel was just too much for him—that was the truth. She was too beautiful, too intelligent, too passionate. Edgerton was scared that he would not be able to live up to her or keep her satisfied. When he'd seen the way she'd kissed another man, he'd realised the well of passion within her, a passion that he could not begin to evoke or fulfil. Sophia was far less daunting a prospect, Richard could see. But if Sir Julian could not live up to Christabel, he knew a man who could. His love for her had made a chaos of his life. It had not let him go for an instant, even when he was denying its very existence. It had always been there and now finally it might have a chance to flourish.

He would post back to London, tell Christy his true feelings, beg her forgiveness once more and ask her to marry him. Again. But this time it would work. His mother would understand his renewed absence when she knew why he was returning to London. She would be overjoyed finally to have the daughter-in-law of whom she'd always dreamed.

In truth, Lady Veryan did not share her son's enthusiasm. She had never wholly forgiven Christabel for the heartbreak she had caused. The catastrophic events six years ago had almost wrecked the deep friendship between their two families and here was Richard intending to ask the girl to marry him once more. Even worse, she had received a letter only last week from Harriet Tallis conveying the welcome news that her eldest daughter was to be married at last to a delightful and highly respected man. Anne would love Sir Julian Edgerton on sight, her friend had enthused. And now here was Richard telling her that this very betrothal, only a few weeks old, was ended. It seemed that Christabel was still adept at breaking her word.

She made no attempt, however, to dissuade her son—she could see that he was determined on his course. Six years of fending for himself in pioneer country had turned him into a decisive and forceful man and she recognised that it was useless to try to change his mind.

Happily unaware of his mother's misgivings, Richard made the tedious journey back to the capital in the best of spirits. He'd been foolish ever to imagine that he could excise Christabel from his heart and even more stupid to embark on a campaign to free himself from her powerful enchantment. Now that her betrothal to Sir Julian was at an end, a future together was within their grasp and he was going to make sure that they seized it. Rather than putting up at Brown's again, he decided he would go straight to the family's London home despite its dilapidated state. It was time to open Grosvenor Square after all these years and make it habitable for Christabel. Everything he did from now on would be with her in mind; for the first time in his life he was absolutely sure of what he wanted and what he had to do to get it.

Nevertheless the condition of the house shocked him when he was shown around by a nervous housekeeper. The family had not occupied it since those dreadful events six years ago, his parents having lost any taste for London life. They could not bring themselves to return to a house which had seen such sadness.

'I'm sorry about the state of things, my lord,' Mrs Moffat apologised anxiously as she accompanied him on a dismal tour, 'but there's only me and Mr Moffat here and 'tis a large place to keep perfect.'

Perfect it was not. The furniture was shrouded in holland covers, layers of dust coated every visible surface and in the darkest corners of each room cobwebs hung undisturbed. Richard's spirits sank a little as he contemplated the mournful sight; the contrast with the house's former glory was painful. So, too, were the images from the past which now rushed back at him: Christabel excited and happy, displaying her latest purchases; kicking off her shoes and curling up on the chesterfield ready to chat; descending the staircase on her way to yet another ball, heartbreakingly beautiful. How young they had been then, how untried and untested. He shook his head in an effort to dislodge such memories and strode to the window to pull back the long brocade curtains. Clouds of dust mounted towards the ceiling and the window panes beyond were grimy and streaked. But the sun was high in the sky, its beams catching at the carved architraves and the marble fireplace, and bringing the tired room to life.

He turned to the housekeeper. 'I realise what an impossible task you've had.' Mrs Moffat bobbed a curtsy at this reassurance. 'However,' he went on, 'could you bring the house back to something like its former condition—with extra help, of course?'

'It depends on how much more help there was,' the housekeeper offered cautiously.

'As much as you need. Hire however many people you think necessary. My only stipulation is that the house should be restored within a few days.'

The woman looked stunned at this demand, but the thought of employing an army of helpers to scrub, clean and launder a house that for years she'd watched fall into disrepair infused her with a new energy.

'A few days? At that rate, we'll be working morning and night. If I may ask, my lord, is there a particular reason for the haste?'

'There is. By the end of the week this house must be fit to welcome the most beautiful woman in the world!'

The housekeeper was alight with curiosity but thought better of questioning her master further. Instead she said with renewed determination, 'It will be, sir. I'll get Moffat on to the hiring straight away. Meantime I'll begin in the basement—we'll be using the family kitchen again and it's certain to need a deal of work before it's straight.'

Richard took a last look at the once beautiful salon and smiled easily. He was leaving behind the old tale of misery and betrayal for a new and happier story. Mrs Moffat and her helpers would bring the house back to life and make it a home fit for the woman he loved. In time there would be renovation and refurbishment, but that was for the future. That could await Christabel's choosing—once she became Lady Veryan.

As she came down the stairs at Mount Street, Christabel heard laughter coming from the hall below. Sophia had returned from yet another shopping trip, but this time accompanied by Sir Julian. Her transformation from the sulky and petulant girl of a few weeks ago to the smiling and agreeable young woman of today had been truly astonishing. Christabel rejoiced that both participants to this frankly odd marriage appeared happy. Nevertheless there was a twinge of resentment; it rankled that Sir Julian should have found it quite so easy to transfer his affections. But it proved what she'd always thought—that he was in love with the dream of Christabel and not with the woman herself. He had never truly known her. She smiled wryly—if he had but witnessed half of her shameful conduct while Richard was in town! Those fevered interludes were ample proof that she was an unsuitable bride for such a model of rectitude as Sir Julian. Sophia, for all her moods, was a pattern of conformity and unlikely ever to transgress.

But Christabel had always been what her father called 'hot to handle'. She had slept away these last six years until awoken by Richard's touch. His return had signalled a release of feelings she had denied for so long. From the night he'd danced with her at Almack's, the passionate, unruly girl had risen into being and the cool, clear-headed Christabel gradually sank without trace. She ached for him. If she closed her eyes, she could see him plainly, their bodies a whisper away as he bid her goodbye: his grey eyes silver in the moonlight, the dark hair falling carelessly across his forehead, the feel of him, the smell of him, the sheer physical joy of him.

She had always loved his energy, his sense of adventure, the way he took his pleasures so intensely. In comparison Sir Julian's were muted; the two men she had promised to marry could not be more different. She almost laughed aloud as she remembered that swim long ago in the cove at Lamorna—the scattered clothes, the mad dash to the sea, the cleaving of their bodies together in the cool water. Sir Julian would have been scandalised. Far better then that he'd changed his mind and escaped a life of vexation. Thankfully only a few people had been aware of their betrothal and though there might be a little gossip, Sophia would soon be married. There would always be doubt in the minds of the scandalmongers as to whether there had ever been an engagement between the elder Miss Tallis and Sir Julian Edgerton or whether rumour had simply fixed on the wrong sister.

'Look what we've bought, Bel!'

Her sister's tone was a little defiant, a little smug. Sophia had not yet managed to accustom herself entirely to the change in her circumstances and was unsure that she liked her sister to be so accepting of the new dispensation.

'Good afternoon, Sophia, Sir Julian,' Christabel said in her musical voice. 'I see you've both been very busy. Come into the drawing room and show me what bargains you've managed to secure.'

Sir Julian beamed. Of all of them, he had felt most discomfort with the alterations to his marriage plans. He still could not quite believe how quickly he had changed his mind over such a momentous decision. His sister, Lady Russell, had scolded him roundly and told him he was a fool. If his feelings were so lightweight, she snorted, he should forget the whole business of getting married. But he had not and had daily been surprised at how comfortable Sophia and he were going on together. She was never out of temper these days, he reflected, and she seemed genuinely interested in the details of his charity work. Even her choice of raiment seemed to have undergone modification. Today she was wearing a soft lilac muslin with cream lace, a modest and becoming creation.

Christabel, also wearing a simple muslin dress, eclipsed her and always would.

Her ethereal beauty outshone every woman he knew, but ethereal could have its problems, he decided.

And he was not convinced that Richard Veryan had finally disappeared from the scene. Sad to acknowledge, Christabel was just a trifle unsteady. Lady Russell had probably been correct all along. Miss Tallis was not the right bride for him. No further proof was needed than the way she had abandoned all delicacy at her sister's come-out ball, kissing another man in public and in such a fashion. He felt himself grow hot at the thought of it. She was smiling at him now, holding open the door, and he followed her swiftly into the drawing room. On the whole, he thought he preferred her as a sister-in-law.

The front-door knocker sounded loudly just as Sophia had begun to unpack her first parcel. Christabel had little time to consider who could be calling in the middle of the afternoon before a footman was at her side with the message that Lord Veryan wished to speak with her privately.

There was a sudden stunned silence among the little gathering until she recalled herself and said as naturally as possible, 'Please show Lord Veryan into the library, James.'

She turned to her companions with a winning smile, 'I must leave you for a moment but I won't be long,' she promised.

'Well!' breathed Sophia as her sister went out of the door.

'Well indeed!' echoed Sir Julian.

She was astonished by Richard's appearance at Mount Street. She had imagined him well and truly settled at his beloved Madron, acquainting his mother with the news of his betrothal and making preparations for Domino to join him.

Why he had returned to town was a complete mystery. His first words did little to enlighten her.

'How can you bear to see that charade?' he flung the question at her, gesturing in the general direction of the drawing room. He'd arrived in a celebratory mood, but the brief glimpse he'd had of Sophia's gloating face had roused him to an angry defence of the woman he loved.

'If you mean my sister and Sir Julian,' Christabel replied coolly, 'I'm delighted they have found happiness with each other.'

'Delighted? Delighted to be rejected for an ill-favoured, ill-tempered vixen?'

She did not reply to the calumny against her sister. His agitation was obvious as he paced up and down the library floor.

'For God's sake, whatever's the matter with the fellow?' he exploded as he came to rest in front of her. The thought was torturing him that he was responsible for the humiliation she must now be suffering.

'As far as I am aware, nothing ails Sir Julian. We simply found that we were not suited to one another,' she replied composedly. 'It was you, after all, who took pleasure in pointing that out.'

'I take no pleasure in what has happened to you,' he growled.

She acknowledged this with a small bow of her head, but then looked directly into his stormy gaze. 'Why are you here, Richard?'

'I met Benedict out riding and he told me the news. I came immediately.'

'But why?' she repeated.

'I have come to ask you to marry me,' he stated baldly.

He'd not meant to make such a stark declaration, but all

his rehearsed speeches had simply melted away. She stared at him, dumbstruck.

'Is this your idea of a joke?'

'Hardly.'

'Then you must have run mad. Or—' and she fixed him with a look of contempt '—you are still intent on distressing me and this is part of your plan.'

'Neither. I am sincere.'

'You expect me to believe you?'

'My conduct has been unforgivable, as I've confessed. I set out to destroy whatever happiness you thought to snatch from your liaison with Edgerton and I seem pretty much to have succeeded. You know that I regret the pain I've caused, but I cannot turn the clock back even if I would.'

She remained standing motionless, silent and bewildered.

'And I would not turn the clock back, because now you are free,' he said with something like triumph in his voice. He advanced closer and took both her hands in his. 'We have both made mistakes, Christy—can we not put them behind us?'

'I hope we may,' she replied in a dazed voice, 'but you need feel no obligation towards me.'

'It's not obligation that makes me offer my hand to you in marriage.' He was finding it difficult to contain his frustration. 'Benedict tells me that the engagement was cancelled after that fool in there saw you kissing another man. Who else could that be but me?'

'Benedict is a silly boy. He knows nothing.'

'But he was right.'

'The engagement was already in trouble.' She sighed wearily. 'The manner in which you chose to say goodbye simply brought it to a swifter conclusion.'

'It was in trouble because of me. Admit it! It was in trouble because of your feelings for me.'

She said nothing, her beautiful face pale and still. The emerald eyes were downcast and she could not answer him truthfully.

'You do have feelings for me, Christy, I know.' He pulled her roughly into his arms, his face buried in the red blaze of her hair.

She pushed him violently away and the green eyes were suddenly shooting fire. 'And what about your feelings for Domino? How dare you ask me to marry you when you are privately betrothed to her! Is there no shame to which you will not stoop?'

'Betrothed to her? Of course I'm not betrothed to her. Whatever makes you think any such thing?'

'You've made it abundantly clear over these past weeks that she will be your bride when the time is right. I believe the clubs have even been running wagers on it.'

'You know as well as I that men will bet on just about anything,' he returned defensively. This was proving more difficult than he'd ever imagined. 'There *is* no betrothal, Christy. I let you believe that I favoured Domino because I wanted to make you jealous.'

'Are you telling me that you have constantly lied about your relationship with Miss de Silva?' she said in a voice tipped with steel.

'I haven't lied. I never told you that I wished to marry her. I just let you think that I was attracted to her.'

'Then you lied by default.'

'You must understand,' he said desperately, 'I thought I'd banished you from my heart, but when I met you again that afternoon in the park, I knew that wasn't true. After all these years, you still took my breath away. You were so beautiful, so desirable. I wanted you for my own and that pompous fool, Edgerton, had you.'

'And that decided you to practise a loathsome deceit?'

'You jumped to the wrong conclusion and, yes, I used it against you. I regret doing so, but there were never any serious feelings on my side. I've never felt anything but friendship for her.'

'And Domino, what of her?' she asked crisply.

For the first time he looked a little shamefaced. 'A mere adolescent fantasy on her part, but it's over now.'

'She is seventeen, Richard, a vulnerable girl, and you took advantage of her to continue a vendetta against me.'

He sighed inwardly; he'd always known that this could be a sticking point. Christabel's strong sense of justice had not diminished over the years.

'She's fine now,' he tried to reply easily. 'There's been no harm done. It was a girlish fancy without substance. I never took advantage of her; I made it clear that I had no interest other than as a friend.'

She was looking shocked and the interview was not going the way he had envisaged.

'A friend? You stand there and tell me that she never once believed you loved her, that she always knew a serious relationship between you was a mirage!'

It was her turn to stride up and down the library, her mass of auburn curls breaking free from their simple band and tumbling around her face.

'You have not been a friend to her. You have been devious, cunning, even ruthless. Not only have you destroyed my peace of mind, but you have treated her abominably. And you dare to come here and ask me to ally myself with you!'

'I thought, hoped, that you had forgiven the mistakes I've made these past weeks,' he said with quiet dignity. 'When we said goodbye at your sister's ball, it seemed as though the slate had been wiped clean.'

'That was before I knew of this further deception. How can I ever trust you?'

Her anguished tone pierced his heart. Abandoning all pretence of dignity, he pleaded with her in a voice husky with longing, 'Christy, my darling girl, I want you, I need you, please come to me.'

His arms reached out for her, pulling her close, his fingers tracing the delicate white skin of her inner arms until his hands cradled her breasts. She felt herself dissolving slowly, longing for his intimate touch, longing for his mouth to pleasure her again. His lips were caressing her hair now, moving down her neck to her bosom. They were hot and all-consuming. Any moment now she would abandon her paltry resistance. But the image of Domino, happy and innocent, rose before her and she pushed him away with a force that took him by surprise. He staggered back.

'I must ask you to go,' she said with as much composure as she could manage, 'and not return to this house. If by chance we should meet again in the future, I entreat you never to mention this matter.'

'Christabel, wait!'

In response she strode to the library door, her expression unyielding.

'Goodbye, Lord Veryan. James will see you out.'

Christabel was left shaken and trembling. She managed to

maintain her self-possession until the front door shut behind him, but it cost her dear. She ought to return to the drawing room and pretend that nothing was amiss, but at this moment she could not face Sir Julian and her sister. Instead she made for her room and cast herself face down on the bed in a paroxysm of sobbing.

It was several minutes before she could regain control of herself and dry her tears. She lay staring blankly into space, engulfed by the jangle of warring emotions: the passion she felt for Richard against his duplicity, the chance of happiness against the likelihood of annihilating failure. Her mind circled ceaselessly. Richard must have returned to London within days of arriving home. When he'd heard of her broken engagement, he'd seen his chance and seized it, retracing the weary miles in order to ask her to marry. It was possible that after all the deceptions he was now sincere in his protestations. But his infamy was even greater than she'd imagined. He'd pretended feelings for Domino to further his own ends. He might have been honest with the young girl, but he'd still exploited her. There had never after all been any understanding between the two of them. The jealousy she'd felt at seeing them together came rushing back as an unstoppable torrent. All for nothing. All that pain for nothing. He'd been trifling with her, playing her like a fish on a line. And Domino, too. She could never trust him again.

Richard made his way back to Grosvenor Square, enraged that she had refused to believe him, enraged that for the second time she was turning him down. But most of all he was angry with himself for making such a mull of things. He'd thought that Christabel was bound to have learned the truth about his friendship with Domino after her rescue mission to Dover. He'd been sure that the enforced intimacy of their journey would have put her in full possession of the facts and she would know that whatever feelings Domino had for him, they were unrequited. Not so, apparently. She had never doubted his pretence and it was only this afternoon that she'd learned his supposed love for the girl was a sham. She was willing to forgive him much, but not this one harmless deception.

But if he were honest, it had been far from harmless. If she truly loved him, his constant intimacy with Domino would have racked her with jealousy. *If* she loved him? But she did, she loved him. When she'd gone to Domino's rescue it had been for his sake as much as for the girl's. She'd thought his reputation would be compromised and she'd not been able to contemplate seeing him hurt and once more the subject of gossip and innuendo. She loved him, he could swear. He hugged the thought to himself, allowing it to flood his body with a powerful energy. He wanted to go back to Mount Street that instant, to hammer on the door, force his way in and simply scoop her up in his arms and tell her that they were wasting time, that they were made for each other and always had been, that he wanted her now and could not wait another minute to claim back his own. In his mind he was with her again, encircling her lithe form in a crushing embrace, imprinting her pale, soft skin with urgent lips, entangling himself in a sheet of fiery curls.

He had reached Grosvenor Square and vaulted lightly up the front stairs to the open doorway. York tan gloves were thrown carelessly on to the battered cherrywood table and a caped greatcoat landed in the arms of the waiting footman. He strode purposefully into his study, calling for coffee to be brought immediately. He had a good deal of thinking to do if he were to win back the woman he loved. He was barred from Mount Street, and trying to thrust his way into the house would do nothing to endear him; he would need to be a great deal more subtle than that. Yet he had to see her, try to make her understand that his dissembling over Domino had been no more serious than the rest of his foolish actions. He must surprise her, create a situation where she was unable easily to escape and compel her to listen to all he wanted to say. He sat down to lay his plans carefully.

Chapter Ten

In the event he could think of nothing else but to intercept her at a time when she was without company and would not be expecting to see him. He knew from the past that she enjoyed riding alone with a single groom whenever she could and he was hopeful that she always hired a hack from the same stables. By dint of a few enquiries he had soon run to ground the mews she patronized, just around the corner from Mount Street. A cheeky stable boy, sufficiently greased in the palm, had let slip the information that a mare had been booked for Miss Tallis the following day. Further largesse elicited the news that the Tallis groom had mentioned his mistress was wishful of enjoying a change of scenery on the morrow and likely to ride in the exclusive but largely unfinished Regent's Park. This had suited Richard's purpose well since there was a good covering of trees running close to the bridle path and he would be able to wait for her unseen by all but the most observant passers-by. The weather had favoured him, too. After recent days of high winds and squally showers, the sun had returned the next morning and he rode out into the balmy air with an excited sense of anticipation.

He arrived at his chosen meeting place close on eleven o'clock. Several groups of people passed by the cluster of trees he sheltered beneath: nursemaids wheeling out their charges to take the morning air, a dowager scolding her companion mercilessly as they made their slow way along the footpath, a lone horseman putting his new mount through its paces. But otherwise the park was remarkably quiet, ideal for the forthcoming encounter. He hadn't long to wait until her trim figure hove into view, the groom keeping a respectful distance behind. She looked sublime in a tight-fitting costume of forest green cloth decorated with golden epaulettes and half-braided sleeves. A tall crowned hat with curled ostrich feathers completed the ensemble. Whatever inner turmoil was ravaging Christabel, the world would see only the fashionable woman they knew well.

As she came abreast of Richard's shelter, he wheeled his mount on to the path in front of her and forced her to come to a sudden halt. The groom moved up anxiously, but she waved him away with her hand. Whatever this ambush was about, she did not want Stebbings to hear.

'A beautiful morning, Miss Tallis.' Richard doffed his curly brimmed beaver, revealing fashionably dishevelled locks. The riding coat he wore was moulded tightly across his powerful shoulders and the palest fawn breeches encased his shapely legs. Gleaming top boots from Hoby and a freshly pressed neckcloth proclaimed him a gentleman of substance. He looked superb and she had to exert every nerve to detach her mind from the impulses of her traitorous body.

The two riders faced each other, their horses gently sidling to and fro until Christabel's mare, growing restive at the lack of action, began pawing irritably at the ground, almost unseating her in its efforts to be gone. Instinctively he grabbed at her bridle and brought their two mounts together. She thought she saw a paleness beneath the lean, tanned cheeks and his grey eyes were crystal clear and piercingly alive. It was as though this was the determining moment of his life.

Attempting to break the tension, she spoke with a boldness she did not feel. 'Good day to you, Lord Veryan. I hope you're enjoying this fine morning. May I ask that you allow me to do so, too?'

Her cold politeness did not daunt him; he retained his hand on her bridle.

'This is crazy. We should not have to meet like this, Christy.'

'The name is Miss Tallis, and you are quite correct, Lord Veryan, we should not. If you would be so good as to release my horse, I will be on my way.'

'Christabel, Miss Tallis, please hear me out. I apologise for accosting you in this fashion, but I've been unable to think of any other way to speak to you. I'll take only a small amount of your time but you must listen to me!'

Stebbings, seated on his mount a few yards distant, appeared increasingly anxious and she sensed that he was getting ready to intervene. The last thing she wanted was any kind of brawl in a public place. Swiftly she dismounted and threw her reins to the groom.

'I shall be back in ten minutes, Stebbings. Please walk the horses until I return.'

'Yes, ma'am, if you're sure,' he replied uncertainly.

She nodded and strode towards the shelter of the trees. Richard dismounted and followed her.

'What is it you wish to say?' she demanded, turning to face him, her tone uncompromising.

All his prepared speeches were once again forgotten. He could think only of possessing the woman that he loved.

'Simply that we are made to be together. You must know that.'

'I know nothing of the sort.'

'You're not being honest, Christabel, either with yourself or with me. Surely we deserve that of each other.'

'I cannot believe you have the temerity to speak to me of honesty! How much honesty have you shown these past few weeks?'

He made no reply and she continued with barely a pause, 'I will answer for you. None. Since your return to England, you have waged a vendetta against me. You have been ingenious, leaving no avenue unvisited. Not content with destroying my plans to marry, you have shamelessly exploited a young girl's feelings in order to hurt me. I think you will agree that you have been thoroughly *dis*honest and succeeded admirably.'

Her voice was metallic and her eyes pools of emerald ice. She was desperate to harden herself against him, to build a protective shell even at this late hour.

Her clear tones sliced through the air. 'Take pleasure in what you have done, for there is nothing more. You have disrupted my life and made me as deeply unhappy as you could possibly wish.'

His dismay that she could think so badly of him forced him to defend himself. 'You must know that has not been my desire. All I want is to make you happy. I've said I'm truly sorry. I cannot do more.'

She looked stonily into the distance and, exasperated by her obstinacy, he spoke what was uppermost in his mind. 'I accept I've caused suffering, but consider also that I've done some good.'

'What!'

'You say that you and Edgerton found you were not suited. And why is that? Because you discovered that you were suited to another man. If it were not for me, you would be contemplating a very unhappy marriage.'

She looked scornfully at him, but he would not be silenced. 'You may deny it, but you know that it's true. And whatever stupidities we've committed, we belong together.'

'As you belonged together with Miss de Silva?' she asked waspishly.

'I've been honourable and straightforward in my dealings with her. You have to believe me. I would never deliberately set out to harm a young and inexperienced girl.'

The expression on her face told him that she was very far from believing him and he burst out in frustration, 'You know what young girls are like, Christabel, they enmesh themselves in ridiculous dreams which are a million miles away from reality.'

'Yes, I do know what young girls are like. Who better? I was one once, remember, and thanks to another man *my* ridiculous dream almost crushed my heart. I survived—just— and now you've come close to crushing it a second time. But I won't allow you to succeed.'

Her face was pale, and though she remained standing tall and proud before him he knew she was in a state of agitation. Her breath was short and irregular and the smooth curve of her breasts rose and fell with emotion. He longed to reach out to her, pull her close to him and let their bodies end the argument.

'I want to win your heart, not crush it,' he said urgently. 'Despite all that's happened, maybe because of all that's happened, I know I can make you happy. We have tested each other to the limit and we've survived. Our love will be fierce and strong and enduring. Give it a chance, Christabel,' he urged. 'Take a chance.'

'I cannot.' In an instant she seemed visibly to shrink into herself. 'I've already suffered too much and all I want now is to be left in peace. Leave me that at least.'

Her sadness fingered him with its hurt. The fight had gone out of her and he was responsible. He had destroyed the fire and the spirit that he had so loved.

'But—' he tried to rally once more.

'No "but", the game is played out, Richard. This is its end.'

She walked slowly away and he watched immobile as Stebbings helped her remount and together continue along the bridleway. He was as certain as he could be that she still loved him, but in the end he had been powerless to keep her by his side. He knew that nothing he ever said would make any difference. The game between them was indeed played out.

He flung himself into the saddle and struck out across the park, his mind tormented by the destructive passions that had brought him to this pass. It mattered not where he was heading—there was nowhere to go. He had striven to convince Christabel of his love: he'd been so sure that he would be able to win her over. But all his energy and resolution had not been enough. He had thought to free himself of her influence for ever and now when he'd come to realise that to be free of her was the last thing he wanted, it was too late. She would not think of a future with him.

Trotting blindly ahead, it was some while before he heard the voices hailing him. A carriage drew up alongside and he slowly emerged from a brown study.

'Good morning, Lord Veryan, how delightful to see you back in town, and so soon! Has Cornwall already lost its appeal?'

It was Lady Blythe with her friend and neighbour, Miss Anstruther, and sitting squashed between them, Domino, startled by his presence, but smiling shyly.

He made no answer and Lady Blythe went on, 'We thought we would explore Mr Nash's new project, but there is a sad absence of company in the park.'

'I imagine most of the *ton* will wait until the Regent's vision is more nearly realised,' he replied, trying for an easy tone.

'As we seem to have the place to ourselves, Lord Veryan, I wonder if you would be good enough to walk with us for a while.'

'Of course, Lady Blythe,' he replied gallantly, though wishing himself a million miles away.

He handed the two elder ladies down from the carriage and they began to walk slowly ahead, still animatedly discussing the topic of the empty park. He turned to help Domino, but she had already scrambled down the steps. Offering her his arm, they followed in the footsteps of her aunt and companion. Neither spoke for some while, but when he glanced down at her, he found her eyes anxiously scanning his face.

'I'm surprised to see you here, Richard. I thought you'd left for home and would never return to London.'

'I thought so, too,' he replied evenly, 'but unforeseen circumstances brought me back.'

She did not feel bold enough to enquire what those circumstances might be, but she was struck by the fixed look on his face. She had never before seen him looking so grim or so dispirited.

'Is there something wrong?' she asked at length and when he did not reply, repeated more urgently, 'What is the matter, Richard?'

He had no wish to unburden himself to a girl barely more than a child, but her sweet face was looking up at him in genuine concern and his heart was sore. He was unable to repress his churning thoughts and found himself describing the recent encounter with Christabel. He was succinct, skimming over his campaign to prove his former sweetheart unworthy and deliberately avoiding any mention of the role Domino had unwittingly played. She must have guessed something of the truth but gave no sign.

'I'm a fool, Domino!' he finished. 'I must not repine. I must learn to accept Miss Tallis's decision.'

She squeezed his arm in sympathy and said impulsively, 'How can you? You love her, Richard. I've always known that. I think that perhaps I knew it before you did. And I'm quite sure that she returns your love. The engagement with Sir Julian never looked likely to stick, or so Aunt Loretta said.'

'Lady Blythe is most perceptive,' he muttered a little sourly. 'But it's clear that Christabel prefers a single life to being with me.'

'I'm sure that isn't so,' she protested. 'Nobody could!' and then blushed bright pink in confusion.

He ignored this telltale comment and said gently, 'Your good wishes do you credit, my dear, but I fear I've made a complete mess of things. There's no chance now that Miss Tallis will change her mind.'

'Then we must make her change her mind,' she said defiantly. He stared at her, his dark brows raised in astonishment.

'*You* must make her change her mind,' she amended quickly.

'I wish that were possible, but it's out of the question.'

An enigmatic 'hmm' was her only response. While they had been deep in conversation, the sky had clouded over and a blustery wind had begun to blow. Loretta Blythe signalled to her groom just as the first drops of rain began to fall. The ladies were swiftly handed into the carriage and Richard bade them a brief farewell. Looking back over her shoulder, Domino saw him riding away in the opposite direction, a solitary figure amid a rain-drenched landscape. She was sorry to leave him so evidently unhappy, but she needed time alone. She needed time to think, to contrive a solution to his difficulties, for she was quite certain there was a way through the maze.

Christabel, too, spent a good deal of time alone in the following days, seeking sanctuary from the prying eyes and listening ears of the household. She wanted more than anything to quit London. The triviality of the Season had never sat well with her and any pleasure she'd had in it was now dust. But she could not go home. Richard was unlikely to stay long at the Grosvenor Square mansion and she could not bear to run the risk of meeting him in Cornwall. She felt listless and unbearably cross. Her mother put it down to Sophia's forthcoming nuptials; the excitement of purchasing bride clothes, planning the ceremony, organising the honeymoon, had taken over Mount Street. It must be a difficult situation for her beautiful elder daughter to bear, even though she had brought this fate on herself.

But Christabel was immune to the upheavals permeating

the rest of the household. If pressed, she would have acknowledged a mild happiness that Sophia was no longer proving
so intractable, but beyond that she had little interest in the
wedding preparations. Instead she was sick to the very heart.
Richard had been right when he'd said that she loved him. His
physical presence shattered her with an intensity of desire, but
this ache, this longing, was more than simple lust. Lust she
knew. It was what had destroyed her first betrothal to him.
This was love. She loved him, all of him. She loved him but
she had no faith in him; that was the nub of it. However much
he protested, she could never trust him again, and without
trust there could be no lasting bond.

Her mind endlessly played out the conflict, trapping her in
a disordered world of her own. It was with only half an ear
that she listened to Sir Julian as he detailed his elaborate plans
for the family to celebrate his new engagement. This was to
include a splendid dinner at his town mansion, followed by
an evening at the Drury Lane theatre where he had managed
to obtain precious tickets to see Edmund Kean performing
in a much-acclaimed *Hamlet*. Sir Julian still felt awkward at
the very rapid transfer of his affections and was hoping that
a dazzling social occasion would smooth any feathers that
were still ruffled. He need not have worried. Christabel felt
only gratitude that she'd been spared a loveless marriage and
her mother was relieved that one of her daughters at least had
found an eligible husband.

The evening's dinner and theatre visit was to be the Season's
last social event for the family. In a few days they would leave
London for Rosings so that Sophia could be introduced to her
new home for the first time. From there they would travel
on to Cornwall to make final preparations for the wedding.

Unexpectedly her sister had rejected a smart London ceremony in favour of being married from Lamorna and it augured well for her new life, Christabel thought, that the city had lost some of its magic allure.

Sir Julian's town house stood imposingly at the corner of Brook Street and their arrival that night was greeted by liveried footmen at its entrance, holding aloft lighted torches. Once inside two more footmen lined the hall and relieved the ladies of their cloaks, then bowed them into a drawing room glittering in the light of a dozen chandeliers, which ran the length of the ceiling. Heavy velour furnishings in the deepest red, ornamented with gold piping, completed the room's opulence. She felt overpowered by so much luxury, but Sophia, relishing these evident trappings of wealth, did a small dance of congratulation in her head. Sir Julian himself handed round glasses of champagne and made ready for a considered but lengthy toast to his future bride.

The dinner that followed was as lavish as the surroundings, one laden course after another. Tureens of soup and a series of entrées were removed for platters of baked turbot and salmon, followed in turn by dishes of roast sirloin and goose with sides of French beans, peas and asparagus. Once his guests had eaten their fill of these delights, Sir Julian's well-trained staff whisked away the starched linen table covering and an assortment of pastries made their appearance alongside a chafing dish of pancakes, creams, jellies, ices and small bowls of preserved fruits.

The room was airless and Christabel ate sparingly while trying hard to maintain her part in the empty trivialities of table talk. It was with relief that she heard the carriage being announced that was to take them to the main attraction of the evening.

At the theatre Sir Julian had ensured that they had seats in one of the most comfortable boxes available, with an excellent view of the stage. Even so she quickly opted for a chair towards the back, hoping in the darkness to be left to her own thoughts. Until the lights went down, though, she must force herself to show enjoyment. She looked around the auditorium at the array of costumes and colours which shimmered beneath the theatre's blazing lights. The buzz of conversation was almost deafening, the noise hanging overhead in the heavy atmosphere. Glancing to her left, she thought she glimpsed Domino de Silva in an adjoining box and was about to remark on it to her mother who sat alongside her when Sir Julian turned to them, holding his finger to his lips.

'The curtain's going up!'

Contrary to her expectation, she had rapidly become immersed in the play. Whether it was Kean's electrifying performance or just that her overwrought mind sought some kind of relief she didn't know, but an hour had passed on wings. Before she realised it, an interval was being called.

Their small party filtered slowly out of the box and into the wide carpeted space which encircled the rear of the auditorium. Many other patrons were already taking a turn and attempting to find a little fresh air. It had steadily become more oppressive as the play proceeded, and a thunderstorm appeared likely. She saw Domino out of the corner of her eye walking nearby with Lady Blythe, both women fanning themselves vigorously. Quite how it happened, she was unsure, but in a trice it seemed that her mother was conversing animatedly with Lady Blythe while she found herself walking arm in arm with Domino. After Richard's admission that the girl had been an unwitting pawn, she felt uneasy in her company. Yet she also felt impelled to talk with her; above all she needed to hear that the young woman had not suffered irreparably from his intrigue.

They were walking slowly along the wide corridor, their steps carefully keeping time, when she ventured her first remark.

'This has been a most enjoyable evening. Such a pleasant surprise to see you again, Domino, and this time in more comfortable circumstances.'

'Indeed, yes,' the girl rejoined quietly. 'Our last meeting was not at all a happy one.'

'And how have you been since your return from Dover?' The question was commonplace, but she could not bring herself to hazard more.

'I've been well, thank you, Miss Tallis.'

The uncertain tone did not match her words. She was evidently troubled and the ghost of Richard rose between them. But Christabel was saved from having to probe further when the girl continued, 'I've wanted to thank you properly for rescuing me from my foolishness. I know I should have called on you immediately, but I felt too ashamed after the trouble I caused for Benedict.'

'You need not worry about Benedict. He got himself into trouble and it's far better that he is in Cornwall learning from my father than racketing around town. You've no need either to thank me.'

'Indeed I have, I can't thank you enough; you saved me from scandal when you could have simply turned away.'

They had once more reached Sir Julian's box and Domino paused her steps. Her planned encounter with Christabel had so far gone smoothly, but there was a good deal more to be accomplished before she could walk away. She touched Christabel on the arm in a gently restraining gesture and said slowly, 'I don't fully understand why you came after us, but I think that it was partly for Richard's sake.'

Christabel made no response. It seemed to Domino that now his name was out in the open the beautiful woman beside her had become strangely paralysed. She appeared unable to move or to speak. She was looking blindly ahead at the theatre box, where the door stood ajar, and seemed to want nothing more than to seek refuge in its shadowy depths.

Sensing that her quarry was about to turn tail, Domino said impulsively, 'There was never anything more than friendship between us, you know. I was infatuated, that's all, a naïve romance—nothing more. Poor Richard, he had much to bear with me, but he always behaved impeccably.'

'I'm glad to know that.' Christabel's voice stuttered into life. 'But after all that has happened to you in London, are you truly happy to be here still?'

'Why do you ask, Miss Tallis?'

'Forgive me, but on the few occasions I've glimpsed you lately, you've been looking a little pale, a little anxious. But that's probably my imagination running away with me.'

'No!' Domino said quickly, delighted that her plan was at last unfolding successfully. 'It's not your imagination. I wasn't telling the truth just now when I said I was happy. Things have not been well with me lately, but it has nothing to do with Richard.' She hoped that she was proving to be a convincing liar.

'What then?'

'May I confide in you, Miss Tallis—Christabel?'

Christabel nodded assent but privately took herself to task. She was sure that she did not want to hear this.

'Since I returned from that stupid flight, I've felt trapped.'

Domino was speaking so quietly that she had to bend towards the younger girl to catch her words.

'Aunt Loretta watches me all the time. I know I can't hope to be trusted completely after my flight, but she spies on my every single movement. I have absolutely no freedom.'

Christabel looked shocked. 'Surely you must be mistaken. Lady Blythe has always seemed to be the most indulgent of guardians.'

'She may have been once, but that escapade changed everything. She is nervous of my father, you know, and desperate to make sure that nothing else goes awry during my visit here.'

'But spying?'

'She observes me constantly. *And* she opens all my messages and makes sure that I receive only visitors that she is aware of.'

Glancing across at Lady Blythe still deep in conversation with her mother, Christabel could not help looking sceptical. Desperate to convince her, the girl threw out what she hoped was a clinching line.

'She says she will even accompany me to Spain when I leave in a few weeks' time.'

'But surely that's an excellent idea. You will need a chaperon on your journey and who could be a more comfortable companion than your aunt?'

'Not at all. She will be watching me closely and then will tell tales to my relatives, so that after her return to London they will continue to keep me fast. I will enjoy no liberty whatsoever.'

'But your father, can he not intervene on your behalf?'

'My father is thousands of miles away and the family has always said that he is far too lenient with me. When my mother died, they pressured him to send me back to Spain to be raised as a "proper" young lady. He resisted and kept me with him. This will be their revenge—they'll keep me locked up, I know,' she finished triumphantly.

'Don't you think you may be exaggerating?' Christabel suggested gently.

'A little, perhaps, but my life in Spain will not be happy. If only I could prevent Aunt Loretta from travelling with me and poisoning minds against me, I might persuade my relatives to believe my story. Maybe then I could enjoy living in Madrid.'

The interval bell rang sharply and it was time to return to their seats. Christabel took the young girl's hands in a farewell clasp, but she felt powerless to help her. The rest of the play seemed to pass in a blur. In some measure she felt responsible for Domino's plight. If she had not intervened in that earlier journey…but she could never have guessed that Loretta Blythe would treat her niece so badly. After their return from Dover, Lady Blythe had certainly scolded Domino soundly, that was to be expected, but she'd seemed too relieved to have her back safely to dwell long on the girl's reckless conduct. It was true that lately Domino was never without her aunt at her side—a proof of their closeness, she'd thought. Surely the situation could not be as bad as the girl had painted.

Yet she had been looking anxious and ailing ever since her return to London and it seemed clear that it was not Richard's perfidy that was troubling her. She had it on Domino's own authority that he had not deceived her and had always behaved towards her as a gentleman. She felt cheered by this revelation. It meant she could think better of him even if she still could not trust him.

Meanwhile Domino had resumed her seat beside Lady Blythe, well pleased with her evening's work. Her aunt looked questioningly at her, but she simply smiled a sunny response. Better Aunt Loretta knew nothing of her intentions. It was time to proceed to the next stage of her plan; only one or two obstacles to clear and it would be complete. The roll of thunder which just then reverberated through the building was a fitting signal, she thought, for the denouement to come.

A few days later Christabel was sitting alone in the drawing room at Mount Street. Her mother and Sophia were busy paying afternoon calls prior to the family's departure, and she had left her maidservant in the bedroom above, packing up her London wardrobe. Earlier she'd tried to decide on which gowns to take with her to Rosings and which would need to be sent directly to Cornwall, but eventually had left it to Rosa to choose, saying she had a headache. She seemed to be using that excuse frequently of late, but hardly cared if she were believed or not. She wasn't agreeable company for anyone, even herself. Since coming downstairs she'd tried reading one of the marble-backed books from the circulating library, so beloved of Sophia, but its silly plot sickened her. She'd picked up her long-discarded needlework, but it made her eyes ache.

She thought she might write to an old friend in Cornwall—she'd been meaning to for an age—but what could she say that would come anywhere near the truth of her life.

For probably the fourth time that hour she wandered over to the drawing-room window, but this time saw with surprise a liveried servant mounting the front steps. In a moment James had knocked and entered the room bearing a crisp, white note on a silver salver. As she took the paper from the tray, she glanced at the signature at its foot; the letter was from Domino de Silva. How strange. With some curiosity she began to read the unexpected message:

Dear Miss Tallis,
I did not want to leave London without saying goodbye or thanking you once more for all your efforts on my behalf. You have been a good friend to me and I hope you will forgive my decision to leave. I find I cannot bear to remain in London a moment longer. My aunt has be-haved very properly and on my behalf has settled the debts I incurred. For that I am grateful. But as I told you the other evening she now keeps me so confined that life has become insupportable. I am desperate to travel to Spain on my own for the reasons I mentioned and have decided to set out again for Paris and ask my father's friends for help to finish the journey to Madrid. This time, though, I am determined to leave England on my own. I still feel very badly that I caused so much trouble for your brother. By the time you read this, I shall be on my way. Please forgive me for not coming to see you at this time, but remember me instead with affection.
Yours ever, Domino

She stared at the sheet of paper for minutes on end, hardly able to comprehend the words she'd read. Since her conversation with Domino at the theatre, a worry had been niggling at the back of her mind that the girl might do something foolish, but she'd come to the conclusion that she was fretting unnecessarily. It was more than likely that Domino had been involved in a minor altercation with her aunt that evening and was magnifying the difficulties between them. But now this! It hardly seemed credible that the girl had fled again and this time completely alone. Without even Benedict's protection, she was exposed to all the hazards facing a beautiful and wealthy young woman on a long, solitary journey. She shivered in fear for her.

This time, too, there was no indication of when the girl had left London or the port she was making for. It was unlikely that she would choose to travel to Dover again for fear of being discovered, but there were any number of small ports dotted along the Channel coast and searching for her would be near impossible. The last rescue had been difficult enough when she'd known where the runaways were headed and when she'd had the faithful Stebbings to drive her.

It was a desperate situation, yet she could not let the girl disappear into a world of unknown danger. She must make some attempt to save her from her own folly. But she would need help and who could she turn to? Certainly not Lady Blythe. She would be even angrier with her niece than before. No, Domino must be found and brought back before her aunt got wind of her disappearance. Sir Julian would assist if she asked him, but he was caught up in a whirl of wedding preparations and would be shocked to the core by the girl's conduct. The image of Richard swam into her mind and was immediately dismissed. But not for long. His name persisted in her thoughts. He'd said just a few days ago that he had no interest in Domino, but it was undeniable that he'd been close to her, accompanying her on the long journey from Buenos Aires, escorting her about town in her aunt's stead. And Domino trusted him. Even if she were no longer in the first throes of infatuation, she must still count him as a friend. If anyone could run her to ground and influence her to return, it would be him. He would know what to do, what and who to ask, and he would be able to ride to the rescue across country if necessary, travelling far more swiftly than any carriage. She must put aside her own feelings and seek him out immediately.

Casting social propriety adrift, she threw on a silk pelisse, slipped out of the house and walked swiftly to the end of Mount Street. With luck an empty hansom cab was passing the end of the road and she hailed it immediately. She had no idea of the fare, but the jarvey seemed content with the few coins she had in her reticule.

Only thirty minutes had passed from Domino's message being delivered until Christabel stood on the top step of the Grosvenor Square mansion and pulled at the bell.

The footman's stare made her realise how imprudent she was in calling on a single gentleman alone, without even a maidservant as company. Discomforted by his obvious astonishment, she assumed a haughty air and commanded him to find his master immediately. The curt tone had its effect and in a moment he had shown her into the drawing room and disappeared to find Lord Veryan.

She walked nervously up and down the room she knew so well. Signs of neglect were everywhere for the house had remained unloved for too long. The blue brocade curtains had faded in the sun and the deeper-blue velvet chairs exhibited bare patches here and there, but it was sparkling clean and a large Venetian glass vase full of sweet-smelling roses and lilies from the garden gave the room a welcoming fragrance. The minutes ticked by and she began to fear that Richard was not at home, or that he'd decided to punish her further with a protracted wait in a room which held such bad memories. Her face flushed with the shame of remembrance and she was almost ready to flee when his tall, athletic figure strode into the room. His elegance proclaimed him every inch a gentleman, but one who could be trusted to take action.

Warm grey eyes searched hers intently, but his face betrayed none of the surprise he felt.

'Miss Tallis, how kind of you to call,' he said smoothly, as the door shut behind the footman.

Once on their own, he moved swiftly towards her, taking her hands in his and studying her troubled face with concern.

'Christy, what is it? What's happened?'

Her eyes filled with unbidden tears. Already she had the sense of a burden being lifted from her shoulders in the presence of this strong and capable man—she had been right to come. Mutely she proffered Domino's letter.

He scanned the sheet of paper quickly, but apart from a puzzled expression on his face, there was no other reaction. Doesn't he understand what has happened? she thought; surely he cannot be so unfeeling that he intends to ignore the letter.

'If you have any kindness for the child,' she broke out in an agitated voice, 'please help me to find her and bring her back.'

He read through the missive again, this time more slowly, and the puzzlement was replaced by a wry smile.

'I realise that I should not be here or be asking for your aid after all that has passed between us,' she began again, her voice brittle, 'but will you not help?'

'Why ask *me*, Christabel?' he asked quietly.

'You know Domino well, you have the power to influence her and…' her voice was hardly audible '…you are the only person I can trust in this difficult matter.'

Again he took her hands into his strong clasp and looked intently down at her.

'The word "trust" fills me with hope.'

'Richard!' She snatched away her hands. 'This is urgent. I don't know when Domino left or which port she's making for. She may have half a day's start.'

He gently stroked her cheek with his hand. 'Stay calm, my darling girl, all is well.'

'I don't understand. And I am *not* your darling girl! You forget yourself.'

'And you forgot yourself in coming here to seek my aid. I imagine that's exactly what Domino hoped would happen.'

She was stunned into silence, thoroughly bewildered by his words.

'Come with me,' he said gently, and she allowed him to lead her by the hand into the adjoining garden room with its tall windows looking out on to a wide expanse of lawn. Beneath the shade of the trees a table was set with a white linen table-cloth and the pretty flowered cups that Christabel remembered well.

Domino and her aunt, looking happy and relaxed, sat chatting and sipping their tea.

She whirled around. 'But I don't understand!' she repeated.

'A hoax, I fear, but one with the very best of intentions.'

'You mean that this letter is false. But why? Why would she wish to upset me so?'

'I'm sure she didn't mean to disturb you this badly. She's very young and not always mindful of the consequences of her actions. But I think I know why she decided on this ruse. After we parted the other day I met her driving in Regent's Park. I was thoroughly downcast and confided to her something of our conversation; I told her that you had lost all faith in me. She must have set out to prove to you that that was untrue, that you still trusted me despite all my attempts at sabotage.'

'But why would she do such a thing?'

'Because she knows how I feel about you. She's always known, even before I realised the truth myself. And she guesses that you feel the same about me. She wants us both to be happy—together.'

She pushed the thought away and instead returned to Domino's deception.

'I really believed she was in danger and was badly frightened for her, quite unnecessarily as it turns out. I don't know what to say.'

'Forgive her, Christy, she's brought us together.' He moved closer to her and she felt his breath on her cheek.

When she remained silent, he said with force, 'Well, hasn't she? My darling, say she has!' And with one swift movement he pulled her into his arms and held her to his heart.

She struggled to disentangle herself. Things were moving far too rapidly. She had to think and her mind was dazed.

'I'm naturally relieved that Domino is safe,' she said carefully, 'though I cannot think her actions anything but thoughtless. Her plan to bring us together was misguided and ill advised.'

'But you're here,' he pointed out, the shadow of a smile flitting across his face.

'I came to seek your help, not to reaffirm my trust in you.'

'But isn't that just what you're doing? Why didn't you go elsewhere, why come to me?'

'Because you are a capable man and you know Domino well,' she answered awkwardly.

'They are superficial reasons. You came to me because you know in the deepest recesses of your heart that I am the one person in the world who is here for you—and always will be.'

He was right. Until her foolish disloyalty had so decisively severed them, he had been her refuge, the rock which had anchored her to the world. But did she still believe that? She wanted to, desperately, but she couldn't be sure.

'And Domino, what of her?' she questioned, eager to change the subject.

'Does she seem to you to have suffered unduly?'

Domino's laugh was ringing out across the lawn. A wasp had evidently interrupted the tea party and she was dancing this way and that to escape its attentions. Richard looked away from this little drama and smiled again.

'Domino and I are the best of friends, but that's all. I hope you can see that.'

Even if she could, Richard remained the cold man who had plotted so adroitly against her. Knowing what he'd done, could she ever really trust him, ever really forgive him?

'Find it in your heart to forgive me,' he pleaded, knowing her thoughts. 'I was shocked when I saw you again, shocked at the way you made me feel. I was wounded and I wanted to escape the hurt which came crashing back at me. I lashed out with this stupid intrigue to prove to myself that you weren't worth the pain.'

But he had failed, she told herself. He might have plotted, but he hadn't been able to go through with it. She thought back to the picnic and the way that he'd looked at her by the lakeside, unable to bear her unhappiness. His campaign had hardly started before he'd abandoned it. Surely it was possible to forgive him.

He was looking fixedly at her, watching her every fleeting expression. Quite suddenly he reached out for her hand.

'Marry me!'

'You don't have to offer me marriage,' she said defiantly. 'I know that you feel you've disgraced me, destroyed my chances. But you haven't. If I stay single, I shall have no regrets.' She almost choked on the brazen lie.

'But *I* shall! Darling Christy, I love you. I've always loved you. I've never stopped loving you. And that love is not going away. And neither am I!'

And once more he seized her in a crushing embrace.

'I don't know what to say,' she repeated stupidly, her mind still blurred, but her body swiftly coming to life.

'Then say nothing.'

He gently nuzzled her face and buried his hands in the disordered mass of red curls.

She began to murmur, but he stifled her protest. 'There *is* nothing more to say. Everything is decided!' and tipping her face he brought his mouth down hard on hers, urgent and demanding.

A throbbing ache of pleasure shot through her body. Her lips sought his with all the hunger that had built up over days of longing. She was inundated by wave after wave of love, coursing through every small part of her, its power at last sweeping away the iron bonds of fear that had held her captive.

She sighed her surrender. Richard was right, everything *was* decided!

Epilogue

It was a perfect August evening when they met on a headland stippled with flaming yellow furze and strolled lazily down the rocky path towards their cove. The languorous air of what had been a hot summer day bathed them in its warm caress. A gentle breeze was blowing now, signalling the turning of the tide, but it barely lifted the leaves of the tall hedgerows on either side of the lane. The scent of dog roses and meadowsweet was everywhere, enveloping them in a cloud of heady perfume. In the distance the surf rolled itself lazily against the rocks, the noise echoing back towards them and gradually growing more thunderous as they made their way downhill towards the beach.

'I thought you might not escape this evening.' He smiled down at the carefree girl who meandered beside him.

Christabel wore the lightest of muslin dresses, almost a shift, her long limbs moving easily in the simple garment. Her hair flowed free, the auburn curls moving in the breeze and flaming in the last rays of the sun. Her smile was luminous. She looked no older than the girl he had fallen in love with so long ago.

'Mama is still fretting.' She grinned. 'She's written and re-written every one of her lists, but she's convinced herself that something is bound to go awry.'

'So why aren't you there, fanning her fevered brow?'

'I'll have you know that I've worked very hard at being daughterly all day. And don't think I didn't notice your quick exit as soon as the rehearsal was over! When Mama began to wrinkle her brow and tap her pencil again, it was clearly time to slip away.'

'So you're not here for the pleasure of my company after all?' he teased.

'What do you think has kept me going all day?' She reached up and kissed the tanned cheek he bent towards her.

'That's much better, a little appreciation is in order!'

Hand in hand they walked in companionable silence to-wards the sea and the setting sun. Words were often unnec-essary between them.

When he spoke again, his tone was pensive. 'I can hardly believe that tomorrow—finally—we will be man and wife.'

'If we hadn't observed the year's mourning, we would have offended too many people, Richard. And the day *has* come at last.'

'Not soon enough for me,' he protested, hugging her close to him. 'These last twelve months since your sister's strange marriage have seemed interminable.'

'Not so strange after all. By all accounts she and Julian are making a success of married life.'

He shook his head disbelievingly. 'Sophia is the queen of triviality and he's such a...' and he struggled to find a word that would not upset his beloved '...a serious person.'

'Admit it, you were longing to say a stuffed shirt. He's a good man and works very hard for his charitable projects.'

'That's what I meant.' He laughed, unrepentant. 'But how he ever thought you would make him a suitable wife!'

'An illusion, I fear. His relationship with Sophia is far more down to earth and that's why it works so well. He really didn't know me.'

'Just dazzled by the exterior, eh? And what an exterior!' He stroked her arm softly and then slipped his own around her waist, pulling her into him as they walked.

'Richard, be careful, someone may come by.'

'They won't—dusk is falling, and do I care if I'm seen embracing the woman I love? No, I don't think I do.'

'You should. You are the lord of Madron and must set an example to your tenants.'

'I'm setting an example to every red-blooded man, not just in Madron but the whole of Cornwall, by marrying the most beautiful, the most exciting, the most enchanting woman in the world.'

They rounded the last bend in the lane at that moment and the noise of the ocean, which had gradually been growing louder, burst fully on their ears.

Waves crashed headlong into the jutting rocks on either side of the cove but between the two spurs of outlying granite, a crescent of white sand lay virginal and inviting. They ran down the last of the path, holding hands and laughing as they almost lost their footing on the downhill slope. The soft sand swallowed their footsteps and prompted them to kick off their shoes. He watched smilingly as she performed an impromptu pirouette, a homage to the heart-stopping beauty all around them: the green headland and the grey rocks, the indigo sea with its white frills of foam and the evening sky now streaked with pink and purples, a harbinger of good weather.

'It looks as though we will have a beautiful day for our wedding,' she said quietly, intensely aware of the solitary beach and his physical presence so close to her.

'Almost as beautiful as this evening.'

His voice was rough with desire as he ran his hands up the white arms and arrived at her shapely breasts. He pulled the ribbon of her bodice undone and began slowly to roll the dress from her shoulders.

'Richard! This is a public place!'

'Do you see any public here? We are as alone as we possibly could be. You didn't used to be so cautious, Christy.'

She blushed at the memory of their youthful indiscretion, but allowed him to continue undressing her, his gaze filling her with an aching need for his touch.

He had soon divested himself of his own clothes and it was her turn to drink her fill. He was beautifully made and she felt herself grow hot and trembling.

He took her hand then, breaking the spell, and they ran together to the sea's edge. For a moment the water's impact took their breath away, but then they plunged headlong into the surf. Richard struck out immediately, powering through the waves towards the darkening horizon and shouting to her to hurry and join him. The cold fingers of the sea crept insidiously over her body and it was a while before the water began to warm her bare skin and slowly bewitch her with its movement. Richard was already far out and she called to him not to go further. She needed to share her delight.

He turned back instantly and was soon treading water at her side. Both of them were laughing with the sheer joy of the moment. The flaming red tresses of her hair encircled him with their ring of fire, challenging the watery environment and setting him alight. His legs slowly entwined around hers and he held her close to him, supporting her body against his, kissing her face, her arms, her breasts in rapid succession. Then his mouth found hers, his tongue tenderly teasing her lips open. She clung to him, exchanging one rapturous kiss after another, but when he felt her shiver, he released his hold and smiled tenderly down at her.

'We should get out of the water before you catch a bad chill—I'll race you back to the beach!'

'You do realise,' she giggled as they tumbled up the sands to reach their pile of clothes, 'that we haven't a towel between us.'

'Why do you need a towel, when you have me?' The look in his eyes was disturbing and she felt her breath catch.

Before she had time to protest, he had spread his jacket on the sand and pulled her down to join him.

'This should keep you warm,' he said softly and rolled her over to lie beneath him, his body covering hers. His voice was barely audible above the sound of the breaking surf, but its passion was unmistakable.

Slowly and inexorably their bodies melted one into another, and a dull ache of pleasure began to permeate her being. Soon her entire body was infused by a heat which spread in ever fiercer waves. It was dark now but for a handful of stars tossed into the night sky and the light of the moon edging the scene with its silver: the empty beach, the constant surf and two lovers, their bodies entwined, lost to the world.

'Think of all the evenings we have to come,' he whispered.

A river of desire was flowing through her and she sighed

with the intensity of its pleasure, arching her body to meet his. His touch intensified and she gave up all pretence of restraint, shamelessly abandoning herself to his lovemaking, her body softening to accommodate the hardness of his form. She wanted nothing more than to give herself without thought or words to this ecstasy. His mouth covered her burning skin with kisses, piling desire upon desire, until she was crying out, swept away by an almost unbearable pleasure.

They lay together, breathless and shaking, Richard's severely crumpled jacket swaddling them in its folds. For long minutes they lay curled in the tightest of embraces while above the black of the distant night sky offered its benign cover. Then he raised himself on one elbow and began to stroke her hair, allowing her tangled curls to flitter lazily through his fingers.

'I can't believe that I've been so lucky, after the mess I've made of my life—and yours,' he murmured.

'We've both been adept at making a mess of life.' She looked up at him tenderly and brushed a lock of hair from his face. 'Do you remember a night like this all those years ago? We came here then to escape mayhem in the house.'

He gave a twisted smile. 'How could I ever forget? It's burned into my memory. If I'd been less of a prig that night, the whole course of our lives would have been different.'

'You were shy,' she excused, 'we both were. We didn't know what to do with such unfamiliar feelings.'

'Not quite so unfamiliar now,' he teased and bent his lips to her breasts to kiss them awake once more.

She sighed her pleasure and scattered butterfly kisses over his body. 'I can't imagine how I ever thought our betrothal meant nothing more to you than a way of bringing our families together.'

He groaned. 'And I can't imagine how I could have been so stupid as to allow you to believe that!'

He tightened his grip, holding her close to his heart. 'What an age it's taken us, Christy, but we've come through.'

Her face was alight with feeling, her eyes an emerald radiance, their lustre warming the moonlit world.

'It was worth the wait.'

'And the pain?' he asked, his voice rough with remorse.

'Love is even sweeter for being so hard-won.'

With one finger she delicately traced the outline of his face, pale and glimmering against the dark of the night, and when she spoke again her voice was not quite steady. 'And it will endure, Richard. For every moment of for ever. Nothing will separate us.'

'Nothing,' he breathed huskily, and took her up into his arms again, covering her face with kisses and meeting her eager lips with his.

* * * * *

DANGEROUS LORD, INNOCENT GOVERNESS
Christine Merrill

Daphne Collingham is convinced that her cousin died at the hands of her husband, scandalous Lord Timothy Colton, so masquerades as a governess to discover the truth. But suspicion and provocation go hand in hand as she becomes the dangerous lord's ultimate temptation…

CAPTURED FOR THE CAPTAIN'S PLEASURE
Ann Lethbridge

Fearsome Captain Michael Hawkhurst lives to wreak revenge on the Fulton family. When he captures Fulton's spirited but virginal daughter Alice, Michael faces a dilemma—should he live up to his scandalous name and take his revenge, or will his honourable side win out…?

BRUSHED BY SCANDAL
Gail Whitiker

Nothing's more important to beautiful Lady Annabelle Durst than protecting her heart. However, when faced with a family scandal, she must risk her reputation and her heart in order to persuade the disreputable Sir Barrington Parker to help..

LORD LiBERTINE
Gail Ranstrom

Notorious Andrew Hunter finds a diversion from his dissolute life in the form of the mysterious Lady Lace. Unable to tell if she is innocent or an experienced temptress, he is determined to seduce the truth from her. But is he ready for the secrets he will uncover…?

Mills & Boon® Hardback Historical

Another exciting novel available this month:

UNTAMED ROGUE, SCANDALOUS MISTRESS

Bronwyn Scott

Passion and scandal in the Ton!

Self-made Miss, Aurora Calhoun, has always possessed an uncommon amount of sense when it comes to men. However, within minutes of colliding with Lord Ramsden she finds herself kissing the incorrigible rogue!

Crispin Ramsden feels restrained by the shackles of his unwanted inheritance. Especially when he is faced with a woman whose impetuous nature ignites a passion that is as uncontrollable as it is scandalous! Society is rocked by this outrageous couple. Can these two wild hearts find a place to belong?

*Another exciting novel available
this month:*

HONOURABLE DOCTOR, IMPROPER ARRANGEMENT

Mary Nichols

A woman worth fighting for!

Dr Simon Redfern has risked his heart—and his reputation—over a woman once before. So when he meets Kate Meredith, who is helping a ragged child, he's shocked to find himself longing to make the warm-hearted young widow his wife...

Despite family disapproval, Kate volunteers to work at Simon's children's home, and her growing feelings for him throw her into confusion. For, longing to have children of her own, she has accepted another man's proposal. But Simon is the only man she can now contemplate as their father...

*Another exciting novel available
this month:*

HIS BORDER BRIDE
Blythe Gifford

Royal rogue, innocent lady

Gavin Fitzjohn is the illegitimate son of an English prince
and a Scotswoman. A rebel without a country, he
has darkness in his soul.

Clare Carr, daughter of a Scottish border lord, can recite the laws
of chivalry, and knows Gavin has broken every one.

Clare is gripped by desire for this royal rogue—could he be the
one to unleash everything she has tried so hard to hide?
Those persuasive urges have stayed safely
dormant—until now…